A KIND OF CATHARSIS

To Ulrike
with love & thanks

A KIND OF CATHARSIS

A TALE OF MORALITY, JUSTICE AND VENGEANCE

ANN CHAPMAN

A Kind of Catharsis

Book Cover designed by Nikki Lundie

Nel Design

Typesetting and Formatting Ithaca Publications

Soft Cover ISBN 978-0-473-51633-8

Published by Gallica Print.

Acknowledgements

My sisters, Gail, Elizabeth, and Jane
who all played a part in this drama.

My husband Lloyd who watched the rise and
fall of my emotions as I wrote.

Renèe, without whose support and advice I
would never have written this.

Penelope Haines whose critiques and
suggestions were invaluable.

There have been others who have
travelled this journey with me.

Thank you all.

COURAGE

Courage is the price that Life exacts
for granting peace.
The soul that knows it not
Knows no release from little things:
Knows not the livid loneliness of fear,
Nor mountain heights where bitter
joy can hear
The sound of wings.

How can life grant us boon of living, compensate
For dull grey ugliness and pregnant hate
Unless we dare
The soul's dominion?
Each time we
make a choice, we pay
With courage to behold the resistless day,
And count it fair.

Amelia Earhart

PROLOGUE

Six Months Earlier

Niall rang her just as she had arrived home after her Zumba class.

'Georgia here.'

'Georgia, can you come down quickly? Brigit has had another accident.'

'How? What happened? How badly is she hurt this time?'

The questions tumbled from her as she booted up her computer to find the earliest flight.

'He said she fell off the back of a trailer while he was reversing, that he didn't know she was there, and she just fell.'

'What does she say?' Georgia was immediately suspicious. Her sister would never get up on the back of a moving trailer. With her Multiple Sclerosis she was always careful of falling.

'Brigit knows she's unsteady on her feet. She tells me she's always careful especially around moving vehicles as she's not so quick anymore,' she added.

'She has concussion and doesn't remember much. When I asked her, she just looked at me and said that she couldn't be sure it wasn't deliberate.'

Niall waited a beat.

'There's more Georgia. She has two broken legs and a broken arm.' Niall's voice broke a little as he spoke. Georgia imagined him running his hand through his hair. He always did that when he was agitated.

'Shit. She's in hospital now?'

'Yes. Surgery is this afternoon. Look, I know you don't like me offering, but I can pay your fare down here.' Niall was tentative in his offer. His experience with his aunt told him she was fiercely independent.

'No, no. But thanks. I can handle it. There's a flight down leaving here at 2.30 which I can make easily so I should be in Invercargill by 4.30. There, I've just booked the flight.'

'I'll pick you up. And …' he paused. 'Thanks George.' He called her by her nickname. 'I'm grateful you can drop everything to come down.'

'He did it deliberately didn't he? And we won't be able to prove a thing or get the police involved. He'll just worm his way out of it again.' Georgia could barely control her anger now that the first flush of concern had passed. She hurled her car keys across the room and doubled over as she tried to control her panicked breathing. 'He's a fucking dangerous bastard,' she shouted into the empty room.

'Yes. And he'll blame her once again.' Niall's voice started cracking and she heard him taking deep breaths.

'Why won't the police act against him? We've given them enough cause to act.' Georgia was almost sobbing in distress as she packed a small bag while speaking.

'Because she withdraws her complaints to them. We just have to accept that Brigit is frightened of him.'

'He'll kill her one day, won't he Niall? We know this isn't the first time.'

'We'll just have to redouble our efforts to get the house sold and Brigit out of his way, safely up in Auckland with you. That's going to have to be our big effort while you're down here with her, Georgia. Get her ready mentally to leave the family home.'

'We can do it Niall. This time we will do it. This time she

must see that she has to leave for her own safety.' Georgia was definite and resolved. She was determined she could persuade her beloved sister to remove her abusive boarder, sell her home and come to the warmth and safety of Auckland.

With a stiffening of her back, a clutch of tissues in her hand, Georgia shut her case, locked up and drove to the airport.

CHAPTER ONE

Day One

At 2.15am he crept like a wraith into her room, pulling his merino dressing gown tight around his big flabby body. He was sure she was asleep; he could hear snoring and her relentless wheeze which so frequented her breathing. Hands in front of him he felt his way through her darkened bedroom. *Don't want to bump anything. Don't want to disturb her yet.* The light from a flickering streetlamp threw a moody gloom into the room through the open curtains and gave him some clarity. He could see her lying curled up, hugging her chest like a child. She liked the curtains open so she could look at the stars and if it were a clear, cloudless night, watch the satellites slowly making their way across the midnight-blue sky. She used to do that at the Observatory when she was a teenager.

He opened the windows. The southerly wind moved in, dropping the temperature instantly.

The only noise on this winter's night in Invercargill was her breath. He listened to the loud laboured breathing of his landlady and he paused, his heart fluttering in anticipation as she struggled for her next breath. Pulling his dressing gown tighter around him, he sat in her darkened room, in his pyjamas, waiting. He thought of her betrayal, and his plans to get even. Ever since she had given him notice his hatred of her had eaten away at him,. *The bitch thought she could get rid of me, did she?*

He knew in this cold, sooner or later she would have one of her attacks. He scowled as he hunkered down, waiting. He needed one of her respiratory arrests to happen now, not tomorrow. Tomorrow would be no good.

He tensed, leaning forward and listening intently, aware now that her breathing was becoming more erratic, louder and the rattle becoming more strained. His eyes followed the trail of mist slowing rising to the ceiling from those frantic gasping breathes. He felt ready.

He had received the call earlier just as dusk was descending, the weakening sun going down over the horizon. 'Tonight.' He understood. That's why he'd opened her windows. He was shivering now, arms wrapped around himself for warmth. That cold southerly wind, a specialty of Invercargill, now infiltrated the room dropping the temperature lower and lower. He went and fetched a rug from his room, grasping it with one hand, and a cigarette in the other.

He had already removed the inhalers from the cabinet beside her, and the increasing cold of the Antarctic southerly which had caused the asthmatic wheeze finally woke her. He was still as he watched her chest heaving, struggling for breath. He sat in the dark, silent, watching as she pulled herself up, groping the side table to find the relief to her lungs. He remained unmoving and unresponsive as she called for him to help her. Brigit knew he was there. She could see the red glow of the cigarette. She could smell the burning tobacco. He remained silent, legs crossed, quietly puffing in her direction, jiggling her inhalers around in his pocket with his other hand.

'Help me.' She pleaded barely able to get the words out. 'Please help.'

He remained impassive, staying seated just watching her, barely visible in the gloom of the room.

She looked at him frightened now, as he continued puffing in her direction, a smirk on his face, his legs crossed, and one leg swinging.

'Please.' She shut her eyes as she forced the word out, the wheeze sounding louder.

He didn't move to help her. She stretched out her arm, patted her weak hand on the bedside table as she tried to reach her phone, but that was also now safely tucked away in his dressing gown pocket. Her eyes were wide now, pleading, hands tightly balled, gripping the bedclothes. Her breath sounding more like a freight train each time she forced her worn lungs in and out. Pushing the blankets aside, she swung her legs around and tried to get out of bed. He watched as she collapsed back on the bed.

And it didn't take long before she took her final desperate breath. He was quivering, a combination of excitement and cold. He smiled. A gentle smile. Dead, and he hadn't laid a finger on her.

The southerly continued its relentless intrusion into the bedroom, dropping the temperature even further downward. Needing warmth and without the need to taunt her anymore, he tightened the blanket around him, hunkering down. He wanted the excitement of his inaction to wash over him in a warm sexual glow, to salivate over her, his final victory. His punishment of her. As he finished his cigarette, he felt an unexpected sexual warmth, one he'd always been denied in this bedroom. He closed his eyes and let that warmth and excitement flow over him. He eyed her dispassionately his breaths coming in rapid gasps, shuddering finally to a stop. He flopped back released. Hands shoved in his pockets his smile widened as he considered his next moves.

Dead bodies didn't bother him. He'd seen enough of them. He took his time as he set the scene. He was in no hurry. He replaced her inhalers and put his smile aside. And only then did he ring the emergency services. The emergency operator answered and logged the call. 4.31am.

CHAPTER TWO

Georgia stepped into the Invercargill terminal, dancing on her toes in excitement. She spotted him immediately, despite the crowds rushing to greet their friends or waiting to board the next plane to Auckland.

He was leaning against the far wall, tall and easy to spot with his blond Nordic hair, and sparkling blue eyes. She smiled to herself as she stuck two fingers in her mouth and caught his attention with a shrill farmer's whistle. She grinned as he spun around.

'Georgia, Georgia,' he shouted as he pushed through the crowds.

'Welcome home. At last.' She felt his arms as they surrounded her. Shaking herself free of his bear hug she gasped for breath.

'So excited to be here again. We've lots to do eh?' George felt her tongue running away with her as the questions tumbled out of her mouth. 'Is she better now? More mobile? Do you think she'll agree this time?' She paused for breath, turning around to him with a questioning look on her face as they strode towards the baggage claim.

'I've sown the seeds gently, repeatedly.. I'll tell you about it over an early supper. I've booked a table at The Soaring Hawk at Otatara, right by the river near the estuary. It's new and a must-visit if you like the wildness of the Oreti Estuary and the abundant bird life.' He grabbed her bag with one hand and arm thrown around Georgia's shoulders, he gave it a squeeze and with a dark look said, 'come on. Let's go.'

He left Georgia standing, a look of amazement on her face. She felt a prickle of irritation at this new, hyped up Niall. She rushed after him and even with her long legs found herself running to keep up with him.

Georgia caught her breath as she tried to assess the situation. She opened her mouth many times to ask questions, but the forbidding look on his face stopped her. She settled back to wait breathing deeply throughout the journey, letting her hurt feelings abate. It wasn't long before he pulled up in the car park with a squeal of tyres and she looked at the swirling birds swooping and diving. For a moment she felt peace, her anger at Niall's abruptness momentarily forgotten. She smelt the salty freshness of the ocean and paused to let the moment and serenity of the scene settle her, and then climbed out of the car.

The small café created an air of intimacy with its comfortable chairs around a much-needed fire on this winter evening. There was a smattering of noisy old guys in fishing garb, gathered around the fire sharing tall stories about their latest catch. 'You know yesterday, the trout were fair roiling the water there were so many of them. You couldn't see the bottom of the river.'

'And you didn't catch a thing, did you?' said one of them as he raised his beer glass. They all laughed as they talked over each other about the size of their catch.

Georgia immediately felt at home. She grinned as they sat down at their table. 'Nothing's changed then. Fishermen and their tall stories all trying to outdo one another. I remember my dad telling the same stories to his disbelieving wife. She'd stand with arms akimbo smelling the tobacco and beer on him. 'You still fish, Niall?'

'No, I gave it up when I set up my medical centre. Being the only doctor for a while was pretty time consuming.'

'You've never wanted to take it up again?' Georgia was

curious about Niall's life down in Invercargill. He never gave anything away about himself. *Is he cautious with everybody or just me?* He smiled in a dreamy way as he sat back in the chair, waiting a moment to roll his shoulders as if to ease some hidden tension.

'Not yet anyway. My general practice is too busy but I'm a bit more settled now. Maybe I'll go back to it in time.'

The waiter approached sidling up quietly. 'Hope the music is not too loud for you.'

'No, it's fine thank you. Anything special today?' asked Georgia as she held her hand out for the menu.

'Blue cod, just in this morning. I'd recommend that.'

'Let's check out the rest of the menu. But would you bring a couple of glasses of the house Riesling please while we decide?' Niall said. They watched him leave before they started talking again.

She looked up a quizzical expression on her face. 'Why did you send me that warning email yesterday asking me to come down next week? You scared me with your description about Brigit and what was happening to her.'

'Let's order first, and I can tell you while we wait.' Niall said.

She gazed out the window at the birds, relentless in their pursuit of prey. The sky was the perfect foil for those white gulls. Their aerobatics showed up against the dark thunderous sky with its threatening clouds looking just like an angry Turner painting.

She stared as the waiter gently coughed, notepad in hand.

'The blue cod for me please, just salad, no chips.'

'Same for me, but with chips please,' said Niall.

Niall leant forward, 'George. About that email,' he stopped abruptly when her phone rang. She frowned as she fumbled around in the depths of her oversized handbag for it. Her eyebrows rose slightly when she looked at it. Unknown number.

'Do you mind if I answer this?' she said apologetically.

'That's ok.'

'Georgia Chappel speaking. I'm sorry I didn't catch who you are.' She frowned. Her face turned white and her hands started to shake. She looked as if she were about to faint, and beads of sweat appeared on her brow.

'What? I'm sorry could you repeat that please?' She listened and then whispered, 'Yes, of course. I'll come right away right away.'

She dropped the phone as if were red hot, her eyes wide with shock, blood draining from her face.

'Police,' she said. 'Brigit is dead. My little sister, your mother is dead.'

She looked at Niall and said bleakly. 'We have to go.'

CHAPTER THREE

It had been a quiet night up until the call came in. Senior paramedic Benedict McGregor took the lead. He'd been working for St John's Ambulance ever since he'd left university and quickly worked his way up through the ranks. It was easy then, Ben remembered as he sped along. I had a clean police record and a driver's license. He smiled in the darkness of the ambulance as he thought of how much he loved his job and the difference he could make to people when they were most vulnerable. He felt at one with the world when he was on night shift. He loved the darkness, the quiet and the soft breathing of his companion. Night meant he didn't have to make conversation. He could just get on with the job.

Ben was hitting 6' 2", the size of a rugby forward, but he was fast on his feet, nimble with his hands. He was safe and steady, and people responded to him.

Ben's wingman this night was a relative newcomer to Invercargill. Tom Forsythe had been there three years now, and Ben was still trying to work him out. Ben could never understand why he never smiled. Ben saw resentment oozing out of him and his surliness soured the mood at the station.

'We're at a loss Ben,' management had said when they

summoned him to a private meeting. 'Can we put you with Tom? Maybe he'll learn from you how to handle himself, otherwise we're going to have to let him go. The others don't like his attitude,' the boss had said.

Ben had shrugged as his heart dropped. He'd spread his hands out in a gesture as if to say, of course. He'd kept his feeling about Tom to himself. *But I don't like it either.*

They were partnered a lot. The novice learning from the master and Tom hated it. *I don't need to be babied like this. Do they think I'm stupid?* His resentment flowed freely whenever Ben advised him. *Patronising bastard.*

'Try not to be so rough, Tom. Patients are frail and often scared. Be patient with them.' Tom had scowled, eyebrows furrowed tight as he eyed Ben. He was silent but Ben saw the glimmer of hatred and resentment in that tall frame. Tom's muscles had rippled through his shirt as he clenched and unclenched his fists.

The more Ben worked with him and observed him, the more he found himself wrestling with his own antagonism for his younger charge. He knew that he frequently fell short of his own standards, in his attempts at creating a working relationship. Tom's arrogance expressed itself daily with his lack of empathy towards his co-workers as well as with his patients.

Tom's mood was no different tonight as they silently raced through the quiet streets towards Chelmsford Street, and the tension was palpable inside the ambulance. In the sub-zero temperatures of a winter's night, it was just as frosty inside the ambulance as the outside. There were no words needed to express the distrust between the two men. Ben's deep breath of frustration as he wove his way around Invercargill was noticed by the ever-silent Tom. Unseen in the dark, Tom's face curled into a tight smile. *Little do you know what you're coming to, you smart arse.* But Ben sensed the change in Tom, that slight movement of his body, the briefest of smirks mirrored in the front windscreen as he shifted slightly. Ben felt the tremor in Tom's forearm as it brushed onto his when he turned the corner. They were greeted by the only brightly lit house in the street as if it were a party waiting for the arrival of the honoured guest.

A man was waiting for them by the door as they pulled up, tousled in his midnight blue dressing gown, hair awry. He fussed impatiently at them, waving them through to the bedroom.

'Through there. Through there,' he was impatient as he ushered them in. 'I'm Rob Bennet. My partner is through there. In the bedroom. Just hurry. What took you so long?'

Ben nodded a quiet greeting, and as they moved through his practiced eye took in the disarray of the bedclothes, the rug on the chair, the window still slightly ajar, and inhalers by the bed. He then focused on the body lying uncovered on the bed as if she were trying to climb out when death took her.

'What's her name?' Ben asked as Tom passed him the stethoscope, the IV needles and the defibrillator.

'Brigit Chappel.' Rob sighed, his breath showing as mist in the air. 'We've been together for five years. I'm not prepared for this.' He fussed, rustled his hair as he watched carefully, his eyes observing every move they made. It was as if he wanted to remember everything, or as if he distrusted what was happening.

Ben found this scrutiny unsettling. He indicated to Tom and said in a whisper, 'will you deal with him?'

Tom looked up at Rob hovering near the body 'None of us are. Please give us some space and wait outside please while we try and help your partner.'

Tom needed to stay close by Ben as he worked on the victim. He didn't want to leave the room. He feared the way Ben could read a situation, could read a person with the ease of a practiced clairvoyant.

They worked quietly and efficiently. They didn't need to talk. Both knew exactly what they needed from one another as they put a mask over Brigit's nose and mouth to try and get the oxygen into those now collapsed lungs.

Tom was quietly pumping the air bag while Ben was doing CPR. His head was down, hidden from view so Tom could not see the eyebrows come together. Ben senses were on fire, and he felt a tingle of surreal prickling running down his spine, that sense you feel as if someone had walked over your grave. They had had many successes before, but Brigit was not going to be one of them. She lay there still and cold.

Ben rocked back on his heels as he raised a hand to stop. He rolled his shoulders. He viewed Brigit's body, and his sense of disquiet deepened. His experienced eye noted her pallor, the slight rigidity. Something was wrong but he couldn't put his finger on it yet. A bell was softly ringing in the back of his mind. His earlier frown lingered as he gazed down, unaware of Tom watching him carefully.

What gave Ben that feeling of foreboding was that although Brigit's body was still flaccid, just a hint of stiffening had occurred, just a slight resistance as they straightened her out. Ben made a mental note of that. Her face was white, waxen, eyes open and cloudy. She was like a porcelain doll, small and fragile. He pressed his fingers against her body to check lividity for any change of colour. He saw the pressure points turn initially white and then slowly revert to a pale blue. He stiffened. *She's been dead much longer than claimed, but not so long as to completely lose all signs of blood still in her veins.*

He looked at his watch, jotting down the time he stopped resuscitation and his observations on time of death on his work sheet. *She's been dead a while, so why was Bennet claiming it had just happened.*

'What are you writing?' Tom asked aggressively.

'Just the time we stopped resuscitation Tom. You know this.' Ben looked at him a puzzled expression on his face.

'You wrote more than that.' Tom grabbed the worksheet and looked down at it, eyes narrowed in the gloom.

'Resuscitation unsuccessful. Stopped at 4.45 after 10 minutes.' Tom read it out aloud, flicked over the page to check nothing else had been noted. Ben was slack jawed as he watched this by-play. *What the fuck is going on here?* Tom threw the worksheet to the ground, stood up and stretched his back.

'I'll go and tend to Mr. Bennet.' He almost sounded normal. Ben nodded, unsure why Tom had acted this way. *He's never checked me before.* He picked up the worksheet and quickly noted down his suspicions on the time of death before closing the folder and packing it away.

Before Rob had called the ambulance, he'd checked everything. On his way to the kitchen he'd cast a quick eye towards the bathroom. It needed to appear as if he'd rushed out when called by Brigit. Yes, the door was open and the toilet lid still up. Brigit's latest painting was askew as if he had brushed it while rushing past on his way to help her. *That's my story. Just need to stick to it.* Her painting of bright sunlight seemed to mock him now that the sunlight had gone from her eyes. Not that they had sparkled for some time. He had always hated that painting. It was as if she had painted it to reject him and the gloom he'd bought to her life and her home. *It will be the first thing to go.*

Tom strolled nonchalantly into the kitchen where Rob was now pacing, fretting as he waited. Yes, he'd had experience about how to make a murder seem like natural causes. But even he could not disguise the coldness of Brigit. And he had been warned about Ben. He knew that Ben saw things an inexperienced paramedic didn't. He'd been warned and now a slight fear was pressing on his temples. He could feel the thud of his pulse thumping. He lit another cigarette. *Would they know she'd died earlier?*

Sweat was running down the back of his neck, cold and sticky like a melting ice block. He jumped at the sound of Tom's voice, loud and echoing in the silence of the house.

'I am sorry. We couldn't save her.' Tom walked into the kitchen as he spoke. He held his hand up as a signal to be careful. He inclined his head towards the bedroom and put his fingers to his lips.

Rob slumped down on his chair still in his pyjamas and dressing gown. He covered his eyes. Tom, put a friendly hand on his shoulder. Squeezed it ever so slightly as Rob made a move to get up and go back to the bedroom.

'Let me make you a cup of tea. It's better to stay here in the kitchen. It can't be easy for you to sit near her body. Ben will cover her up and attend to the details. You just stay here with me while he clears the room,' Tom said.

Rob sighed, struggling to play the role of grieving partner. He muttered to Tom, 'the doctor needs to sign this off quickly and not send her to autopsy. They should do that. She'd been to see her doctor just this week. He knows she hasn't been well'.

Tom nodded thoughtfully, 'I'll see if I can manage that. But it'll be Ben's call as senior paramedic.'

'Undermine him then you fool,' Tom was surprised at the venom in Rob's voice.

They were sipping their tea, each with their own thoughts when the sun started to filter though the curtains. The angle of the sun's rays, still low in the sky hit Brigit's picture through the doorway radiating false warmth throughout the house. They were silent as they waited for Ben to finish.

Tom's thoughts were rushing like a tornado, swirling around. Ben may be treating him like a rank novice, but Tom knew much more about the job of an ambulance officer than he let on. He also knew much more about the business of murder. He had spent an interesting time in Auckland before moving to Invercargill. He had changed his name and invented an ex-wife in an attempt to remain unknown. This was the start of a new chapter. He couldn't stop a smile appearing as he looked out of the window, watching the dawn appear.

Ben appeared silently in the doorway, watching them with a heavy frown on his face, casting an even deeper chill to the already cold room. Tom had his hands in his pockets taking no notice of the man beside him. They were separated by distance and thought. *Why didn't they put a heater on? Why isn't Tom taking care of this man? Are they deliberately aloof with each other? Where's the care for a bereaved man, Tom?* It was as if a swirling mist had seeped into the kitchen with menace and fear despite the emerging sun, its nascent rays flickering gently. Ben shivered, his regulation gear no match for the stygian gloom that now seemed to penetrate the house.

'I've called the police,' he said eventually as he watched Rob shrewdly.

Rob reacted instinctively getting to his feet in alarm, spilling his tea down his dressing gown.

'Damn it. Look what you've made me do, creeping up on me

like that.'

'Don't lose it,' Tom muttered as he put a restraining hand on his arm.

Rob looked at Ben.

'Why? She only saw the doctor last week and he saw how sick she was. No need for the police because that's how she's been for ages. Our doctor will know that. Wait for him. He'll tell you. That's why we don't need the police. You only need them if somebody's not seen their doctor for ages. Brigit's there getting checked up all the time because she's so sick.'

Rob was aware he was sounding desperate, babbling like a fool. He gulped and continued more reasonably.

'That's why we don't need to involve the police. She was always expected to die soon. Her doctor warned me she could go at any time.' Rob slipped right back to the grieving partner as easily as a snake moved through the grass.

'I don't want this hanging over me. She wanted a quick funeral, no fuss or bother. We'd talked to her doctor about it. He'll know there's nothing unusual about her dying.' Rob sat, head in hands sniffing. 'There's really no need, is there? After all, she simply died of an asthma attack. She had them all the time especially on cold nights.' Rob made a show of wiping off the spilt tea from his dressing gown as he spoke.

'It's a requirement in law to call the police for unexpected deaths.' Ben said quietly.

Rob sank back down into the chair, hands over his face, a picture of despair.

'But this wasn't really unexpected. She often had asthma attacks in the night. You all know that because I've called you lot before and you've got her to the hospital in time. And this time you're too late and she's dead. It's all your fault for not getting here quickly enough,' he whined.

'The police will need to know.' Ben explained patiently. He had remained by the door as if unwilling to enter the room where the chill seemed deeper than the temperature outside. 'Her death will be classified as 'unexpected'. Also, we need to call for a doctor to issue a death certificate who will confirm time of death.

Then the doctor will decide whether to call for an autopsy and advise the coroner. But these days that's pretty standard.' He looked for a change in Rob's demeanour when he mentioned time of death. He wanted to see any reaction to satisfy his suspicions. He hid a smile when Rob jumped back up again, alarm clearly showing on his face. From the corner of his eye he saw Tom move quickly over and put a steading hand on his arm.

'Autopsy?' Rob protested. 'Brigit never wanted to be cut up. She wouldn't like that. We talked about it. Catholics don't like the body desecrated. I don't think I can agree to that.'

'It's the law Mr. Bennet. And an autopsy always gives relatives peace of mind that they did all they could. Although you could protest, you would have to do so in court. They might wonder then if there is something you want to cover up. Is there?' The question was posed seemingly innocently. Ben noticed the look of amazement in Tom's face and that he coughed quickly putting his hand over his mouth to cover his confusion. Tom put a hand on Rob's shoulder again as he tried to warn him to be careful.

'Was she religious?' asked Tom. 'The courts may listen to that argument, but it is unlikely.' Tom, the consummate character actor, was playing his part in the coverup of this murder, and trying to move Ben's scrutiny away.

'Catholic.' Rob muttered into his hands. 'What do I need to do? While we wait for the police that is.' *Hope it's an inexperienced young copper this early in the morning. Perhaps one I've already bribed. Maybe that Brendon fella.* He began picking at a stray thread on his dressing gown as he worried.

'Nothing Mr Bennet. We'll stay with you until the police arrive. Don't be afraid that we'll leave you alone. Is there anybody we can ring for you?'asked Tom. Rob looked up at his solicitous tone and smiled gratefully.

'No. I'll ring my daughter. She'll come. But she will have to arrange care for her kids.' He rang Topaz.

'Brigit's dead. Can you come over? The St. John's people haven't been able to save her and they've called the police.'

Ben looked on, his mind clicking furiously as he wondered what the real story was here. There was no apparent sign of grief.

Rob's call was curt almost to the point of rudeness. Rob was still as he listened, turning away from the paramedics so they couldn't see the expression of anger on his face. He controlled the tone of his voice.

'When can you get here?' he whispered. 'And Topaz, make sure that the grandkids have someone to look after them before you come. I'll be ok because the police are still to arrive, and the doctor. And then there's the undertaker.' He listened until he delivered an abrupt 'goodbye then.'

He stood up and stretched. 'I need a leak,' he said plaintively and wandered into the bathroom. He checked his watch. Exhaustion swept over him. Exhaustion and fear mixed with a deadly chill. He couldn't help the shiver as it ran down his body. His hand shook as he thought about Brigit's last desperate plea. He pictured her face as he stood there. He was surprised that he felt of sense of remorse worming its way into his consciousness. He remembered the desperation, the whiteness of her face, the wide-open eyes, the clutching outstretched hands as she cried to him for help.

He ran his hand through his thinning blond hair and turned his mind to his new love. The past is done. The plan successful. Onward. The beautiful and ever dutiful Topaz. God, he couldn't get enough of her body. He needed her now, to have her arms wrapped around him, seeing to his needs.

His smile soon turned to a frown as he remembered their telephone conversation, her comment, and the shock in her voice. Her disbelief at what he'd done. His fists tightened.

CHAPTER FOUR

'Would you like some time alone with your partner Mr. Bennet? We can stay in the kitchen so you can be alone with her.' Ben was solicitous while Tom just stood there silent, the perpetual glower on his face.

'Ok. I'll do that. It'll be a chance to remember all the good times we had together.' He smiled faintly as he said it. Ben and Tom watched the swagger.

And so here he was sitting with his memories in the cold silent grey early morning. His body was present, as he hunched over, arms resting on his knees, hands together, thumbs twisting around each other, as he looked at Brigit lying small and cold and still in the filtered dawn light. His mind was elsewhere, and his face was empty of any empathy or compassion. He didn't feel guilt anymore. His feelings for others and the effects of his actions on him had once caused sleepless nights, but no longer. Guilt he'd learned was a wasted emotion causing too many sleepless nights, and he liked his bed for sex, planning and sleep, in that order.

He remembered how he came to be here, sitting in this cold room. He even started to smile slightly. In the silence of the room he settled into the memories. The two of them had had such fun together when he first arrived, suitcase in hand in answer to her advertisement for a boarder. He pulled the blanket tighter around him. He'd hoped they'd become a couple one day. She'd enjoyed his company so much, laughed at his jokes and welcomed his help. That all changed when he first bought Simon home to meet her. She'd rejected him, and their attempts to use her place to deal drugs. The happy friendship and seduction stopped. The angry and noisy conversation between them along with Simon's overbearing and threatening presence changed the happy camaraderie into a crackling fiery tension.

Well, I'd changed by then anyway. That's why I started feeling my way further afield to greater delights. It's what drugs do to you. New friends. New loves. New opportunities. Perhaps if I hadn't been so desperate to get Simon on board, we might have worked things out. But no, Simon never misses an opportunity and the silly prick had scared her.

Now he was sitting in her domain, the place she'd called her sanctuary. The place he had never been invited into, unless he was called to help. Her bedroom. He'd wanted to come in often enough when he was feeling horny, but she'd always rebuffed him. *Silly old bitch. If you'd allowed me to do you, you might still be alive.*

After Rob left the kitchen, Tom exploded. 'What the fuck are you thinking of Ben? There's no need for the police here. A simple case of an asthma attack leading to death.'

Ben turned angrily to Tom, face tight and confused.

'You know the law Tom. Besides something doesn't seem right. She's too cold. The house is too cold. It doesn't add up.'

'You think you know everything Mr. Smart Arse. Trying to be all things.' Tom turned his back and gazed out the window. Ben felt his heart drop. *Tom is even stranger than usual. What's going on here?*

Rob was barely aware of the argument, his mind recalling everything past. He heard Tom's voice as a faint irritant and shrugged. *Let him deal with Ben. I've got enough to worry about now.*

Invercargill was to have been a new beginning for Rob. He'd

first moved to Bluff, the home of his wife Blanche. His face curled into a sneer. Bloody little Blanche. He was almost settled in that small coastal village on the edges of Foveaux Strait, until she booted him out. He'd almost set up a deal which would've been the making of him, and he could have quit her anyway. Her father disliked him and refused to have him on his fishing boats. He couldn't get around old man Hunter at all. Couldn't even get work from him. He remembered vividly the conversation he'd overheard. The conversation which had turned his face forever away from Blanche and Old Man Hunter.

'No Blanche,' Hunter had shouted. 'He's got no history with boats; no experience fishing and he would be a liability for the rest of the crew. Besides he's a sleazy bastard and I don't understand why you ever hooked up with such a criminal. He's a jailbird and a bloody nark. He only came down here because no one wanted him in Auckland. I don't want him around.'

He and Blanche had the mother of all rows when her dad had announced he had to go. That was when Rob discovered that his wife was a fair-weather wife only, and his anger soon changed to greed when the old man bribed him to leave his daughter and move away. Rob did, with land in his name that he could sell, and a future planned in drug dealing. He might not have the ear of the old man anymore, but he did own the first mate.

He felt that old anger at rejection sweeping over him again. He scowled. Once handsome, his face was now damaged by drugs, drink, and prison, a face now turned into a gargoyle as he remembered how she'd kicked him out the minute he had to rely on the benefit, and the odd theft, to keep them in any style at all.

'You can't chuck me out now that I'm on the bones of my arse,' Rob had shouted. 'You wanted to be around for all the good stuff though, didn't you? Even when I risked everything and ended up going to jail for you. Where the fuck will I go with no home.'

'I'm so over you Rob. Life's just too much trouble with you. I never know where you are, what you're doing or if you'll be in jail tomorrow.' Blanche snorted at Rob's pitiful 'no Amanda' comment. 'You never wanted Amanda around anyway. You always dismissed her because she was a girl and no use to you.'

'Always bought you expensive shoes and perfume though, didn't I?'

'Yep. Perfume for sure when you could nick it. You never actually bought it though, did you? It was always second hand. Stolen from the latest poor sucker whose home you and your thugs raided.'

Blanche stood tall, facing him off. 'You know when we came down here, when you got out of jail, you promised to go straight.'

'And I did.'

'Yes, but then you slipped back to your old ways again. Didn't you? Met some new friends. And it went all downhill again.'

He'd stared balefully at her knowing she was right.

'You're a chameleon Rob. You change like the wind to blend in with whoever you're with. I'm tired of it. Tired of trying to keep up with your ever changing moods. I'm tired of wondering if you're going to be home tonight, or whether you've been nicked, or if you're with her. You flick the switch on and off at will and I'm tired of it. I want rid of you.'

'I can change again. Get rid of Simon and Nigel. We can be a family again. You know I need you. Need a family.' He sounded whining, grovelling, and he hated himself, and her, for it.

'You need a family for cover. Maybe sex. That's all. I know all about your affair. You get your sex elsewhere anyway, so you don't even need me for that anymore. And you have no references, so you can't get a job, so you just need to bugger off, Rob and leave us to get on with our lives.' She turned her back, rigid as she fought back her tears of anger.

So, he'd left and found himself on the street with precious little hope for the future.

He pulled himself up with a start as the noises of the house broke into his memories., Tom and Ben shouting in the kitchen. Louder this time. The longer he sat there, the bigger his sense of entitlement became as he looked around Brigit's gracious bedroom. He'd always found it feminine, warming and welcoming the way she'd arranged the pictures and ornaments. He eyed Brigit, moved closer to her and he pulled the sheet off her face as he whispered to her.

'I was grateful to you initially though. You got me out of a tight spot. And we could have been a great pair. But you rejected me, and I turned against you. You didn't know that did you? I covered my feelings well. I was glad you got MS and got so sick. Meant you couldn't check up on me. The opportunity didn't take too long for me to get even. No-one ever rejects me you bitch, and that Blanche is soon going to find that out as well.'

Five years ago, he'd found hope in Brigit's little advertisement for a boarder. He saw it in a nearby grocery shop and set out to charm her. 'Boarder wanted. References required. Preference for a professional woman.' So, he'd phoned her.

Their first meeting went well. Brigit was cautious of a male boarder, she usually had women. She was a single professional woman and she felt safer that way, even though she was well used to living and travelling alone. She had recently been diagnosed with Multiple Sclerosis and knew that she would become increasingly frail. She was won over by his easy manner and claims he was a builder. His references looked good and his work with the Beneficiaries Union was a good sign. Her Catholic upbringing and inherent Christian kindness imbued in her throughout her childhood, worked well to his advantage and eventually led to her death

He thought about that shared lunch together, and the laughs they had as he described his carefully sanitised life. After a few wines she decided. *Maybe a man would be better in the future.*

He arrived later that day with his suitcase, and a bottle of bubbles.

'Thought we should drink to a blossoming friendship.'

'That's nice, Thoughtful. Thank you.'

His seduction of her was so subtle that she was barely aware of it or his increasing use of her home as a base for his new business. Her house rang out with the sounds of activity, hammering, new fences, another greenhouse, painting the bedrooms. He painted Brigit's a soft apricot and his bedroom a steely blue, a colour which suited his nature. He furnished it, moved a desk in and rearranged the house as he gradually took over. His bedroom also became his office and the new locks on the door caused an argument with his landlady.

'This is my house Rob. You can't just lock me out of part of it.'

'I pay for this room. It's my place and my business so keep out.' Brigit's reaction to his terse reply was curiosity rather than anger. Her anger came later when she realised what his business was. Ever short of money for his lifestyle, Rob reverted to what he knew best. Drugs. The dealing and selling of them. *Good job she didn't know at first. Too stupid to even suspect where her rent money came from.*

He'd seized the opportunity as the debilitating effects of MS on her mind and body became more and more apparent. She became more and more dependent on him and her ability to move about the house became more limited. He used the gradual deterioration to spread out as she retreated, and he started to plot. He knew how to play the long game. He'd long since stopped enjoying her company, and she became confined to this room. He looked around again. How he loved the sense of peace it gave him. This beautiful room with the large windows giving spectacular views of the garden. Her domain, and it left the rest of the house for him, his business, and his friends as Brigit became isolated into her own world. Rob found it easy to stage all the accidents. But they proved to take too long. She always recovered.

He'd been icily calm as he waited earlier that morning as he watched her die. He'd plotted as he waited. I need to make sure the doctor knows to just sign the death off as natural.

'You had it coming bitch,' he had said aloud, leaning closer as he stroked her face, finger tickling over her cold skin. 'Thought you could kick me out, did you? Not when I had my eyes on this house. No-way would you get to do that.' He pinched her hard before he moved away. *I'll need to paint it quickly, get rid of anything to do with her.* He drew back away from her and turned his back as he watched the world come to life out of the window.

The home was grand. Grander than he'd ever lived in before. He loved the large rooms and the sense of privacy in this elegant suburb. *And it's all mine now, mortgage free and big enough to expand the business.* And then that damned sister had appeared intent on getting Brigit to sell and move north.

'I have to move Rob,' she'd said. 'The house is too cold. Invercargill is too cold, and my lungs just can't cope. I need the warmth.'

'But what about me? What about my plans? My life down here? Doesn't that mean anything to you?'

'I'm sorry Rob but you'll have to find another place to live.' Brigit had been adamant. 'Georgia is coming next week to help me prepare the house for the market. You'll have to be gone before it's listed.'

It was the anticipated arrival of her sister which had moved his deadly plans forward. Once Brigit was dead he would claim the house. His business would continue without any worries that she'd find out.

'The house is due to me', he'd whispered as he moved back towards her. Wrapped in his blanket, eyes closed the sounds of the dawn and subdued voices of the two ambulance officers filtering into his awareness. It wasn't long before his reminiscences were interrupted.

CHAPTER FIVE

Topaz felt the early morning chill deepen, worsened by the sweat prickling her forehead like shards of ice. Time seemed to slow down as she stared at the phone. She felt the thumping of her heart, so loud and fast she feared she would faint. Her breath sounded as if she had run a marathon. She could barely get the words out, the flowers of her bedside table almost invisible to her wide opened eyes. Their beauty lost to her blank gaze. Their fragrance now of death.

Rob's voice whispered in her ear. 'Get over here now.'

'What the fuck are you talking about?' Topaz heard her voice at a distance. Her breath shuddered as she listened, her hand turning white around the phone. 'You didn't kill her? Tell me you haven't. Please tell me you haven't.' Blankets now strewn across the floor, and her long legs flailing as she tumbled out of bed. She slid to the floor, phone falling from her hand, tears now running down her face.

Forgotten were the good times, the unrestrained parties she'd enjoyed, wine running free. The heady throb of music blaring as she threw off the shackles of her childhood, shaking her long black hair free, tossing it wildly as she danced. Unconstrained she'd thrown herself into hedonism. She danced, rocked, and rolled the nights away with him, his hands grasping her long hair swinging around her shoulders. She'd egged him on with her wildness, loved how he'd preened when he was with her. It made her forget all those letters of rejection. It made her forget those nuns. Made her forget her parents and their disappointment in her.

That was a world away now, Rob's phone call a juddering stop which threatened to overwhelm her. Her mother's voice, and those of the nuns of her childhood came back to haunt her with their stories of hellfire, and damnation. Her mother reinforced them every time she saw her, and her words echoed in her mind as she gazed out of the window of her tiny flat. The scenes she usually enjoyed were gone now. She no longer saw the life beneath her, people scurrying like ants, cars whizzing by, or the night-time curb crawlers. She saw only greyness, walls creeping in on her, and in her mind heard the sound of police sirens.

She'd met Rob at the local bar when she was feeling low. She'd been gazing into a near empty glass feeling sorry for herself when he sat down alongside her.

'Looks like you need some cheering up. Would another drink help? My name's Rob.' He smiled at her. 'What's up? A beautiful woman like you shouldn't be drinking alone. What's your name?'

'I'm called Topaz and I'm drowning my sorrows because my CV was returned again,' she said. 'Employers always ask for a photo and when they see my brown skin I'm always rejected.'

'Oh, I know all about rejection,' Rob smiled at her as he continued. 'My wife's a bit of a snob and I get rejected all the time. Her father doesn't like me, so I'm not introduced to the family friends. I've got a daughter who doesn't want anything to do with me either. She's a mummy's girl. They're all down in Bluff and I'm here on my own.'

She saw a good-looking man, slightly older than her and thought it wouldn't hurt to just talk to a stranger who expressed a kindly benign interest in her.

'Topaz is an unusual name.'

'A made-up name from my modelling agent. I was wearing a

Topaz ring when I first modeled for her.'

'I like it though. It suits you. There's almost a flash of green in your brown eyes, A bit like a Topaz.'

His eyes slid over he and she sensed his admiration. Surprisingly, she found a need for such open lustful admiration. His mouth was parted, moist, eyes glittering in anticipation as he poured her glass after glass of champagne. She was warm and glowing, her face flushed, and she responded. Stretching like a cat she leaned back against the bar, legs crossed, and brushed her hair out of her eyes, thrusting her chest out as she did so. His eyes were fixed on her as he regaled her with his stories, and she sat back in the bar listening as he entertained her with his stories of adventure and fun.

An easy mark. Rob was controlled as he held her tight against him as he drove her home and tumbled her into bed. When she woke in the morning, he was sitting beside her, cup of coffee in his hand looking down at her, a quizzical expression crinkling his eyes.

'Good morning my beauty,' he'd said as he put down his cup and moved quickly to silence the questions on her face and the realization of what had happened. Forestalling her embarrassment and her attempts to get up, he lay down on the rumpled sheets and covered her mouth with his. His touching of her that morning when he saw the confusion on her face was gentle, seductive, and considerate, and she felt alive again. She didn't realise how much she missed the touch of a man, the caressing of hands. Her body had responded and arched towards him in pleasure. The early days of their relationship were a joyful reprieve from her loneliness.

Now on this cold morning she stood in the bathroom, hardly aware how she'd got there. There was a woman in the mirror looking back at her. One with wide dark eyes in a ghostlike face, mascara ruined by rivers of black down her cheeks. How had this happened. *How did I come to be here involved with this man, this stranger, this chameleon who'd turned so quickly from loving to control?* Her face in the mirror looked back at her silently. The mirror had no answer. She was on her own. And her mother's words came back to her.

'You'll be dammed for your evil ways,' her mother had shouted.

'Just leave him,' her dad had pleaded.

'I can't. He'll kill me,' she'd sobbed. 'I've tried before, but he's always dragged me back.'

'Well you obviously didn't try hard enough,' her mother had said, stone faced.

'You don't understand. I need your help and support to leave him.'

'No. You got yourself in this mess get yourself out of it. You are a shame to us, a failure.' Her mother was unyielding.

The river of tears continued to flow, and she made no attempt to stop them. She had crossed an invisible line. from one world to another, that had no exit or return. It was a reverse metamorphosis from butterfly to grub. And that grub wriggled its way from her dislike of him, to a hatred. She could no longer just brush off his domination of her, or the lechery of his friends or his laughter at her distress and his refusal to help brush away Simon's groping hands.

Hunched over the bathroom sink she asked the shadow looking at her. 'Why was I unable to escape?' She wiped her face, dried her tears as she thought about her life. 'Because I have nowhere to go, and my parents have wiped their conservative hands of me.'

Topaz could see no way out. *I have to leave. I have to get out for my sanity and safety. I should run. Just run.* She steadied her breath and closed her eyes. *Be strong. Be calm. You can get through this.* She tried to smooth the deep worry lines from her forehead as she put on her makeup, dressed carefully and, with a final sigh looked around her neat and tidy flat and walked out the door, back stiffened, like a soldier ready to face the enemy.

She wore flat shoes and jeans in case she needed to run. It's what she did these days.

CHAPTER SIX

Still in his PJs, and dressing gown Rob slumped in the chair, eyes half closed, his breath floating on the air like little puffs of white candy floss. He sensed Ben and Tom back in the room with him, as they moved lightly around. Legs stretched out in front of him, he listened to the sound of the police arriving, suddenly aware by the look on Ben's face that his incessant sniffing irritated. He suppressed his smile.

'Shall I fetch some tissues for you?'

The mask on Rob's face slipped slightly, the sneer about to erupt from his mouth when he controlled himself.

'Nah.' He fished in his pockets for another cigarette, lit up again, inhaled deeply, relishing the aromatic taste of tobacco on his tongue. His senses became alive, a tingling to his fingertips, the stupor dissipating. The shot of nicotine was like caffeine to him. A drug which his body craved to feel alive. He wiped his face with his handkerchief and inhaled deeply and sighed.

The medics eyed each other. Ben shrugged at Tom, eyebrows questioning as he observed Rob.

Tom wandered over, squeezed Rob's shoulder. 'OK mate?'

Rob sniffed and nodded, looked at Ben.

'When can I move her? When will the undertakers come and

take her away? I don't like looking at her.'

'We'll have to wait for the police to come.'

'I'm getting cold. And I can't get dressed with you lot in here.'

Tom turned to Ben to find him frowning.

'What are you thinking Ben?' Tom probed.

Ben hesitated, opened his mouth, but the sharp rap, the door opening, and the arrival of the police stopped his response. He turned in surprise as his friend DI Craig Arnold walked into the room, looking disheveled as if he'd just tumbled out of bed. He nodded at Ben and Tom, turned, hands shoved in pockets and waited for Rob's reaction. He noticed Rob's eyes widen, the scowl deepen, and his lips being licked. He opened his mouth in surprise as if about to ask a question.

'Good morning everyone. For those of you who don't know me, I'm Detective Inspector Craig Arnold and this is Senior Sergeant Philip Adams.' He turned and indicated at his colleague. 'We're here answering the 111 call from earlier this morning.'

Craig's casual greeting was a surprise to Ben who turned to see SS Philip Adams lounging against the door frame, watching and listening like a predatory bird, observing the looks of amazement on both Ben's and Rob's faces.

'In explanation to your unasked question Rob, we have recently set up a new unit devoted to gangs and the supply of drugs creeping into Invercargill. Your name is on the list of suspects which indicates a call to a senior policeman.'

Craig never discussed his work, so this piece of information was news to Ben. Although he knew nothing about Rob's past, Ben felt that maybe his disquiet at the scene had some basis after all. Tom looked stricken.

'Mr Bennet has just lost his fiancé, Inspector. He's in shock and that statement and your aggression cannot help. Please respect his loss.' Tom said pompously.

'Detective Inspector if you please.' Craig said.

Tom puffed himself up. Ben hastily pushed him by the shoulder towards the door.

'We'll be off now Mr. Bennet. You take care of yourself and give yourself time to grieve.' Tom shook Rob's hand.

Ben did not say a word, simply turned and picked up his bag. Tom looked at him questioningly as he strode out the door without a sound. There was none of Ben's usual gentle farewells to the families he'd attended.

Tom whispered to Rob, 'be careful,' and rushed to catch up, worried by Ben and Craig by the door.

'We need to talk. Usual place?' said Ben. Only Craig heard him, and he walked slowly and thoughtfully back into the bedroom.

'Something's worrying Ben,' he muttered to Philip as he passed by.

Rob stifled his beating heart. Took deep breaths as he turned to look at the policemen standing there. *I can still pull this off. Nothing to see here. But holy hell they've sent the double A team.* He'd made himself familiar with the staff at the Invercargill CID. He'd got to know who was who, whom to watch for and whom to work with. Arnold and Adams had proved to be two coppers he couldn't work with. But there was nothing to be seen or found here. Everything looked normal. Just two sad middle-aged people in a messy house. Nothing more normal than that, except one was now dead.

'Let's go into the kitchen where we can talk more comfortably Rob.' Craig said, standing aside and ushering him through the door.

'Fiancé, Rob? When did that happen? Tell us.' Phillip lounged by the doorway.

'Never mind that just now. What exactly happened? Step by step please.' Craig was straight on point.

'Can't you see I'm in shock? This was nothing to do with me. She had an asthma attack and I couldn't help her.' Rob felt an icy prickling on his forehead as he flopped down, elbows on the table, defiance on his face.

'Why not? You've never had a problem getting help before. What was different this time?' Craig joined him at the table while Phillip remained propping up the door.

'Couldn't get to her in time. I was having a slash. And I didn't have my hearing aids in so I couldn't hear her at first.'

Rob's answer are short, sharp, defiant and irritated. Philip noticed a bead of sweat appearing on Rob's forehead. *Is he getting rattled?* Rob got up, paced back and forth and, as if in distress, he brought a sob to his throat. The detectives just watched him.

'Why so agitated Rob?' asked Craig, watching the movements become rapid and jerky as his hands went up and down like a puppet as he puffed furiously. It was almost like a scene in a Charlie Chaplin film. The black, grey, and white of the early dawn, the grimness of the unkempt setting, the main actor pacing back and forth smoking furiously and, on the side, two unpersuaded (unbelieving) cops observing, questioning. Except that this was no laughing matter.

'Why are you giving me such a hard time?' Rob whined. 'Her asthma's been getting worse over the years and she's become very unsteady on her feet, what with her MS and all, having a man about the house has been good for her.' He sighed unaware of the exasperated looks between the two policemen.

'We're just asking routine questions Rob. What really happened?' Craig didn't sound as if he was losing patience, but he was. He was as disbelieving of Rob's muddled account of the events that night as he was of the story of love and marriage.

'I've told you already. Why do you keep harping on? You're just like her with her endless questions. Her wheezing and coughing woke me, and I got up to see if I could help.'

'You said earlier you were in the bathroom.'

'Yes, I was. At my age you need to go urgently. I left the door open so I could hear her if necessary. She was coughing something dreadful. Much worse than I'd ever heard before. I heard her trying to get up and then there was a crash as she tipped over the bedside table. Her inhalers and other stuff went scattering everywhere. By the time I'd finished and rushed in she was lying across the bed. I tried to move her, but she was too heavy for me and I couldn't do mouth to mouth easily.' He paused for breath, shuffled in his pocket for the inevitable fags.

'You told the telephone operator she was all curled up and you couldn't help her.' Philip continued while Craig went prowling back into Brigit's bedroom.

'Yes, she was but I managed to straighten her out a bit. Then I had to open the door for the ambulance lads and that's when she stopped breathing. I wasn't even there for her when she died.' Rob choked, head down in his hands. He didn't notice the raised eyebrows and Craig leaving

Craig soft footed, entered Brigit's room. He'd learned how to remain aloof; of being part of the scene while not appearing to be in it, or even aware of what was being said. But his mind was buzzing, and his eyes kept looking. Seeing the chaos of the bedroom in what was once a gracious room. The mess of the bed. The clothes scattered around. The smell of mould in the damp room. The aroma of tobacco. The ash scattered on the floor by the solitary chair. The feeling of an unkempt, unloved house. He noticed the open windows, felt the southerly, wrapping its arms around him. He shivered into himself, hands shoved in his pockets as if to keep the tentacles of cold air out.

Rob was relieved to hear the doctor arrive and jumped up sidestepping Philip in his rush to the door. He stopped in surprise to see it was a young woman.

'Where's our usual doctor? Who are you? I want our usual doc. He knows us. You don't'. He stood there in the middle of the door blocking her entrance.

"Out of the way Rob.' Philip came forward. 'Good morning. I'm Senior Sergeant Adams. The victim is through there.' He pointed to the doorway.

Rob shuffled and jostled, 'is there anything I can do to help?'

'No. I'll do this. Please leave me to do my job.'

'But surely you need me to tell you what happened? To be with my darling when you examine her. Don't you need my permission?' Rob managed to keep the alarm out of his voice, and instead sounded petulant.

She looked up at him and said, 'no I don't. And I prefer to do my job on my own.' Formal and aloof.

Of the two policemen, Philip was the precise one. He was a stickler for systems and procedures. Nothing got past his fine eye for detail. Tall and ascetic he could have easily passed for a monk of any of the Benedictine orders. Except he was anything but. He was blessed with a fine sense of humour, pithy comments associated with a loud raucous laugh. He enjoyed his life, his wine, his wife, and his daughter. Those who knew him well weren't worried at his apparent aloofness. But equally, his cool thin face with an aquiline nose and high cheekbones seemed to scare people he questioned. They usually quailed under his austere gaze.

Rob found himself falter when Philip said, 'we'll wait in the kitchen Rob. DI Arnold can assist the doctor if necessary. Come now.' The firm grip of his hand on Rob's elbow was enough, and they moved back, away from the action. Rob looked over his shoulder, back towards the tableau in Brigit's bedroom.

Doctor Chloe Cook nodded to Craig as she went over to the body. She noticed the inhalers on the bedside table.

'Is this all of her medication? Have you moved anything?'

She turned to look at Craig for an answer, paused and then looked again at the body. Chloe Cook recognised her.

'Are you suspicious?' Her question, out of the blue, was asked conversationally and surprised Craig. Chloe noted the widening of his eyes, the raising of his eyebrows and added quickly, 'more for background information than an implication of anything untoward.' She was too soon into her examination to make any assumptions.

'I haven't moved anything and yes, I am suspicious. We have close contact with the women's refuge. They always advise us about women at risk. This is Brigit Chappel and she's been a regular at the refuge, but she always come back here.' Chloe nodded to herself when she heard the name. 'She argued that it was her home and was worried that she'd lose it if she left. So, when her name came up on the 111 dispatches, along with the red flag against his name, Philip and I were called.' Craig continued.

'What's his story?'

'That her coughing woke him up, that he had to go to the bathroom first. He could hear her coughing and wheezing and said that she must have collapsed while he was still in there.

He says he tried to move her, but he couldn't manage mouth to mouth. He says he called the ambulance, and that she died when he let the paramedics in.

Craig didn't sound convinced. Chloe heard the doubt in his voice.

'But?' said Chloe.

'There are discrepancies with his story now, and the story he told the 111 operator. And I don't think the timeline works.'

'OK, I'll do what I can here.' Chloe turned back to Brigit's body.

'I know you'll make a note of everything. But I want to hear about anything that appears even slightly at odds with Rob's story. I'm treating this as unexplained and unexpected. Any problem with us photographing the scene while you're working on her?'

Chloe rested her bag next to Brigit's body. 'No that's fine,' she said as she crouched down and put her small hand gently against Brigit's pale waxen face. Craig looked on, not saying anything. *I wonder how Philip is getting on with Rob.*

As he watched her working, he tried to get a sense of what the scene was telling him. He let his mind wander, taking in everything. Even the most trivial observation could mean something important. It was cold. The windows were wide open. The table was upright with the lamp still standing on it, Brigit's latest book opened on it. He picked it up, 'The Readers of Broken Wheel Recommend.' *Strange title.* There were many books around. An eclectic mix of best seller thrillers, Nordic Noir, and some more literary ones he noted. *What's Jane Eyre doing amongst thrillers?* He remembered someone had said she was a teacher once. Perhaps it was Philip.

He started wondering aloud. 'How on earth did she get involved with someone like Rob?' He was aware that he was talking aloud but Chloe barely registered it. He needed to hear the sound of his voice. It helped him think. 'She either became too afraid to move, or too worn down to try to remove him.'

Chloe took her scalpel and with a deft nick of the skin pushed the thermometer it into Brigit's abdomen for a reading of liver temperature.

'When did he say this happened?' Chloe interrupted Craig's thought.

'Less than a couple of hours ago. We got here promptly after the paramedics called us in. That would have been around 5am. They'd been here 20 minutes or so by then.'

Chloe looked at the temperature reading, cocked her head and frowned.

'It doesn't gel.' Chloe had picked up the local lingo from her kids. 'The body temperature is far too low for that short amount of time and rigor mortis has started. She died much earlier than that. He's not telling the truth.'

'Hmmm. Noticed anything else?'

'Bruising, old and fresh. The autopsy will tell us more. On the face of it, it does seem like cause of death may well be an asthma attack, but because of her history I'm uneasy.'

'Will you arrange an autopsy and the removal of the body? What about the death certificate? Will you issue one?'

'I'll note that I was called 6.30am and that I certified her as dead at 7am. That her body temperature was 31degrees, and that rigor was on its way to be well established which would mean she died before 3am. That time doesn't fit with his story, does it?'

'No. We were called by the paramedics at 5am and they had been here about half an hour. The 111 call was lodged at 4.31am.'

'Well the process of rigor mortis starts between two and six hours after death. It starts with what is called 'primary flaccidity'. The body goes absolutely slack, and then the muscles start to stiffen beginning in the eyelids, neck, jaws, travelling downwards to the rest of the body. If you crouch down beside me you can see that the limbs are beginning to stiffen, especially the arms. With this amount of rigidity and coldness of the body there is no way she could have died only two or three hours ago.' Chloe was talking to herself almost as much as Craig.

'If you look at the colour of her skin you can see the darkness of the pooling of blood as it flows down towards the part of the body where she's lying, but it's only visible after two hours postmortem.. There's now quite a lot of liver mortis showing – much more than could be explained by a death only about two and a half hours ago. It has not yet reached maximum stage which occurs after eight hours. The room is cold which slows down rigor, but she's very, very, cold.'

'So, she's been dead longer than he claims?'

'Yes. In simple terms the body loses 1.5 degrees centigrade of heat every hour. So, in four hours her body temperature would be around 31 degrees and given the ambient temperature of the room, that is what I would expect.'

'What was that temperature again?'

'31 degrees.' Chloe looked at Craig frowning. She felt her professional integrity was now at stake, but she also knew that if this went to court her testimony would be critical.

'I'm confident she died much earlier than this man claims. Over four hours ago.' she said looking at him. She finished packing her bags and said, 'I'll note her death as unexplained and unexpected. That should alert the coroner. I'll request an urgent autopsy.'

He looked down at Brigit as he spoke. 'I can't arrest him yet, not without an autopsy or coroner's report. I'd like to get him down to the station for questioning, but I want him on his own just now without the assistance of that shyster lawyer Jack Olds. Olds is the reason Rob's stays out of jail. He's a crafty number, our Jack.'

'I can't prove this woman was murdered, but I can safely say this death is unexplained. Asthma medication is so effective these days you don't get many deaths. Get a forensics team in.' Chloe stood up to leave.

'Will do,' said Craig. He walked out with her, giving a cursory look at Rob, sitting in the kitchen, cup in hand while Philip looked stoically down at him, his nose wrinkling in distaste.

'Go have a shower and clean yourself up will you Rob. You smell,' said Philip.

'I'll do that when you're all gone. I don't want to shut myself away while you're all here fossicking around here. I need to keep an eye on things.'

As Craig saw Chloe out, the forensics team arrived. Knitted out in their white plastic overshoes and overalls, they hustled past him with their bags. They suited the mistiness of the morning as they moved with purpose towards the bedroom.

'Good morning team,' said Craig. He picked up Chloe's bag and like a butler to an aristocrat, he escorted her to the door. 'I'll just see the Chloe to her car, and I'll join you in a minute. Philip's still inside and he'll advise you of the situation.'

'Thanks Chloe,' Craig opened her car door. He watched her go, turned and frowned. He noticed a natty black BMW parked outside. *That wasn't there earlier.* He filed it away and returned inside to direct proceedings.

CHAPTER SEVEN

'Why now?' Topaz asked herself. 'Because she gave him notice to leave, and he's got nowhere else to go.'

Slowing driving round and round the block, knuckles white on the steering wheel, foot soft on the accelerator, her heart still thumping, she crept forward dreading the moment of arrival. *I'll just drive round and watch. I won't go in yet. See what's happening. There may be a way out.*

The sun rose pale on this dawn morning as she sat, engine idling, shivering from fear as much as the cold, her eyes on Brigit's house. It was a soft morning with the slowly dissipating mist gently swirling around the trees. The rising sun flickered through the dark clouds as if desperately seeking a pathway through them to lighten the day. She hated winter and it's short dark cold days. She wanted the spring, with buds bursting and daffodils smiling through the cold. She wanted the signs of life that spring bought. The soft green buds on sleeping trees and bushes that heralded the warming of the days. It not only lightened the days but also the spirits. And hers were now at an all-time low. She felt her chest heaving and her heart rate accelerating when she saw the bevy of cars outside the house. All was still in the dank gloom, the street illuminated by the slow blue and red strobe lights from the ambulance, police and hearse neatly parked across the road stopping any passing. *I'm an accessory to murder. Oh God, oh God. What will I do?*

She'd seen the two sides of Rob. The hedonism and fun alongside the temper and ruthlessness. She knew he cultivate people as easily as he culled them as soon as they crossed him. She remembered his sudden temper at any signs of weakness, and signs of dissent. How quickly it rose. He was as mercurial as a thermometer, would change from charming and companionable to vicious as quickly as a rat darting to safety. People vanished, done away with as easily as he'd got rid of Brigit. If she still had a church to go to, she would have flown there for sanctuary. But as it was, she had left the teachings of the church a long time ago.

She gasped when she saw the two paramedics leave in their crisp St John's uniforms. *What the fuck? Him? How?* Her breath stopped mid-gasp when she recognised Tom. *How had he ever become a paramedic? Didn't St John's do reference checks?* Unseen she watched mouth open, horror souring her taste buds as they loaded all the detritus of their attempts to save Brigit.

Ben noticed her car parked outside with its engine running. He saw the profile of a women with long hair before she ducked down. He frowned puzzled. What was that about? Why was someone watching the place this early in the morning? It was the partly opened window in her car that clicked in his brain. *That's what the problem was. The bloody windows in the house were wide open. But why? That's why it was so cold, and what was wrong. You wouldn't have that many windows open on a winter's night if you suffer from asthma.*

He braked and turned his head to look back. 'What?' said Tom.

'Nothing, I just thought I'd left something behind back at the house, but no it's there in the back.'

Topaz saw the brakes flash on, the ambulance pause and then drive off again. She let out a long breath, and unconsciously started chewing her carefully manicured nails. *The police are in there a long time. Why were the police still there if Rob had made this look like death by natural causes?*

She remained parked in her watching spot. Unnoticed by her, Ben had slowed the ambulance as he came to the corner, checking the car in the rear mirror. It didn't move. She didn't get out. *Strange.*

Topaz waited a beat, fingernails well mauled and ragged. *I'm out of here. I need time. Should I just cut and run? Not even front up to Rob but just disappear quietly and quickly to Dunedin.* Headlights off, she drove away, heading towards her thinking place. A spot by the river which no-one knew about. The place with the Kauri and Rimu where bird life sang troubles away accompanying the soft burble of the water. Once around the corner she turned the lights on, sped up and drove into the early dawn.

As he drove back to the ambulance base Ben thought about the car waiting outside. 'Did you notice that car parked there with a woman in it?' he asked Tom.

'No. Why?'

'It was fogged up, window slightly ajar and a woman sitting there watching the house.'

'What's up with you? You behaved very strangely inside. Called the police instead of just the funeral director. Warned me off saying anything and you were awfully terse with the deceased's partner. What's going on?'

'The scene jarred. It didn't fit with his story. Something was just a bit off and I couldn't put my finger on it.'

'And now you notice a random car in the street. I think you might be seeing problems where there aren't any.' Tom forced a laugh.

'Maybe, but I've just figured out what was has been bothering me. The windows were all open.'

'So what? What's significant about that?'

'It made the room cold and besides if you suffer from severe asthma as she did, then you wouldn't have windows open on a cold night. The room would be heated, and it wasn't. You'd be dressed warmly, and she wasn't. And finally, there were no signs that he'd done anything to help her. She was just lying there. Not covered. No sign of panicked activities even though he sounded panicked. No sign of any care or any attempt to cover her up and make her look decent. Nothing rang true.'

'Well I did notice the nosy neighbours peering out of their windows.' said Tom segueing into safer territory. 'They were looking out the windows and looked as if they had been there for a while. So perhaps there is more to that household than meets the eye. Maybe you should check it out with them. Maybe they keep an eye on what's going down in the street. Maybe they're part of Neighbourhood Watch?'

Ben brooded, lost in his own thoughts, not taking much notice of what his partner was up to. He didn't notice Tom's anxious side glances, the slight drumming of his fingers on the side of the ambulance door. The clenching and unclenching of his fist.

They remained silent until they returned to the station, logged their reports, and then left for the day. Off duty finally, after a troublesome night, Ben got in his car and considered his options: home to bed or return and observe the scene. *I'll never sleep. I'm going back. I need to see what that woman was up to. See if she's still there.*

CHAPTER EIGHT

Tom went straight home with an easy conscience. Had he been the lighthearted or singing type he would be singing now. *Gone without a hitch so far.* He needed to shower and rest before Rob called him to discuss the rest of the plan. First, they had to get through a police inquiry, a coroner's hearing and then deal with any fallout with Brigit's family. *Bloody nuisance, but it must be done so everything becomes legal.*

Fast action was needed to claim the house. Rob had to do that before Brigit's family arrived. He thought over the plan. Once entrenched and settled into the house, they could then start recruiting. He imagined the outbreak of gang warfare when he and Rob muscled in to take over the drug trade in the city. They had already arranged the source and systems, and he smiled at the thought of the upheaval it was going to cause. It'll keep the cops so busy they won't be able to see what's really going on. The trial run at Bluff had worked - identified some problems but now that was sorted with the old man bribed to participate. Now emboldened, they would start on the destruction of the other city gangs one at a time.

As he showered Tom, thought over the events so far, working just like clockwork and with Simon and Nigel under Rob's thumb the future was looking good. It was a bold, far reaching plan and was sure to have some casualties along the way.

His hand smoothed back his hair, ran down his naked warm body and he twisted and moved to admire himself. Those muscles glimmered in the steamy room as he flexed and preened. *We'll build a gym when we get the house. Then I won't have to share with the plebs.* He flexed and rippled his belly muscles. *I'm an Adonis.* He wiped the mirror, and watched his muscular body emerge out of the steam and felt the tingle of pride and admiration at the sight. He was Rob's successor, the brains, the beauty, the entrapper. Rob was grooming Simon to be the hard man. The enforcer. *And they don't even know I exist yet.* He smirked.

The other key element to the master plan was keeping his identity and past hidden from his workmates. He was safe now and his role in Rob's life remained unknown. Thoughts flittered through his head as he shaved. *What should they call themselves? Rob's Mob? No, it needed to be something that lasted after Rob's death, whenever that may happen to be. It couldn't be anything already taken down here or the name of any other New Zealand wide gang. Southern Slickers maybe? Invercargill Ignobles? Invercargill Invincibles? That's better. Invercargill Invincibles it'll be then. Must tell Rob.* He laughed out loud in his small empty home, patted aftershave down his smooth chiseled face.

He looked around his digs. *Hate it.* The plan he and Rob had hatched up was for him to live at Brigit's house with Rob. It couldn't happen soon enough. There was plenty of room down the back for the greenhouses they planned to build. No-one would ever think they were growing dope and not tomatoes. Not in this gentrified suburb. And he knew, because Rob had told him, that garden was productive with good soil. Well cared for by Brigit. *Just need to get through the next few days without anyone knowing.* Tom's eyes were empty, glazed, looking vacantly to the future, absent from the present, while Ben was feeling antsy, restless, stalking around, tidying up and unable to settle. *I need to check that house.* He arrived at Chelmsford Street, crawled around the corner, and parked. The smart car was gone. He noticed the neighbours at their window, sitting together, cups in hands peering out through the net curtains watching everything intently.

Tom was right. They are still there watching. I might just go and say hello. Wonder if they'll talk to me or if they consider that an ambulance officer shouldn't be poking his nose into police business. Give it a go.

He smiled wryly at his attempts at being a sleuth. What would Craig make of him overstepping the mark? But his curiosity had been piqued and throwing caution aside he sauntered quietly up to the neighbour's door and knocked. He heard the sound of shuffling feet.

'Hello?' A querulous, fearful answer greeted his knock as an elderly gentleman opened the door.

'Forgive me for intruding. My name is Ben McGregor and I'm an ambulance officer. I noticed you were watching the house next door when we were called earlier this morning and wondered if there was something worrying you?'

Stephen Tait looked at his wife Moira, then at Ben. 'We're the Taits. We've lived here forever and knew poor Brigit well. Always looked out for her, we did. Didn't we Moira? Took her cakes and stuff. Moira's so good at cakes and scones. She should have opened a wee shop. She'd have done good at that. We were awoken by the noise. All that coming and going of ambulances and the police. Poor Brigit. She's always had a terrible time since that man moved in. They often had such arguments. We've called the police before, but nothing has ever come of it.'

'Something's not right,' added Moira. 'Is she alright? Has he had a go at her again?'

Before Ben could answer Moira has started speaking again.

'I don't think the police will do anything though.' said Moira. 'They never have before when we have called them with all the comings and goings on in there.'

Stephen and Moira were on a roll. They told Ben that they had lived there all their married life. They'd always liked Brigit and had shared meals and gardening tips with her over the years. They'd helped each other in the garden and divided up their surplus vegetables between them.

'She was always better at gardening than us though, because she's was younger and fitter in the early days and would mulch with her compost.' Moira looked as if she'd chatter on until Stephen intervened.

'Think you better come inside rather than stand on the doorstep in the cold,' he said as he gently ushered his wife inside. Ben followed.

'It all changed when he arrived about five years ago. He took over her life,' Moira said.

'He didn't like her talking to the neighbours,' Stephen added, 'Almost kept her a prisoner, he did.'

'Yes,' Moira interrupted. 'She'd try and wave when she was outside but always sneaked a look to see if he was watching.'

'Never was though. He used to spend all his time in bed watching TV. All those awful reality shows and stuff. Just like Lord Muck he was.' Stephen said.

'We noticed when she had to go to the hospital after he'd had another go at her.' Moira was pensive. 'We worried about the changes. There were shady types visiting. We weren't allowed into her garden anymore. We used to share things from the garden but then the wheelbarrow disappeared.' She sighed. 'That was odd. Of course, he denied he took it.'

Stephen nodded, 'Brand new and expensive and we never saw it again.'

'Wheelbarrow?' Ben caught himself before he laughed. 'Why would anybody steal a wheelbarrow?'

'She didn't have one. Couldn't afford it. Saw him pushing it out to a van, we did. Tipped something heavy into the back of it.' Stephen turned to his wife. 'Middle of the night it was, wasn't it dear?'

Moira and Stephen went completely off topic and Moira told Ben about Brigit's wonderful garden. She was sipping tea, talking, waving her hands about almost in excitement as she readied the table. She was a whirling dervish compared to Stephen who just sat watching her, a companionable grin on his face at her antics.

'She had a real talent and could get anything to grow. She had wonderful roses. Her sister had an old rose nursery and she got a lot from up there. It was such a picture in the spring. A real chocolate box garden. It was the talk of the local gardening club and they often arranged trips to visit it. Brigit had been generous like that and had prepared wonderful produce like Kasundi and pickles and amazing blackcurrant jam.' She stopped for a breath before she continued.

'You know,' Moira bent forward and whispered, 'Her Kasundi chutney was named after her brother who died. He was a Buddhist and it was called after his Buddhist name. How lovely is that?' she sighed. 'It all stopped soon after HE got here.' She nodded in the direction of the house.

'We never knew what it was in our wheelbarrow or saw it again. We used to joke that it must have been a body.' Stephen carried on the conversation as if his wife had never interrupted.

'The police weren't interested anyway.'

'You know,' Stephen said conspiratorially. 'It happened just after there were reports of that woman gang member disappearing about three years ago. They never found her either. Perhaps I read too many crime books, but I did wonder. There were often dodgy looking people next door after he moved in.'

'You sure it wasn't just weeds?' asked Ben. 'You've told me about her great garden.'

'Phiff. You don't get rid of weeds in the middle of the night and she always composted anyway which is another reason she didn't have her own wheelbarrow. Besides weeds aren't heavy and he usually didn't do anything. Just sat and watched TV or entertained his friends. Street used to be cluttered with cars. So, it was very odd him wheeling it in the middle of the night.' Stephen paused for breath and his wife continued.

'You know, your other ambulance officer looked very like one of them. Funny that. The police weren't interested anyway. Thought Rob was a do-gooder as he worked in the beneficiaries' organisation, helping people get the right benefit and what's owed them.'

They are an odd couple and repeat themselves all the time.

Can't have much to do in life. Ben felt a bit sorry for them. Old now, and a bit frail but at least they were so used to each other they finished each other's sentences. *That at least is one of the more comforting things about growing old together.*

'We never saw it again.' Moira went back on topic.

'Or that van,' added Stephen.

They sat at the window watching, listening. It had been an exciting and curious night for them. Being the local busy bodies, they needed to know what was happening. They'd been here so long that they felt it was their right to know, as the guardians of the street and stalwarts of the local Neighbourhood Watch. They remained there, upright in their chairs, leaning forward towards the window, eyes straight ahead, barely looking at the fresh date scones as they moved slowly from plate to mouth.

Finally, Brigit's front door opened, and the police stepped outside. A few minutes later Brigit's body was wheeled out to the hearse. There was no sign of Rob. Moria flopped back, tears flowing down her wrinkled weather-beaten face. Stephen put his arms around her, his face tight as the gurney was wheeled to the waiting hearse.

'Bloody bastard,' he muttered. 'Always worried that he'd do something but maybe Brigit just died, natural like. She might have though Moira. It might have all been natural. She was poorly, you know.' He pattered her back.

'Maybe not,' sniffed Moria. 'If she had, why are the police there?'

'Perhaps we should go in and see how things are. Try and cheer up Rob until someone gets here. He's sure to have rung his mates or his girlfriend. Offer some tea or breakfast or something. What do you think Moira?'

'I Think we should wait a while. The police are still there aren't they? Didn't see them leave. Best wait till they've gone and Rob's alone. Maybe he'll talk to us then. Tell us what happened, and we can ask if he needs any help.' Moira voice quavered.

'These things seem to take time, don't they?' Stephen asked Ben as if he expected Ben to know all about what went on in a home after someone died.

'Sometimes they can.' Ben was non-committal as he sat still waiting to see if his suspicions would be validated. He barely heard Moira and Stephen anymore as he wondered at this unlikely couple who, even though they seemed to despise Rob Bennet, were prepared to go and help so they could get the gossip on what really happened. All for the sake of validating their lonely lives spent looking out the window.

Craig and Philip appeared at the front door, buttoning up their jackets against the cold. 'They're about to leave,' whispered Stephen as if the police would hear him. 'Not long now before we can go in.'

Ben looked in despair at these two nosy parkers intent on other people's business no matter the circumstances. *Don't think they've many friends they can gossip to.* He waited a beat before turning and carrying the tray of empty cups into the kitchen. When he returned, he simply said, 'I'll leave you two now. Thank you for the tea and scones. They were delicious on this cold morning.'

The odd couple turned back to the window and waited for their opportunity to be good neighbours.

CHAPTER NINE

'I need to be here for when my daughter arrives,' he said petulantly. 'Topaz will expect me to be here. You can take my statement here.'

'It won't take long. The forensics' team is here to let her in when she arrives.' Philip smiled at him.

'I need to be here and keep an eye on you all.' Rob said aggressively. Bullying was his default position. All through his life he'd found that people were scared of him. He glared at them. Their insouciance was annoying.

'It's better to take you away to get your statement written up, while the team's doing the forensic work here. It's easier for them when there's nobody hanging around. Don't want to create any friction for the family when they arrive,' said Craig.

'Nothing to worry about. Just routine,' added Phillip smoothly

'Routine. My arse. I've just lost my fiancé. You've whipped her away.' Rob was working himself up to a fine old tantrum. 'I haven't even had time to give instructions to the funeral director before they left.' he complained loudly.

'There'll be plenty of time for that. She'll be going to the hospital mortuary first. Then there'll be an autopsy, then a coroner's hearing. Besides, it will be Brigit's family liaising with the funeral directors not you.' Craig was standing aside watching this little byplay between Philip and Rob.

'I don't want an autopsy. That's unnecessary.' Rob protested loudly. 'Nothing to see.' *Except for the bruises.* 'Beside I'll need to tell them about her falls and the she always bruises when she falls. The MS you know. The pathologist will need to know that. What with her history and all.' *Easy to use MS as an excuse. No one could disprove it. The broken legs and wrists were easily explained away before.*

'You'll have no say in it. The coroner and the doctor will decide,' said Philip.

'We'll advise the family.' Craig said. 'So you don't need to bother them.'

'I'm her family. There's no one else.'

'Her sister and son Mr. Bennet. They've been to see us in the past when Brigit has ended up in hospital after her accidents. At least that's what you called them. Accidents. Like falling while carrying the washing. Falling from a trailer while moving rubbish.' Philip said needling him.

'That awful sister. She's always meddled in our business. Brigit never wanted to have anything to do with her. We disowned her. Brigit didn't have any children, so I don't know why you think she has a son. That's a lie. She'd would've told me. I'm all the real family she has. It's my job to arrange her funeral and deal with our things.'

'Why do you think she never mentioned her son, Dr Niall Smithson to you?' Craig spoke in his gruff drawl. Baiting. He knew Brigit never told Rob about Niall. It was the safest thing to do. She hadn't wanted Rob interfering with his life or threatening him in any way. Niall on the other hand knew all about Rob, who was sitting there, legs wide apart, eyes wide open in shock. He closed his mouth and clamped it shut. *I need to warn Tom. Always knew I could sort the sister, even if he pretended she didn't exist. But a son? Pity, I could've put the screws on him for drugs. Maybe could've got rid of her earlier. Too late now. I'll just have to deal with these cards. But he's a real joker in the pack all right.*

Philip, ever the man for details focused on Rob's statement, looked down his nose in distaste and interrupted Rob's thoughts.

'*Our* things? Really Rob. There's no, *our*. We know exactly your position in *her* house. She was explicit that there was no relationship with you and that you are merely a boarder.' Phillip was deliberately trying to provoke Rob. He knew he'd get a reaction if he referred to Rob as 'merely' anything.

The strategy of good cop/good cop was working. Rob was unsettled. The two policemen looked at each other. Their excessive politeness was designed to provoke Rob into making a mistake. Rob wouldn't know how to handle politeness and he may just slip up.

'You keep describing the deceased as your fiancé Rob. Why?' asked Philip.

'Well she was. We were going to be married soon.' Rob fussed, wondering where this was going.

'But you've still got a wife,' said Philip thoughtfully. 'You were never divorced. Which leaves me, as a police officer, wondering if you were contemplating bigamy, Rob?'

Craig stood silently, a slight smile on his face. Rob looked at him wondering what was coming next. Nothing. Craig remained inscrutable. He just stood, still as the Easter Island statues.

Philip continued the relentless questions, mildly delivered so softly Rob could barely hear them. 'So how have you supported her? Money from the ex's dad? Drugs? A little tidying up after him?'

Rob's life was like a tapestry with strands intertwining together. A bit of good, some bad, some caring, some brutal, a bit of love and a lot of hate, a mixed childhood, and a wandering adulthood, all woven together over the years. And now it was beginning to unravel.

'He gives me a bit as alimony to keep me away from Blanche and Amanda. Thinks I'm trouble. Wants to protect them from me. Little does he know about them two, silly old fart. Mother and daughter are as bad as he is, that old man of hers. That's what I used to help Brigit.'

'Never thought of Blanche's old man being generous Rob. Did you know that Philip?' asked Craig turning slightly. Philip shook his head, shrugged his shoulders, and raised his hands.

'Go have your shower and get dressed Rob,' said Craig impatiently. 'We need to clear the house to let the team get to work.'

'Not likely,' Rob snarled. 'You'll have to arrest me first and drag me down to the nick in my PJs. That'll be a good look for you wouldn't it.'

'We may yet do that,' said Craig mildly.

'Meanwhile, I am wondering, Rob,' said Philip, 'with the money you got from your father-in-law, why did you steal from Brigit's account? You might think about that on the way to the station.'

'Don't need to think. She said I could use it.' Rob looked at them defiantly, refusing to move, unwilling to leave them alone while he showered.

'No, she didn't, and she laid complaints about money disappearing from her account. We traced it to her card, but it seems she was always in hospital when the money disappeared,' said Philip.

'Good job you didn't know about her private escape fund, Rob. She set it up after you were taken in for questioning about those rapes you were accused of. You'd have emptied that as well. Her son and sister put money into it. The deal was you were never allowed to know about it. They knew you'd steal from it.'

Rob snorted at the mention of Niall and Georgia. 'I don't believe you. Brigit would never have made statements to the police. She hated you. Besides, I was always with her at night to help her. In case she stopped breathing and had to go hospital. So, I couldn't have done them anyway.'

'What makes you think they happened at night? Did we say anything about night?' Craig looked over at Philip. Again, the shrug.

'But you're right. They were night-time events, although I'm curious as to why you assumed they were.'

'All this is bollocks. A load of crap. You're just winding me up hoping I'll slip up and confess to something I didn't do. I'm not saying anything else until I get in touch with my lawyer.' Rob was now shouting at them.

'Why do you think you need a lawyer Rob? Done something you need his advice about? You think Old's going to protect you again?' asked Philip.

'Enough of all this. Let's get to the station.' Suddenly Craig was all business. 'We need to get your statement written up before you forget what happened here. And the team's here to work through this crime scene for evidence.'

'It isn't a crime scene and they'll find nothing.'

'Go and have a shower Rob. Can't have you down at the station looking like that.' Philip looked down his nose at Rob.

Rob glared while Philip indicated with an abrupt flip of his hand towards the bathroom. They waited to hear the sound of water.

'Let's have a look around while he's in the shower,' said Craig. 'There may be something he's missed that will shed some light on this.'

Philip went out the back. He was sniffing the air when he came back in. 'Harvest's been done I reckon.'

'But where's it stashed?' Craig stopped when Rob appeared.

'Quick shower.'

'Put on a coat Rob. It's cold outside,' said Philip.

The two policemen went out the door, stopped on the porch, turned back to look, and waited in the cold. To the puzzled Tait's next door, it seemed as if they waited for a long time but in reality it was mere minutes.

'What's happening? What does this mean? Are the police leaving?' asked Moria.

'No, they're just waiting. Is he being arrested?' said Stephen. 'Good job if he is.'

They watched until a freshly dressed, Rob finally appeared, wrapped up in a coat, wet hair combed down.

'Leave it unlocked Rob. Forensics are still in there,' said Philip.

He stared straight ahead, and with the police on either side of him, he walked down the path and stepped into the waiting police car.

The journey to police station was in silence, Craig driving and Philip in the back with Rob, trying to keep some distance between them. When Philip started humming to himself Craig smiled. An old trick to try and unsettle people. Pretend to be nonchalant.

'You walk in the middle Rob, between us,' said Craig. 'The path to the station is slick with ice.'

Rob hated that feeling of being flanked by the cops. He hated more the fear that was snaking into his belly. This was more than butterflies. They took him into an interview room. It was cold; the station hadn't awoken from the night and although the offices were warm, the single bar heater in the interview room was no match for its dank chill. He shivered.

Rob had sat with his mouth clenched shut, hands between his legs throughout the ten-minute trip and only spoke again when he was taken to the little room, furnished only with a small table and two hard chairs. A pad and pen were resting on the table. There was a single bright light hanging from the ceiling with no shade. He knew these rooms. He could feel the fear emanating from the walls. He'd been here before; knew how they'd operate. *Breathe deeply, stay calm.*

'Cup of tea?'

'Phone.' he demanded.

'You haven't been arrested Rob. You're just here, to make a statement, helping us with our inquiries as we try and gain a complete picture of how Brigit died,' said Craig mildly.

Silence. Craig and Philip nodded to each other and left. Outside Craig said, 'We can wait. Plenty of time. And the more information we get from forensics first the better, so let's slow things up.'

'OK. I'll write it up and you go and see if you can find Ben. See what was bothering him.' said Philip.

Craig nodded and walked off. He and Ben had often worked together informally. Craig recognised that Ben, as the first responder to a scene, often saw things that the police might miss. He didn't always like working with outsiders. It was a bit irregular, but this seemed to work.

CHAPTER TEN

Craig Arnold drove down Queens Drive deep in thought, his belly rumbling. He could almost smell the bacon at their usual meeting place, a place where they often went to discuss things, like rugby, food, fishing and sometime the latest case. The grace and charm of the old stone buildings in the city were lost on him this morning. There were lots of Oamaru stone buildings, built when times were good, and the sheep farmers kept the entire country in funds.

Just past Queen's Park he saw Ben's car parked near their favourite cafe. The food was good, solid Southland food with a touch of continental flair. It had become so popular you often needed a booking to get in for lunch. Women liked to come here with their kids. There was a small room adjacent filled with toys so kids could play while their mums had a catch up over good coffee. Ben had been gazing out the window when Craig strode into the café, nodded to Ben, chucked his coat on the chair as he went to the counter to order. 'The usual please. But I'm desperate for a coffee so I could have that first please.'

He picked up a glass of water and wandered back to Ben. 'Want to talk now or later?' he asked.

'Let's eat first. I hoped you'd get here before I had to leave,' said Ben.

Craig sat down opposite Ben and near the roaring fire. He eyed Ben and said, 'At this time of the morning we can talk without being overheard. When you've been up half the night dealing with a suspected murder and a known crim, it's amazing how comforting that smell of bacon can be.' He sniffed the air and his tummy responded in anticipation. *Ambrosia.*

'You know, I could never be a vegetarian. Love the smell of bacon too much.' Ben grinned, his saliva flowing freely in expectation of the taste of crispy bacon and deep orange runny eggs. 'And greasy eggs on toast with hollandaise sauce. Coffee's good as well,' he added, eyes lighting up at the sight of the steaming plates just arriving.

'Enjoy your meals,' said the smiling waiter.

They ate in silence and after their second coffee Craig settled back in his chair, wriggled his shoulders, stroked his chin, and smiled.

'Tell me. What's troubling you?'

Ben told him.

Craig nodded. 'I noticed the open window too.'

'I don't know why but I feel unsettled about this one. Nothing quite adds up. There's nothing I can put my finger on. Just a feeling.' Ben stirred his coffee thoughtfully.

'Does Tom feel the same?'

'No, he just thinks I'm seeing things where there's nothing to see. He just laughs at me. Says I'm now cynical and just see the worst. I've been in the game a long time. He hasn't.'

'It's called experience. Don't undersell yourself. I can only tell this much.' Craig filled Ben in with the basics. There were some things Craig omitted even though Ben had proved trustworthy in the past. *It's a bit like Holmes and Watson.*

'We've got Bennet down at the station to give a statement.'

'Has he said anything yet?' Ben asked.

'No, he's waiting for a phone to ring Jack Olds.'

'He's going to be waiting a while then. I heard he's gone to Bluff to deal with a drug problem down there. Something about a fishing boat not fishing for oysters if you get my meaning.'

Craig laughed, 'the price of oysters is better than the price of pot these days. Of course, Bluff is where the old man Hunter, Rob's father-in-law, operates his fleet.'

'Not pot. Cocaine this time. They're upping their game. Going for the big time and the big money. It's the drug of choice amongst the upper classes these days. I suspect P will be next once they've cracked the cocaine market.'

'Really? In Bluff? Why are they using that port rather than the ones nearer the main centres? The traffic's better up there, people are richer and there are more of them, harbour's much safer than Foveaux Strait. Homicide usually gets to hear from the drug squad when something is going down. Why haven't we been told? The station's not so large that the different departments don't get to hear what's going on.' He looked at Ben keenly. 'How do you know this?'

Ben shrugged. 'People trust us. We hear a lot while we're out and about on jobs. People talk when they're nervous. It's as if they won't notice what we're doing if they talk. We always pass any relevant information along,' he added and segued into a different topic. 'Do you know the next-door neighbours in Chelmsford Street?'

'No, not personally. Why?'

'I had a chat with them. According to Tom they were looking through the windows at what was going on, so I thought I'd find out what they saw. I wanted to ask them about the car I mentioned earlier. The one parked down the street with the windows half down. It probably didn't have anything to do with Brigit's death, but it was odd. And you know me with my curiosity, I had to poke my nose into things.'

Ben recounted the conversation of an old married couple finishing each other's sentences and imagining wild conspiracies.

'Are you turning detective now? Or social worker?' Craig laughed. 'Have you thought any more about my suggestion about joining up? You'd be able to do it for real then.' Craig said turning serious. 'One day you'll get yourself into trouble Ben.'

'Nah. I'm just uncomfortable about tonight's events. My mind's a bit too active. Maybe I should do as you suggest and become a copper instead of a paramedic. But my degree is better suited to this job than a policeman.'

'Intuition is what you've got Ben, You've used it before to help me, and you're smart enough. Intuition is what makes or breaks a case and you've got it in spades. If you don't like the idea of joining the police, think about a psychology degree. I think you'd be a natural at that.'

Ben just shrugged. 'Maybe.'

'Did you ask the neighbours if they called the police? We might be able to get a time frame if they did.'

'Asked them but they said the police were not interested anymore in their calls. Too many false alarms with Brigit always saying everything was ok when they visited.'

'I'll go and talk to them. Did you get the make of the car? The number?'

'It was a black BMW, quite modern. And no to the number plate. It was too dark, and I was a bit too quick, but the driver saw that I'd noticed her. She was the only occupant. She looked as if she was trying to hide. The door was open, and it looked as if she had been about to get out but stopped when she saw us. Did she come into the house while you were there?'

'No. Curious at that time of the night, or should I say so early in the morning. Rob had rung his daughter so perhaps it was her. I'll check with the neighbours.'

Replete, they finished their coffee, paid up and went their separate ways both engrossed in their different thoughts; Ben on the strange woman in the car and Craig on how he was going to tie all this together to get a conviction. He returned to the station to observe the interrogation of Rob.

CHAPTER ELEVEN

Rob started tapping his foot, checked his watch and glared at the door. *Why were they leaving him alone for so long? And what about my phone call?*

They couldn't hold him long without taking his statement. If he kept stalling they would run out of time and let him go. *Where's my mole? He should be here helping get me out. Can't be on duty yet. Perhaps they keep them robbery coppers separate. He'd better be along later.*

'I know you're keeping me in here alone to unsettle me,' he yelled. 'But it isn't going to work.' The small table jumped when his fist banged down on it. 'I'm wise to your tricks.' His nostrils flared as he stared through the window.

He fidgeted, crossing and uncrossing his legs, cold and tired, he needed a slash. It had seemed a long night waiting for Brigit to die, and the cold hadn't left his bones yet. He'd watched her struggling to breathe. It had seemed to go on forever. That rattle. The desperation. For a moment he became calm, coldness forgotten as he flashed back to that bedroom scene. *Such a good plan using her ill health against her.*

He swiveled round in relief, jumping up expectantly when he heard the key turn in the lock.

Barbara Johnson strode in with a mug of tea. ‘I understand you have milk and sugar.’ She placed it on the table and sat down opposite Rob.

‘I want to pee. I’ve been sitting here for ages. It’s against the law to leave people alone this long. I’ll report you for cruelty.’ He looked down at her, legs crossed, belly sucked in.

‘Will you? Who will you report us to?’ she said pleasantly.

‘Where can I go to pee?’ He jumped up knocking the table, tea sloshing around. ‘Now,’ his voice whispered, low with menace.

Barbara remined seated barely moving as he stalked around the table to her.

‘You realise I’ll have to accompany you?’

‘What about those two male coppers? Where’re they? Why can’t they take me?’

‘Out making their enquiries. Talking to the forensic team. Setting up the autopsy. Talking to the pathologist. A myriad of things to do with an unexplained death. Speaking to witnesses. Writing their reports. You know, all the usual stuff we have to do with a suspicious death.’

Rob looked at her, assessing her. ‘Have we met before?’ he asked eventually sounding confused.

‘No. Shall we go? Then you can have what’s left of your cuppa in comfort while we chat.’

She walked slowly in front of him and with a flick of her head indicated which way. She held her hand out blocking the closing cubicle door.

‘Sorry Rob. Can’t have that. We don’t know what you could flush down.’

Colour rose up his face, his mouth tightened, the glare like an unblinking fox. He turned abruptly, his embarrassment and anger only showing in the stiffness of his shoulders.

‘You can wash your hands over there. Towel’s clean.’

He massaged his hands with soap hot water running through his fingers taking deep breaths, the hot water soothing, eyes glinting in the mirror. His mouth was a tight line when he returned to the interview room.

‘Don’t you need two of you here?’The aggression now barely

controlled, his glare bullish. Her coolness as she gazed upon him without a flicker of interest was unflinching. Cold and dispassionate. He felt an involuntary shimmy snaking down his back.

'That's just for a formal interview once someone has been charged. This is just a friendly chat. I'm Detective Johnson. Take me through what happened.'

It was an easy open question, quietly delivered. He had to strain to hear, leaning forward towards her in an almost intimate movement, head cocked to the side as he listened. She sat opposite him looking straight at him a quizzical expression on her round face. She had a cute bob hair cut framing her face, dark glossy hair. *He was sure he recognised her from somewhere. But where?*

'I've told the other two already what happened. I've nothing more to say without my lawyer present.'

'Well, usually lawyers are only needed once someone has been charged and we haven't charged you. Yet. But you know all this, so why do you want your lawyer?'

'I don't trust you lot. You've tried to stitch me up before and I'm now wise to your tricks. Call my lawyer or release me.'

'You can walk out of here any time Rob. You're not under arrest.'

Rob rocked back on his chair, hands on the table and started pushing himself up.

Detective Johnson murmured quietly, 'but leaving now without giving us a statement will not look good. We'd just go to the court and get a warrant to arrest you for failing to give a statement when requested.'

Hand still primed to push himself up, he hovered. She looked back at him in silence. *I'll call her bluff.*

'You can't get a warrant for that. I'm leaving. You already have a verbal statement. The other two coppers both heard it. Get them to write it up and I'll sign it if I agree with what 's written. That's what you get paid for isn't it. I'll sign it if they bring it home.'

Barbara didn't move.

'I've got things to attend to. Need to arrange a funeral. Clean up the house for visitors. I'm expecting my daughter and can't have her walk into a mess, can I? I'm going back there now so if you want me to stay then you'd better arrest me. But you have no evidence of a crime, have you?'

Quick as a fox on the hunt, he jumped up, gave her the fingers, and strode purposefully to the door. He glanced back, winked and opened it.

Craig stood there. He was a big man, tall and powerfully built. He stood unsmiling, arms folded across his chest, legs wide apart. His attitude and stance saying, 'don't mess with me'. He looked at Rob.

'Going somewhere?'

Rob faltered. Although he was also tall, he certainly didn't carry the bulk and muscle of Detective Inspector Arnold. He thrust his arm into Craig's chest and shoved hard in an attempt to push him aside. Craig didn't move. Rigid and impassive.

Barbara Johnson got up smirking. *Gotcha.*

'Mr Bennet. I'm arresting you for assaulting a police officer. You have the right to remain silent. You do not have to make a statement. Anything you do say will be recorded and may be given in evidence in court. You have the right to speak to a lawyer without delay and in private before deciding whether to answer any questions. We do have a list of lawyers if you need to speak to one for free.'

His mouth dropped open. *Fuck.*

CHAPTER TWELVE

'It's a set up. You bastards. My lawyer will have you for this.' Rob faced off Craig. They shuffled together, two grown men jostling as Rob was manhandled backwards into the room, Craig's arm pushed straight on Rob's chest as Rob stumbled over himself.

'Come back inside and sit down Mr. Bennet.' Barbara said. 'As you are now formally charged with assault would you like to call your lawyer or perhaps discuss last night's events with us? Which would you prefer?' She waved his phone at him, just out of reach waiting until he either grabbed it or calmed down.

'You bastards provoked me deliberately. Give me back my cell phone.' He thumped the table. 'I want to ring my lawyer. Alone. Get out.' His face showed the signs of sweat beads trailing down from his hairline. The cool arrogance had deserted him.

Craig and Barbara observed from the one-way window as Rob phoned his trusty lawyer, Jack Olds. Recommended by a mate in Auckland as the right kind of lawyer for him, Olds had worked for him on a retainer ever since he arrived in Invercargill. He had great faith in Old's ability to keep him out of jail and he had proven his worth and his high retainer fee time and time again.

'Jack. I'm in a spot of bother, at the police station and a jacked-up assault charge against me. You won't yet know but

Brigit's dead and they think I killed her. So that's something else to handle. When can you come?'

'Sorry Rob. I can't help you now or ever again.' Olds sounded distracted, distant, and excessively formal in his reply. The pause and sudden crinkling of his eyes, the stiffening of his back showed the watching policemen that all was not going Rob's way. Craig smiled grimly. Barbara looked at him in unspoken question. Craig put his fingers to his lips. They could now hear Rob shouting; they could sense the disbelief in his tone.

'What? What do you mean? You're on a retainer from me. You come when asked. You've dropped what you're doing in the past when I've called. What's so different now?'

In the silence that followed they observed Rob get up, pace around hand through his hair. What do you mean you've been retained by someone else and that conflicts with my interests?' Boom. A fist came down on the table. 'You dealing with old man Hunter? That shifty bastard. You can't do that to me. I know too much about you and…'.

To the waiting police it was a pantomime, a one-sided conversation for them to fill in the blanks.

'Why are you acting like this? What the fuck's going on?'

Nothing. Rob looked down at his phone, an angry flush creeping up his neck to cover his scowling face. *What the hell was happening down in Bluff? Was this to do with his first deal in Bluff? The shipment on one of the old man's boats? That shipment was secure. The only people who knew about it were the courier, the captain and him. Even old man Hunter didn't know.*

He stood up and faced the one-way window scowling. He mouthed at them 'I know you're watching. Get me the fucking duty lawyer.'

Barbara walked back into the room, file ready in her hand.

'You want the list of duty lawyers do you Rob?' Barbara paused a while as she looked in her files and handed him the list. Rob snatched it suddenly suspicious.

'You have it ready? Why?' He demanded. 'You knew something didn't you? Knew that my solicitor was unavailable?'

'Not at all Rob' said Barbara reassuringly. 'We just like to be prepared for all eventualities. Is Mr. Olds not available?' She smiled innocently.

They're bloody well up to something. And that woman, why did she seem familiar?

'We'll just leave you with the list to go through and wait until someone is available to help. We've got to go and interview Brigit's son and sister now. We'll be back later when you've found a lawyer to attend to you.' Barbara said as she turned away.

'Hey. That so-called son. I want to see him. I don't believe she had one in spite of what you say.'

'That's not going to happen Rob. He's busy dealing with his mum's death.' Barbara said mischievously delighting in his reaction.

'So far so good,' quipped Barbara to Craig as they walked away. 'Good feeling to have one up on Rob. Now the only cloud on the horizon was the meeting with Brigit's family. That's going to be the difficult task. Talking to the son and sister.'

'I don't think they're going to take this well.' Craig said.

'No. I've spoken to Brigit's sister by phone. She'd just landed and was to see her sister later today. She's devastated. The son, Niall, was picking her up, so now he knows as well.' Craig picked up the files.

'They all apparently only met a few years ago. Niall's adoptive mother always knew who Niall's birthmother was. Not quite an open adoption but both mothers kept in touch. Let's get coffee Philip. I think better with a cup in my hand.'

'Anyone know about him? Apart from the fact that he is a well-regarded doctor.' Philip asked.

'He was adopted as a baby by the Smithsons. He was a former mayor of Invercargill and as I understand it, couldn't have kids. The adoption went through quickly and without any problems. Niall's had a fortunate upbringing. Much better than he would have had with Brigit being a solo parent.' Craig had all the information at her fingertips.

'How did they manage to adopt so quickly?' asked Philip

'A private adoption. The Smithson's parents were friends of

the Chapels,' replied Craig.

'Who's his father?' Philip paused as he asked.

'Unknown. Or at least not listed,' said Barbara looking at the file.

'Brigit's mother was a devout Catholic. Full of virtue. The daughters both rebelled.'

'How do you know that Craig?' asked Philip.

'My parents knew them. Just the odd comment I overheard now and then.'

'I've made the small conference room available for them.' Barbara was now business like as she ushered them to the door.

Niall and Georgia were sitting in silence, both pale and hunched, a picture of misery, and Niall with his arm around her shoulder. The marks of tears were still visible on Georgia's face and now they sat together unified in grief. The anger was just simmering.

Georgia had travelled from the warmth of Auckland, leaving early, so felt the chill of a southern winter. She still remembered that feeling of cold to the bones from her childhood, but years of living in the north had now left her unprepared. Her thoughts bounced around, memories flooding in. The tears flowed readily again as she remembered her golden days with her partner Maureen. That flush of youthful excitement as they set out on a new life totally removed from the controlled one of her childhood. *I wish Maureen were here now.*

Instead she had to turn her mind to the grim reality that Brigit was dead. She and Niall had to try and find out what happened. She was sure this was no coincidence. She was sure that Rob was involved somehow. She just had to hold it together and find out how.

She straightened up and turned to Niall.

'He did it, didn't he? He wanted her house. I thwarted him by getting Brigit to agree to sell up and come to Auckland with me. So, this time he succeeded in killing her. It was his last chance.'

'No proof of that yet George. Let's wait to see what the police say and what the autopsy shows.' He took her hand and held it as he sat close to her offering what little comfort he could. She'd known his mother all her life. He, on the other hand, had only become part of Brigit's in the last few years.

CHAPTER THIRTEEN

Alone again Rob settled back to relax into the wait. Legs propped up on a chair, he rocked backwards stretching his arms above his head, his mind trawling through his past. He smiled to himself as he remembered the way he'd had people running after him doing his bidding. He was a lazy sod. The thinker, the manager, the ideas man rather than the doer. The veneer of the cultivated man hid his cruelty and his temper well. But those who thwarted him learned the hard way. His reputation for violence was based on fact not myth. His father had taught him well. His own mother had learned the hard way. Rob has taken his father's lessons to heart and perfected them.

He'd loved the way Brigit ran around after him. He just needed to sit there and click his fingers and she'd come scampering to do his bidding. *Pity she wanted me to leave, she and that sister.*

The second lesson he'd learned from his dad, after seeing what threats could achieve, was to have a copper in your pocket. There's always one who needs a little extra cash, or has a dark secret he doesn't want broadcast around. And he had one here, and he needed to get to him. It was payback time.

While Rob waited in the small, cold room, eyes closed and reminiscing, Craig and Phillip retrieved a rather large paper folder from the now little used filing room. Craig held it up, hand estimating its weight.

'You still prefer paper to computers?' Philip asked.

'Yes. Old habits. I like them as a book. Able to leaf through it. I see more on paper than a computer. I see patterns emerging. That's harder on a computer. This is a pretty large file.' Craig bounced it in his hands.

'Yep and although it shows a history of suspicious activity there's never been any arrests or convictions since he arrived down here,' Philip said flipping through the pages.

'Both the drug squad and serious crimes were onto him in Auckland though, even though they couldn't ever pin anything on him.' Craig was frowning at the file. 'There's mention in here of his Invercargill activities, but nothing definite.'

'Well, we know he's involved in drugs and we do suspect he gets his money from theft even if there's nothing in this file,' Philip said.

'Brigit Chappel must've become a hindrance to his activities. What do you think Philip? Anything there we can use?'

'There's nothing here. No proof. Our suspicions aren't enough to take to a judge, Craig.'

'No. His past history in both Auckland and Australia isn't enough. Damn. Rob's file is heavy on supposition but not a lot of facts.' Craig observed as he scratched his head in frustration.

'Word on the street,' he continued carefully, 'is that the gangs always viewed him with contempt mixed with more than a bit of dread. He was not the leader for nothing. Craftiness laced with amorality and a disdain for others had projected him to being one of the most feared gangsters in Invercargill. People gave him wide berth. They danced to his tune and his close colleagues, Simon Smart and Nigel Butler made sure that the dominant emotion when Rob walked into a room was fear. At least that's what our mole said.'

'We have a mole?' Philip was surprised.

'Yep, I inadvertently almost let the cat out of the bag when I stumbled upon him and some mates drinking up large in a pub. I had been called by the barman as they were getting a bit raucous.

Recognised him and just stopped myself in time from asking what the hell was he doing there. Drug squad had him there watching. It's because of him we they were able to stop a couple of big deals going down.'

'Hey,' said Philip. 'Look at this article about Rob and Mr Asia in The Listener. There he's described as *'having extensive criminal history and has convictions which led to the New Zealand Police describing him as a thief, burglar, car converter, abortionist, sex offender and false pretender.'*

'And that reputation is why he's successfully recruited prospects down here,' Craig said as he put his mug of coffee down, his mouth puckering. 'This station coffee is really dreadful.'

'Here's another article in the Sydney Morning Herald, about the Commission of Inquiry into Drug Trafficking. Listen to this, *The Commissioner assures the public they can have every confidence that everything will be done in a fair and proper manner concerning Mr Bennet or any other informer.'*

Philip stopped, eyebrows raised in surprise. 'Now that is really interesting. Puts a new dimension on Rob doesn't it? He must have been really young to be criminally active then.'

'Yes. A prospect perhaps. Earning his stripes and young enough to get caught and take the fall. So, he finally became an informer? That explains the remarkably light sentence he got compared to the rest of the Mr. Asia gang.' Craig looked up eyes focused, fingers drumming as he thought about the information.

Philip clicked his fingers.

'Earth to Craig. Earth to Craig come in please.'

Craig laughed. 'Sorry off on my mind trips.'

'Further down it says, *'in new allegations Rob Bennet is the police informer and was a former associate of Terry Clarke, the leader of Mr Asia.'* Phillip's finger was scrolling down the page.

'Well this file does identify an extensive criminal history in Australia and Auckland, but not down here. It talks about large scale cannabis dealing and we know there is a problem with that. All good information but nothing here we can use to help us.' Craig suddenly felt irritable, his usual calm deserting him. His hand clenched. 'There must be something.'

'And look. He also claims that a senior police officer was corrupt in Australia.'

'Police corruption. Hmm. He'd know how to arrange that then.' Craig continued, 'you know, what has always frustrated me about this man is our inability to get anything concrete on him. He's a slippery bastard. He comes and goes, unseen and untouchable. Yet we all know he's at the heart of many of the robberies and other gang activities here.'

'Are you thinking what I'm thinking? That piece of information puts a different aspect on him never being arrested,' said Philip.

'Yes. And I'm surprised that this is in his file. It's hasn't been reviewed for some time going by the front cover. Look who signed it out last.'

'He's viewed this file more times than anybody else, as well,' said Philip.

Craig stood up suddenly. They looked at each other. Philip nodded and in silent assent quickly photocopied the file and replaced it without signing for it. No-one should ever know that they had viewed it.

'I'll keep these at home. Any conversation we have now about anything other than this case must be off-site. Agreed?' Craig said looking grim. His face had paled, and his mouth had lost its usual soft lines. His tread was heavy as they walked back.

'Absolutely. This is a real worry. Who do we trust now?'

'Not Serious Crimes for sure.' Craig said. 'We need to keep this secret for now while we gather more information. This looks like corruption to me.'

'Do you trust Barbara?' The question was sudden from Philip.

'Yes, she's as honest as they come. I would stake my career on that.'

'Ok, I agree. So, we tread carefully then.' Philip looked at Craig as he asked, eyebrows raised in question.

'Yep. Ever met her partner?'

'No,' replied Philip. 'She keeps her private life quite separate from her job here. He never joins her at any work functions.'

'That he's in Serious Crimes is an issue. And the fact that he was the last to sign the file out. Do you think it's complete?'

'I don't know. How would we know? We need to do some discreet investigating of him, don't we?' Philip asked warily.

'Yes, Very quietly. Barbara shouldn't know of our suspicions about him. And that's all we have. No evidence at all.'

'Yet,' said Philip.

'Why do we think there's something there? Is it because he keeps away from us? There could be many reasons for that.' Craig suddenly started thinking aloud, his mind jumping from one question to another, trying to answer himself.

'Yes, there could be. The conflict of interest thing. Keeping what's going on in each division relatively separate until the need to talk with anyone about the investigation. Keep the evidence chain from being corrupted. All of the above. No reason we should suspect anything really.' Philip was quick with his answers.

'Except?' Craig was non-committal, his face closed as he gazed through a window as he passed by at Rob, cool confidence plastered over his face.

'Cocky bastard.' muttered Craig. 'Thinks we won't get him.'

'Well he may be right again. But this time it's us investigating, and not anyone in Serious Crimes.'

As they walked back into their squad room Craig added, 'When we're sure of our facts I think I should talk to Barbara alone, off site. You ok with that?'

'Sure,' said Philip. 'Trust no-one. Wasn't it Stalin who said, 'I trust no-one, not even myself?' Philip smiled grimly as he said it.

With a wry smile Craig replied 'Well there's no hurry yet. Nothing that can't wait. Especially if what we now suspect has been going on for some time. Let's crack this one first.'

CHAPTER FOURTEEN

Georgia shivered, clutched Niall's hand. 'Bloody horrible room. Can't they do better than this?' She straightened her back, stretched it with a yoga stretch. Her face slowing turning from a picture of misery, to one set with anger. Her thoughts raced from her childhood to Brigit's death, rolling the decades through her mind like wagon wheels. The room at the station was uninviting, hard chairs and little natural light. Nothing to relieve the overpowering sense of gloom.

'This feels like a room where bad news is delivered, where people grieve. It isn't a room for peace and solace.' Georgia suddenly needed to fill the empty space with sound. Her voice reverberated around the empty room sounding harsh and unnaturally loud. Her outburst relieved some tension. She slumped back onto Niall and became quiet again. *I need you Maureen, and my piano. I need us playing together again.*

Niall remained silent as if taking his cue from her. He knew from his patients when to talk, and when to wait for them to collect their own thoughts. They both jumped suddenly when Barbara and Philip walked in.

'Morena.' Philip nodded to them. 'I am Senior Sergeant Philip Adams, and this is my colleague Detective Barbara Johnson.

You spoke to DI Arnold yesterday by phone. We're sorry to bring you here at such a time but we needed to talk to you about Brigit.' Philip started the conversation quietly indicating that they should all sit down.

'I am sorry for your loss, and I understand how difficult this time is for you. For now, we're treating Brigit's death as unexpected and unexplained.' Barbara said as she sat down opposite them.

'Unless there is any further evidence of foul play then there's not a lot we can do. I'm sorry if that reality is hard for you,' added Philip.

Georgia nodded numbly. 'We don't think she just died, do we Niall?' she looked up at him for confirmation. 'We've always had our suspicions because Brigit was always having accidents.' She raised her hands to signify speech marks. 'Even though I've always been afraid something like this would happen, it's still such a shock. It's why we were planning to get her away from him and move up north. I'd come down to finalise things.' Her voice quavered. Her eyes welled up once more. She hunted for a tissue.

'What do you mean Georgia?' Philip asked. 'What do you mean by accidents?'

'He tipped her into a concrete bunker at the refuse station last year. That time she ended up having two broken legs and a broken arm.'

'And concussion,' added Niall. 'She couldn't be certain that he did it deliberately. So we couldn't do anything about it. We just tried to persuade her to be more careful around him.'

'You didn't advise the police?' asked Barbara.

'No. Brigit was too scared and wouldn't let us,' said Niall.

'Then there was the time she fractured her femur while bringing the washing in. She thought she'd tripped that time, but she wasn't sure.' Georgia continued her hands twisting around each other.

'Again, another concussion,' added Niall.

'So, when we planned for her to sell and move up to Auckland, we both warned her not to tell him, but I think she must have.

I think she told that bastard just before Christmas that she was going to sell up and that he'd needed to make other arrangements. She said his attitude towards her changed then. She thought it would give her time to clean up the place, and for him to find a new place to live.'

'She thought she was doing him a favour by giving him three months' notice. And then suddenly she's dead? It's much too convenient for me to believe he didn't have a hand in this. I expect the bastard to be dealt to. If you can't I will.' Niall exploded and rubbed his hands through his hair. He was usually so calm, patient and quietly spoken. Barbara's eyebrows shot up while Philip dropped his hand to the desk and stared at them. It was like a sudden volcano which ruptured the sense of solemnity in the room. Philip saw the bitterness and anger becoming more and more apparent. It threatened to overwhelm him. He looked at them both, his statement a challenge. For a moment, the police were at a loss for words. Barbara swallowed and recovered her gravitas with a quietly delivered question. Niall's statement was noted, but initially ignored.

'In what way did his attitude change?'

'She said he'd become quiet and thoughtful and almost kind towards her. He didn't lose his temper with her as he usually did. She said he kept watching her with almost an almost quizzical look on his face. Occasionally he went silent on the phone when she walked in. Usually he didn't care if she heard what he was talking about. This time it was different. But he still seemed to keep her inside most of the time, under his thumb where he could watch her.' Georgia continued.

'She noticed him watching her all the time. Quiet and still like a cat waiting for a mouse. Those were her words.' Niall added.

'She said his attitude freaked her out and she was suspicious of it as it was so unlike him.'

The two policemen looked at each other, silently reviewing what they had learned so far, putting it altogether in their minds along with their suspicions and their impression of the scene.

'You said earlier that there didn't appear to be anything suspicious.' Niall was curious at their questioning. 'Have you changed your minds? Do you know something you're not telling us? Can you now take this seriously seeing there is a pattern here?'

'There are a number of reasons we are leaving this open as an unexplained death.' Philip marked them off with his fingers as he stated them; 'Brigit's history of injuries and her frequent trips to hospital; some discrepancies in Bennet's story; the timeline and finally the scene. The doctor says Rob's timeline doesn't fit with her estimate of the time of death.'

'And then there's his own shady history.' explained Barbara.

'We know about that,' said Niall.

'Where was he? What was he doing when Brigit died?' Georgia asked.

'He claimed he was in the bathroom and didn't hear her until it was too late,' said Philip.

Georgia nodded sadly. 'I don't believe him. I knew he would do something if she told him she was leaving. Why didn't she wait longer until everything was arranged?'

Nobody had an answer.

Barbara went back to Niall's outburst. 'While I understand your comments Niall, and the feelings behind it, we need to gather sufficient evidence before we can charge him, and that evidence needs to be robust enough to convince a judge and jury.'

Barbara was direct. 'We don't want you taking the law into your own hands. Please just sit tight and let us complete our investigation.'

Philip was alert to the nuances of the conversation. 'We don't want you to jeopardise a potential arrest and conviction if we manage to get that far.'

He stood up suddenly as if the interview was finished. 'There are things you can do to get you through the next few days. Find a lawyer in case you need one. Secure the house. Here are the keys.' He passed them to Niall. 'They were returned to us by forensics after they finished up. I don't think you should stay there, at the house, Georgia, because Bennet may have to be released in the short term. Were you intending to stay there?'

'No, she'll stay with me,' said Niall. 'I'll arrange a locum to cover my clinics in the meantime, so we'll deal with this together.' He then started his own rapid-fire questioning, just like a machine gun.

'Where is my mother's body? Will there be an autopsy? When will the coroner hear the case? When will the body be released to us? Do we need to wait till the coroner has determined cause of death before we can bury her?'

He stopped for breath and Barbara leaned forward to reply.

'The autopsy will be completed today, and the coroner will receive the report. A decision will be made tomorrow about if, and when there is to be a hearing. After that, Brigit's body will be released. Do you have a preference for a funeral company? We'll notify you when Brigit is ready to be collected. You'll need to notify the funeral directors of either her instructions, or yours if she hasn't left any.'

'Affinity Funeral Home was her preference when we last spoke about this eventuality. She liked that it was run by three women.' Niall was thoughtful.

'She wanted to be cremated and have her ashes scattered from the Cromwell Bridge like our brother's,' Georgia added. 'Except', she paused, 'after your phone call to me, I looked at the death notices in the on-line Southland Times I wanted to see how they were written.'

Her voice rose in anger. 'I was stunned to see that her notice was there already with Rob as her partner. He appears to have arranged a funeral for Friday and the funeral directors are Singer and Co. How the hell did that happen? He's been in your charge all morning, hasn't he?'

They all looked at each other all thinking the same thing,

'Yes, he'd been with someone since the ambulance arrived. He hasn't had an opportunity to do that since, but we did return his phone when he asked for a lawyer.' Philip sounded puzzled.

'Actually Philip. It reinforces our concerns about his time frame. Remember you told me that Doctor Cook said she thought that Brigit had died much earlier than the 111 call at 4.31 would suggest, at least four hours prior to her examination. He must have organised that in the hours before he called the ambulance,' said Barbara clicking her fingers.

'So that canny bastard was setting his own agenda and writing his own script. Making it known publicly that Brigit is his partner.' Georgia was silent for a minute. 'Confirms my suspicions.'

They all looked at each other as the realisation dawned on them about how well-planned Rob was.

'This was not a natural death.' Niall was now pacing, long legs stalking the little room.

'He wants Brigit's assets. No other reason could explain why he's suddenly naming himself as her partner.' Georgia added for emphasis. 'It's a million-dollar property in the best part of town. He wants her money the bastard.'

'And he killed for it. Killed my mother for a house.' He looked at them, his face twisted in anguish, barely seeing the concerned looks on Barbara and Philip's faces.

Neither Georgia nor Niall were interested at the prospect of having Brigit's assets. Until now they had never thought about them. But that simple notification in the Southland Times confirmed to them Rob's intentions all along. He had motive.

'No way is he ever going to have her things. Most of them came from the family anyway so there is no legal way he can say anything is his. He came with just a suitcase for god's sake. He owned nothing,' said Georgia. Her voice was rising, anger now in every word.

'He must have got in contact with the paper online while waiting for us this morning.' mused Barbara. 'I'll get in touch with the newspaper and see when he lodged the call or the email to have it online so quickly. This may be interesting from the point of view of his timeline especially as we think that there were some hours unaccounted for.'

'Don't worry,' Philip said, 'we'll make sure she goes to Affinity after the autopsy. You just advise them she's coming tomorrow. You arrange the funeral how you want it and keep Bennet out of the picture. There's nothing he can do about it. You are her family and have prior rights over him.'

Niall helped Georgia up and, arm around her shoulders, led her out to his car.

'Poor bastards,' muttered Philip. 'They're in for a rough time.'

CHAPTER FIFTEEN

Once inside the house, they felt Brigit all around them. Her fragrance wafted around, hanging subtly on the still air. Georgia still felt that lump in her throat, the one which had been there ever since Craig's phone call to her that morning. She held onto the hall table swallowing, trying to hold back the tears still welling in her eyes. Nothing could disguise the bleakness of the home, the messy kitchen, the unwashed mugs left at the table. Her walk into Brigit's bedroom was the only thing which calmed that sense of despair. She sat on the bed looking around. It was clean and tidy except for the unmade bed and a rug flung on the chair. The pool of ash on the floor the only jarring note. Her heart slowly thumped in her chest. She could feel the rhythm of it, a steadying force in this turbulence. She heard Brigit's whisper, help me, please help me. She felt her fear and panic.

Georgia sat for a long time, waiting for her resolve to harden. Here in Brigit's room she had her epiphany. Here was the space she needed to determine her next moves. It was here with Brigit surrounding that she found the strength to voice her determination.

'I'll do it Brigit. I'll avenge you,' she whispered. Her thumping heart settled to an unsteady flutter as she drank in the remains of her sister. The southerly front took the opportunity to quieten its rage and the wind dropped its force to that of a mild zephyr.

Niall watched from the door, arms folded. 'We need to start George,' he said softly. 'Before he gets out.' When she looked up he saw the light of determination in her eyes rather than the tears. He saw the firmness of her chin, jutting out as if to challenge him.

'We need to do as Sergeant Adams suggested and take what's important before the rat comes back. I suspect they're not going to be able to keep him locked up for much longer,' said Georgia. 'This may be the only chance we get before the police have to release Rob.'

Georgia restrained herself from kicking something, her mood now of icy determination. Her hand idly caressed the tabletops, brushed the spines of books in the bookcase and straightened the pot plants as she wandered around. In touching these memories, she remembered her parents, her brother, and her childhood here amid these things. Things of her childhood safely kept in Brigit's care.

They found a bag and stuffed it with some of Brigit's papers lying on top of her desk, her jewellery, and the photo of their late brother. Georgia picked it up and looked at the smiling image, tears threatening her again.

'Can't leave that here, not in this place now.' Georgia said to Niall. 'Brigit adored him. He was the one nearest to her in age and probably understood her best. You're very like him,' she added. Georgia paused, looking around and thinking. She picked up a glass vase, observed her parents' pictures on the walls, and the silver tea service in the dresser.

'Niall, we weren't happy as kids. This stuff means nothing to me. Time to get rid of it. Beautiful they may be, but too many bad memories. I never understood how Brigit lived with it all. Take whatever you want, 'cos I'm going to get rid of it all. I'll call in Todd's Auction Rooms to take the lot.'

'Just this photo of your brother, my uncle. It speaks to me but nothing else does.'

'Good.' Georgia sat down. 'We need to plan what to do. I'm

nervous. I expect the worst to happen. He's going to get off with this unless we can find some real evidence. He'll come back here and make our life hell when the Will is read, and we claim our property.'

'I know. We don't want a long court case and it will be long. It'll be dirty because that's the only way he plays.' Niall was thoughtful as he gazed at Georgia. 'It's all too distressing. We also need to check with the bank to close her account down. He'll be into that as well given half a chance. He'll raid it for sure. He's done that before when Brigit's been in hospital.' Niall added. 'In fact, I'll do that right now.' He picked up a bank statement and rang Brigit's bank.

Georgia frowned. 'It's so unexpected all that's been happening. I feel I can't properly grieve for my little sister while all this shit is flying around. But Niall, sitting in there in her bedroom with her ghost still hovering around me, I became resolved.'

'And I know he'll get to come back here, and he'll never let us have the place. He has nowhere else to go. Brigit told me that his former wife won't have him back and his daughter doesn't want him. He'll fight to the death to keep this house.' Georgia felt her resolve crumbling. She put her head in her hands to cover up her welling eyes.

Niall finished his call. 'That's all sorted. They've put a temporary stop on her account and want us to come in with the Will as soon as we can.'

Georgia nodded. 'Thanks for thinking of that. He'll have taken her bank card. I can't see it her in her purse.'

Niall joined her at the kitchen table. It was her mother's kitchen table, an ancient Baltic pine one, scrubbed clean but with that wonderful patina of age which brought a mellow buff coloured glow to it. Niall ran his hand over it thoughtfully.

'I've been thinking, and there's no easy way to say this but if he doesn't leave, we have to make him, one way or another. On his feet or in a box.'

Georgia straightened, mouth opened. She had in that brief moment in Brigit's room, resolved to do away with Rob, but never expected this from Niall.

'We need a plan in two parts George. An action plan. First, plan A - the legal one, the long expensive court battle to have him evicted, and the place legally determined to be ours. And then plan B if necessary.'

'Plan B?'

'The box option.'

'The box option?'

'Yes, a coffin, feet first.' Niall grimaced. He rubbed his eyes. 'I always knew I was adopted. That was never hidden from me, but I still don't know who my real dad is. His name's not on the birth certificate and Brigit refused to tell me. She said there was no point as he was a Norwegian sailor she'd met at a party in Bluff. He doesn't know I exist. I was happy to just get to know her at first, and maybe later my father. She said I got all this blond hair from him.' He ran his fingers through his hair. It was a habit of his when he got agitated; he'd automatically do it, rustling it up until it looked messy.

'I'd never blamed her for having me adopted and I understood why she never told anyone about me. You didn't even know until a few years ago did you? She worried that if she told Rob he'd cause me trouble. But over the last couple of years, I saw her deteriorate and my heart just ached for her.' Niall couldn't bear to mention Rob's name, 'I saw her go downhill quickly and wondered why. She'd never discussed him until the last couple of 'falls' she had. Then the full picture of his abuse came out. He drained the life out of her. She'd told me lots about her life when a student and then as a teacher, and her travels as well. She was such a feisty woman when she was young. I wish I had known her then.'

'Yes, she was always the wild unconventional one.'

Georgia watched him, his face crumbling, shoulder tense until he shook himself and set his shoulders straight.

'Of the two options,' he waited a beat, 'I prefer plan B. I want to kill the bastard and I plan to. Not only for my mother's death but also for the way he treated her over the last couple of years.'

They stared at each other. Thoughts tumbled around Georgia's brain. They collided as the battle between morality, justice and murder fought for supremacy.

'Niall,' Georgia cried out. 'Oh God, that's just what I was thinking. A few moments ago, in her room. I sensed her need for revenge. What are you suggesting?'

'I'm suggesting murder George. Murder. Something against the fibre of my being. Something against my training and my love for my work as a doctor. Something against my oath to help people. Oh God almighty, George. I can't get the thought of killing him out of my mind.' He looked down at her. 'I'd wanted a bit more time with her George. I wanted to make up for all those lost years. I wanted to see some happiness in her life.'

Niall finally broke down and sobbed. Georgia went over to him and put a tentative hand on his shoulder. She stood mute and shocked as she stood there, tears streaming down her face until he finally calmed.

'I need a drink,' she muttered.

Niall laughed bitterly. 'Later.'

'How would you do it?'

'I've been thinking ever since we were told. I could go and buy a gun but that would be too obvious.' Niall said it with a grimace. 'I'd never wanted to own one, but now? I can feel my trigger finger twitching.' He held his hand out trigger finger primed.

'We need to think of the legal route first. And we need to be certain that he is going to claim Brigit's property before we do anything. We need to make sure that that's what he's planning on doing.' Georgia was being cautious, her words were slow, her voice deep. 'We'll need a lawyer.'

'Yep and I know just the person.' His face suddenly lit up.

Georgia laughed. 'Ah Sam. Of course. The new woman in your life. Good. Will she do it?'

'Yes, but now's not the time for philosophical discussions about the rights and wrongs of our courses of action. That'll have to come later. We need to get cracking here.'

Silently they hustled from room to room, brows furrowed looking for memories. Then one final glance around them, relieved to go back out into the sunlight, they left before there was any chance that Rob would appear.

Justice, morality, or murder?

Which would win?

CHAPTER SIXTEEN

'I hope Niall has taken note of Barbara's comments about not taking justice into their own hands,' said Craig. Philip was standing by, coffee mug in hand fidgeting and shuffling as they waited for Rob's lawyer to arrive. Craig smiled to himself as he watched Phillip itching to move on.

'They'd be silly not to. Besides they're not stupid and they're too busy just getting through the day, hour by dramatic hour,' replied Philip.

'Barbara,' Craig said as she walked into the room. 'We were just discussing the case. Any sign of a lawyer yet?'

'Yes. She's just arrived. Samantha George,' she said. Craig whistled and laughed. Philip's head shot up and Barbara raised her eyebrows in surprise.

'Do you know something we don't?' asked Philip.

'Want to share?' asked Barbara.

'Not yet. Later.'

'He's not happy,' Barbara nodded towards the interview room.

'Tough,' said Craig.

They moved toward the interview room. Barbara led the way followed by Philip. Craig watched from next door.

'Your new lawyer's here.' Barbara said as she walked into the room.

Rob glowered. 'I didn't want her, but she was the only one available. Mine's busy in Bluff. Must be doing something for old man Hunter.'

'Bit of action going on down there. But then you know all about it don't you? Bit of snitching going on as we speak.'

Silence.

They moved aside as the duty lawyer, Samantha George who had been behind them, stepped forward and intervened. She turned to the police and said. 'I'm not here to discuss what's happening elsewhere. I'm here to get Mr Bennet his freedom. This is a trumped-up charge and you know it.'

She ignored Rob and focused on the police.

'From what I've read you have nothing to go on. The assault charge will be thrown out of court with the judge admonishing you for wasting the court's time. As for any suggestion of murder, that's laughable. You have no evidence to present to a Preliminary Hearing. Leave us. It's my client's right to speak to me in private.' She stood, tiny, firm, arms crossed and gazed steadfastly at them. Rob sat with mouth wide open at this.

She confronted both the police and Rob, all business here. Both Barbara and Philip could sense the steel in her as she gazed coolly at them. But privately all she wanted was to get away from this creep as quickly as possible. *This was someone who needed two lawyers on hand if his reputation was anything to go by.*

Philip leaned against the door as if reluctant to leave. Barbara nudged him outside.

'Nothing we can do just yet,' she muttered to him. 'Wait for forensics and the autopsy. Then we'll see what we can do. In the meantime, I suspect he'll have to be let go for now.'

They could hear Rob shouting as they walked down the corridor to meet up with Craig.

'Well that's not going well.' Philip snorted with laughter. 'I think they know each other. There may be some history there. Ready to tell us yet Craig?'

Craig could barely keep the grin off his face.

'I happen to know that Samantha's mother went to school with Brigit, and they were best buddies. No doubt she'll have met Brigit through her. So maybe Samantha knows some of her background from her childhood.' Craig said. 'That's why I laughed when I heard she was the duty lawyer.'

He turned towards them when they got to his office. 'Not only that, but she was the lawyer for that lassie who accused Rob of rape a few years ago. The one who went up to Nelson. Love to be a fly on the wall. It's not going to be a pretty interview.'

'But she'll do her job and he'll walk for now.' Philip said mouth curling downwards.

'Yep,' said Craig. 'So, let's discuss if we can charge him with anything.'

'If not for murder, maybe failure to provide the necessities of life?' said Barbara.

'I don't think we even have enough for that unfortunately,' Craig said.

'OK then, let's look at our options, work on some strategies while Ms. George talks to Rob.'

They'd barely started when Samantha knocked on their door. A polite little rat tat tat.

'Can I talk to you?' She walked straight in with confidence, put her cards on the table and they listened impassively. They gathered around, Philip with hands shoved in his pockets and head down, Craig looking straight at her and Barbara with a deeply worried frown on her face.

'You know you can't keep him. You have no evidence of a crime. You can only hold him for another couple of hours but then you must let him go. As duty lawyer I must argue his case for now, but I'll refuse to take his case if it comes to court. I know he's a scumbag and so do you. If you let him go, he may trip himself up and do something stupid. He's already threatened to go to the ombudsman and claim unfair and illegal treatment.' *And if he knows I'm in a relationship with Brigit's son he'll go ballistic and so will you.*

They nodded and sighed. Maybe next time. There's always a next time. With that Samantha walked out the door.

'She's right,' said Barbara.

'One day we'll nab him. He's getting old. His mind can't hold up forever. The booze and drugs will have made that a certainty.' Craig sounded wistful as he flopped in a chair.

'He's slipping through our fingers again.' Barbara jumped up with hands in the air.

'And there's always the promise of the young ambitious prospects coming up behind him in his little gang,' said Philip. 'And who knows what he'll do with the property, and Georgia and Niall. Maybe he'll slip up there.'

'And he's just lost the support of old man Hunter who is down there in Bluff fighting his own little legal battle over the importation and distribution of cocaine.' Craig observed.

'And that seems to be something he hasn't yet told his son-in-law,' said Barbara.

'Well the old man never knew Rob was using his fleet,' said Craig. 'Besides Old man Hunter is never going to forgive Rob for the abuse of his daughter and granddaughter. He would sing to save himself. And maybe, just maybe, we can get Bennet that way.'

Craig heaved himself out of his chair, shook his shoulders and with determination said, 'onwards.'

Rob walked free into the soft early afternoon sun. 'By the way Rob,' Craig called as Rob was about to walk through the door into the bright and rare sunshine, 'keep away from Brigit's family. They have rights that you don't have.'

Rob gave Craig the fingers as he sauntered off down the street.

He was in no hurry. He needed to think, to walk off the fury which threatened to overcome him. He found himself clenching and unclenching his fists, frustrated that there was no-one to punch. *Slow down. No hurry, just pace yourself. There's time enough to deal with them. Bloody coppers, deliberately trying to do my head in.*

He stopped abruptly. *I need a large drink to settle me down. That'll do the trick. A drink always calms me down and sets the old brain on an even keel.*

He went to the nearest pub for a lunchtime drink. He propped himself up at the bar, hunched forward, hands propping his head up.

'Pint and some chips. Large.'

He mentally listed the things to do. First get the gang together and if need be, they can knock a few heads together for me. They need to scare the sister and son away. Drag them to see me if necessary so I can stare them down. Sort out with Si what he can do to them. I'll click my fingers and just watch. They'll then know who's in charge. They'll know who's boss then. They won't expect anything like this. And that Si. His look is enough to scare anyone away. Si and Nige standing with me will be enough.

He grinned to himself as he imaged the scene. Si cracking his knuckles, those big arms covered in tats. The old knife scar down his chin. Georgia trembling behind Niall. *Enough to scare anyone and they'll learn that I can, and will do anything to them if they get in the way of what I want. They'll understand why Brigit did as she was told.*

His mental image of a scene of terror made him laugh out loud. *Yes, that'll be it. I'll be back in my element. Just like the old days. Then I can get down to business with them out of the way. Arrange Brigit's funeral. Get hold of her Will. Find out who her lawyer was, get to my lawyer and file a claim on her property if necessary.*

'Would have to be that new one seeing Olds has let me down,' he muttered to himself unaware that the young men next to him moved out of the way, their distaste showing. He took another sip and shoved some more chips in his mouth. *Might need some more of these, those bastards took me before I'd had any breakfast. He snorted. I'll bloody well have to get my own meals now until I can get Topaz in. She'll be waiting for me at home by now.*

His thoughts bounced around racing from one to the next in no logical order. He continued his list. Get Topaz to clear out Brigit's shitty things, sort out what to sell and then she can move in. Quicker that's done the better for me. He mentally ticked it all off in his head. Find out from the Taits what they saw. *They'll tell me everything I need to know or else. Don't need to worry about what the nosy neighbours think. They're so old they're almost doolally. File a claim against the police for improper arrest. Might get some money that way. Sort out the Bluff thing and put a contract out on Olds. That bastard's not going to get away with refusing me. And finally sort out old man Hunter and what the fuck's happened to my consignment of coke.*

By the time he left the pub, well fed, and mellow with drink, he almost felt he was on top of his game. Good grub and beer and a plan of action. What more could he want? Maybe some sex in Brigit's bed. He laughed out loud at that thought. *Bonking on Brigit's memory.*

He whistled as he walked home. Brigit's home. His home.

And Topaz had better be there when I arrive. Little blue pill and a beer to the ready.

He wasn't about to wait until nighttime to cement his authority. He had the entire afternoon and evening to enjoy himself.

He was ready for action, light on his feet as he whistled a passing cab. He'd got away with it again.

CHAPTER SEVENTEEN

Ben wasn't in the mood for phone calls. He'd turned his phone off and shoved it in his back pocket. He didn't care, wasn't on duty, so it didn't matter. He'd said all had he wanted to when he met Craig this morning at breakfast. After all the sleuthing he had done, he'd eventually gone home and tried to have a brief sleep.

Once up after his siesta, he just needed to punch a few bags at the gym and pound a few kilometres on the treadmill, before having a few quiet drinks to put him in the mood for sleep that night. The time at the gym he used to wrestle with the demons that were bothering him. Even the mental picture of Rob's face superimposed on the punch bag didn't help his mood. No matter how hard he tried the picture of Brigit kept creeping back.

Then hopefully, after a few quiet wines, he'd be rested and ok for his shift the following morning.

Freshly showered at the gym, bag slung casually over his shoulder, he sauntered into a bar. From the outside it looked just like the Hopper painting 'Nighthawks' with its bright yellow walls and wide windows. It also had that same sense of moodiness despite the yellow, perhaps because of the subdued lighting. It suited him this evening. It wasn't rowdy or busy, and the music was soft jazz, Ella Fitzgerald. He was greeted by a scene of peaceful tranquility. A solo woman was at the bar hunched over, dark hair hiding her face as if she didn't want to be seen. A group of businesswomen were saluting themselves over a glass of wine and another couple sitting closely together, lovingly looking at each other as they spoke.

He wandered over to the bar. 'Dry white please. Riesling if you have it by the glass.' He'd thought he might only spend half an hour here before going home, just winding down. The gym tired his body sufficiently even if it hadn't solved the mental gymnastics still going on in his mind. He leaned on the bar waiting, looking around at the artwork, posters, and the other clientele. There weren't many. He sipped his wine as he looked around when his shoulders went into spasm. He rolled them around to relieve the sudden radiating tension when he recognised the lone woman sitting on a high stool just along from him nursing a drink.

He held his breath and moved over slightly. *I need to know.*

'Mind if I drink here? I won't bother you.'

She turned towards him. Their eyes met. Her eyes widened as she remembered the ambulance, the cold waiting outside Rob's place and the two ambulance officers driving away.

'I don't mind at all.' She swallowed a gulp of wine nearing choking on it. 'I could do with the company.' There was desperation in her eyes as she faced him. 'You were there this morning, weren't you? With the ambulance. I know you saw me. You slowed the ambulance and kept looking at me as you drove by.'

He propped himself up beside her, elbow on the counter and took a long sip, rolling the wine around his mouth. He studied the glass, observed the light-yellow tinge of the wine, swirled it around, sniffed it and took another sip. *Central Otago always does a good Riesling.*

'Yep. Who are you? What were you doing there?'

Topaz looked down at her near empty glass. 'My name's Topaz. Stupid name but it was given to me by my modeling agent way back. I was wearing a Topaz ring when we first met.

Yours?'

'Ben.' He raised his glass in encouragement. Topaz considered what to say. In the end she decided to let the drink do the talking and to hell with the consequences. She liked the kind look on this man's face and suddenly trusted her gut. She had already had enough wine to let down her habitual guard and it all came out in a rush as she gabbled her words, fearful that she would stop.

'Well, Rob, he's the man at the house this morning where that woman died. We've been having an affair and he thinks he owns me. He rang me to tell me that Brigit, that's her name, that woman you attended, had died, and demanded that I come over straight away. He calls and demands my attention, or he comes to my place anytime, and expects me to jump.'

Ben leaned back in his chair, brooding dark eyes looking steadily at her.

'But anyway,' she continued, 'his call this morning was so early I was confused. He woke me up. He said to come, but to be careful as the police and ambulance officers were still hovering around. So,' long pause as she took another sip, 'I waited outside until everyone had left. My heart was thumping, and I was in a right panic. I couldn't believe he'd killed her.' She'd barely paused to catch her breath as the words all poured out of her.

'That's what he did. He killed her. He'd always joked about it so we could have her place. I never thought he'd really do it. And now I'm terrified.'

'So, what did you do?' Ben gave nothing away, but his curiosity was renewed and really wanted to know why she was there at that time so early in the morning. He'd thought about her during the day, in an entirely abstract way of how she fitted into the picture he'd gathered at the scene. Now his curiosity was suddenly more personal, not the removed professionalism as he saw her beauty and vulnerability close-up. His heart kept giving little nudges as if to try and gently awaken him out of years of slumber. *Settle down.*

She paused. Was her need to talk going to override the caution that she'd developed in her dealings with Rob? She'd become much more secretive since she'd hooked up with him. It was a mixture of fear and shame that she'd started to feel some time ago. A hot flush swept over her. She put her head down to hide it and that glossy black swirl of hair covered her face. She took a deep breath and once she started speaking again, her troubles seemed to pour out of her. It was as if she was afraid that if she paused to think she would stop.

'I don't know what to do. I don't know what to do. So I just came here to get pissed so I wouldn't have to think anymore. And now I've had too much to drink while I've worried about it.' The words just blurted out like the Rotorua geyser. Her eyes filled with tears.

Ben didn't rush her, just waited, slow sipping, relaxed and non-threatening until she was ready. People needed to talk in their own time. *Psychology 101.* He noticed other people looking at them, so he moved closer and whispered in her ear.

'Speak softly so others don't overhear what you're saying. You don't know who's here. Pretend we're friends.'

She shuddered and looked around at everybody. There were not many in the bar but the sight of a beautiful woman in distress with a rugged man was getting attention. Just in case. She didn't recognise anybody. She smiled at Ben, raised her glass.

'Thanks for your support. It's been a bad day.'

It was surely that, one of the most difficult days she'd to face because she now had to confront a question of integrity. *Should I be brave and endanger myself by reporting my fears to the police?* She looked at him through her thick black eyelashes.

'I think I'm in too deep with him now. It used to be cool hanging out with him. He was such fun at first. I always felt safe and no-one pestered me. At least in the beginning but lately he's been egging on those two creeps he hangs out with. Simon's the worst, and creepy little Jono. Nigel's quieter. He's a bit more respectful. A bit more watchful.' Another pause for a strength giving sip of wine.

'Rob was just reeling me in like a prize fish, keeping me to himself until I had nowhere else to go.' She paused, steadied her hands on the glass. 'Dirty, sexist creeps,' she spat the words out, fingers curling hard around the stem of her glass.

'I don't know how to leave. Gang girls don't leave, they just disappear. I heard them joking once about a girl who tried to leave a few years ago. One time one of them joked that he screwed her and buried her, and Rob was pleased. I think that was Simon. He's always the de facto leader when Rob's not about. I think he has designs to be the boss. Heaven help me when Rob dies and he takes over. He's one brutal bastard.'

She stopped suddenly as if she remembered something. It was something that had been hovering at the edge of her mind and she couldn't quite place it. It was a fleeting thought which had eluded her all day and now seeing Ben she remembered. 'That paramedic with you. Who's he? Has he been with you long?'

'That's Tom. He often partners me. Been down from Auckland a few years now. He was a paramedic medic up there and transferred down here. Said he had family here. Why?'

'Nothing. I just thought I recognised him from somewhere. But probably not. Probably a doppelganger and it was a bit dark anyway and he was side on to me.' She fossicked in her handbag for a tissue to wipe her face now streaked by her tears.

'Another one?' He nodded at her glass. He couldn't help but feel sorry for her but more worryingly he felt a growing attraction as he watched her.

The barman was suddenly busy, not keen on serving Ben.

The barman finally acknowledged Ben and whispered as he passed over two more glasses of wine. 'I'm watching you mate. Just go easy there with that lass.'

'She's a friend. Just had a bad day. Someone close to her has just died. I'm helping her relax.'

'Yeah right bro.'

Ben grinned, raised the glasses to the barman, 'I'm ok mate. Relax.'

'I really felt sorry for him initially.' Topaz carried on as if she'd never stopped. 'He told me his dad was a cop and that he had a sister who he hadn't seen since he was a kid. I was surprised he couldn't remember her name. His father had kicked the mum and sister out of the house when he was about 10. His dad had wanted Rob to stay with him. He reckoned he had a great life with his dad, Eddie, I think his name was and he never missed his mum and sister except....' she slowed down wondering if she should continue.

'Hang on I'll just get us some water and then you can carry on,' said Ben. 'Here you are. It'll refresh us both. Have a glass.' He had decided that he was prepared to hear her out however long it took but didn't want either of them to get drunk. *I'll leave after making sure she gets home safely.*

'We should have something to eat. Shall we grab some fish and chips here? Soak up the alcohol. There's a restaurant area just back there.'

'That's a great idea,' she said as she got up and Ben admired the grace of a model. As they settled down he asked, 'Has talking helped you come to a decision?'

'It's helping for sure but there are things about his life I simply don't understand and that's why I feel sorry for him as well as being scared of him. It's very confusing.'

'What don't you understand that makes you feel sorry for him?'

'I don't understand how anyone could just let their mum and sister vanish from their lives. Never try and find them again. You know he never saw them again. Didn't know where they went. He just supposed they went to her mum and dad. They were rich. He was a QC or something. His dad never wanted him to have anything more to do with them. Sometimes I think he regretted that.'

Over their meal Topaz loosened up even more and they relaxed into each other's company.

'I was a model for a while. Never in the big league, that'd never happen in Invercargill. But I had dreams of becoming a famous model. An agent found me soon after school and encouraged me. I was successful at first and then a beauty pageant finally crushed my ambition.'

She looked into space, face vacant as she remembered.

'Why? What happened?' Ben prompted her.

'I lost out to a blond white girl and realised that I'd always be up against racism.'

The words Maori and Bluff usually sent a shudder through the god-fearing white folk of the Deep South. Ben remembered his father telling him he could bring anyone home except Maori, and he'd turned his face away from him after that.

Topaz continued her story, 'life was a bit difficult after that and as I got older and the look people wanted changed. I couldn't get work. There were no further opportunities for me.' Without bitterness she raised her glass of water and said, 'cheers to old age,' laughing as she said it.

He liked the way her nose twitched when she laughed, the early tension now gone.

'This pub grub is better than most. That blue cod was simply the best I have tasted for a while.' Ben said as he wiped his lips. She looked over her napkin at him and giggled as she said with a mischievous twinkle in her eye, 'probably came from Rob's father-in-law's fishing fleet.'

At the mention of Rob, they suddenly ran out of things to say and in the quietness of that slight pause the background music suddenly filled their void. With the words of Norah Jones' moody blues song 'Come Away With Me,' they looked at each other, her eyes filled with tears. Their hands brushed together, and their eyes met. 'What if?' he said. 'What if will do nicely.' she replied.

He was gentle and unhurried at first, kissing her softly. She responded, unbuttoned his shirt first and then his trousers. He picked her up and laid her on the bed and undressed her. He kissed her as he removed each item of clothing. First her shirt, soft kisses on her shoulders, then her bra, harder kisses on her breasts. He took a long time over her nipples sucking and biting until they stood proud and erect. He moved on to her trousers and knickers. Caressing and kissing her all over. Then he went onto little teasing motions with his fingers. She'd never felt so desired or ready before. This lengthy passionate foreplay was new to her. She enjoyed it as she stretched out tingling at his touch. He hadn't let her touch him yet and she moaned as she tried to grasp him. She could feel him strong and hot and he let her stroke him slowly at first and then more forcefully. 'Now.' she whispered as his fingers reached a frenzy and he slid inside her.

She sighed, wanting more but exhausted so she just snuggled down against his chest and slept. Ben wrapped his arms around her and looked down at her beautiful face. It finally looked peaceful, the earlier tension in it long gone. *The therapeutic effects of sex.* He smiled to himself as be remembered her willingness and abandonment with him. He couldn't explain his feeling. *What the hell was he going to do now? Encourage her to go to the police? Or maybe just leave things alone and let the police do their job.*

His mind was like a hive. *I could try and talk to Craig. Pretend I had this information from somewhere else, but he'd rumble me as soon as he saw Topaz with me.* Because this much he knew, he was going to see her again. No one had ever made him feel this alive since his beloved Phoebe died.

Thoughts buzzed around, his mind unquiet, busy in his attempt to make sense of her story and his now undoubted feelings for her. *Never believed in love at first sight before. Maybe it's just lust at first sight?* He smiled at the memory of their lovemaking, wide awake as he cradled her to him.

It was nearly dawn by the time he went to sleep and that was rudely stopped short by the ring of Topaz's telephone.

She sat bolt upright confused, grabbed her phone as she wildly looked around her. Without thinking or checking who it was, she blinked rapidly in the soft morning light and answered it.

'Where the fuck are you?' Rob shouted at her. 'The lads say you're not at your place. I expected you to be here at my home waiting for me. Not out gallivanting around. I've been waiting all day and night for you. People have been rummaging around my house and I'm pretty pissed off with everything. You'd better have a good story.' he added darkly. 'Better get over here now or you'll be in for it.'

'H-h-hello Rob.' she quavered. She looked at Ben and without wasting a second to think about the consequences said, 'I'm not coming back. We're through. You murdering Brigit has made me think again about being around you. I don't want to be part of that, or your lifestyle with all those creeps who surround you anymore. I won't talk and you can just leave me alone. Don't call me again.' She paused for breath and went to press the off button.

But before she could switch it off, he said, deadly quiet and so softly she almost didn't hear him. 'You'll pay for this. No-one ever dumps me you fucking bitch.'

She looked at Ben eyes wide open in fear. He held her, rocked her back and forth until the trembling subsided. 'It'll be ok. It'll be ok.' He kept whispering until she went limp in his arms. She finally stood up if not quite ready to face the day at least to start thinking about what she needed to do.

'I have to be at work soon. Do you want me to call in sick?' Ben hugged her.

'No. I'm going to have to face this sometime. He can't do anything, and besides the police will be watching him.' She sounded more confident than she felt.

'Go home, get some gear and come back here. I'll give you a key and we'll work something out tonight.'

They lingered together in the shower exploring each other again. He groaned into her hair, arms tense with the efforts of holding her tall strong body up. She giggled as the hot water cascaded down their bodies. They soaped each other clean, rubbed shampoo in their hair, and were as intimate with each other as they had been the previous night. They dried each other and dressed slowly. They were both reluctant to leave the warmth and security of Ben's home to face the unknown.

It was a misty morning that greeted her as she stepped outside. She breathed deeply and sighed a contented sigh. She straightened her back and went to her car. She'd have to give the car back, but she could do this. With Ben beside her she could do anything.

They were waiting for her when she arrived home.

CHAPTER EIGHTEEN

Day Two

It was a surreal scene when she arrived home, parked and looked around. All seemed quiet. *Safe.* In the dawn mist they appeared, from behind the adjacent trees. She knew these men. Simon, Nigel, and Jono clad in leather jackets, muscles flexing, jaws jutting, arms swinging as they surrounded her with arrogance and aggression. At first, she looked startled, then scared. They blocked her pathway.

'Rob sent us to get you,' said Simon.

'I'm not going. I've told him we're finished.'

'He sent us to get you.' Jono said voice raised. Simon just stood flexing his muscles. Nigel shuffled his feet, looking uncomfortable.

'Hey, go easy there you guys,' he said.

'Let's go.' Simon reached out. She shrugged him off.

'I'm not going anywhere with you. I've told him already we're through and there's nothing more to say.'

'He told us that, but he wants you to know that nobody messes with him.' Simon spoke through clenched teeth. She tried to push past them into her house. They straddled the driveway like a rugby front row, legs apart, fists clenched and heavy scowls on their faces.

Topaz felt fear snaking around her belly. She turned her head around around in desperation to see if there was anyone around to help. She swung her bag at them. Simon laughed.

'Great weapon. Think that'll help you?'

All was quiet. Husbands and wives had already gone to work, and children safely delivered to school, babies sleeping after their morning feed. She opened her mouth to scream when Simon was ready, reaching for her before she had time to utter a sound. His hand clamped around her mouth as he held her in a headlock.

'He's not happy sweetheart,' he whispered into her ear. 'Expected you yesterday and you didn't show up when he called you. And then he found out what you'd been up to and that made him mad as hell. Didn't think he'd find out, did you?'

'We're pretty pissed off as well,' said Jono. 'He had us driving all around last night looking for you. He knows all about you now. You're a fucking slag. Didn't ever want me, did you but yet you run off with that ambo guy for a one-night stand.'

'We're to teach you a lesson,' said Simon. 'So you're coming with us now. We do as we're told. Pity you didn't. You wouldn't be in for it now if you had. Get in the car.' Simon leered at her licking his lips.

Her breath came in gasps as she tried to escape from him. She knew of Simon's reputation, and it terrified her. She looked them, 'please let me go. I'll disappear. You don't need to tell him you've let me go.' She was sobbing now. 'Please.'

'Get in the car quietly of we'll just pick you up and throw you in.'

'Simon, go easy. You don't need to do this. Tell Rob you couldn't find her.' Nigel put his hand on Simon's arm. 'Just tell him she's disappeared or even tell him that you've sorted her. He doesn't need to know you let her go.'

'Stop being such a wuss Nige. Just get in line.' Simon shook him off. 'Just get fucking into line will ya. I've told what to do so back off and let me do my job.'

Topaz choked back a terrified breath.

She struggled to reach her phone. Simon grabbed it, threw it to the ground and stomped on it. 'Boyfriend's not going to help you now you stupid bitch. Did you think Rob wouldn't find out what you were up to last night?'

'We saw you last night in that boozer. Rob sent us to find you. Then we followed you to his house.' Jono piped up. He was dancing on his toes, barely able to conceal his excitement.

'Rob was not happy when we reported back.'

'Not happy at all,' sniggered Jono. 'Here I'll open the door for you.'

She twisted her head enough to loosen the hand covering her mouth. She bit down on it, tasting the salty flavor of blood. Simon gave her a vicious blow to the head as he yelled and looked at his hand. Her teeth marks were already drawing blood.

'You fucking bitch.'

She felt his menace, saw the glint in his eyes, her stomach was heaving. She could barely breathe.

'I'm going to have you good and proper for that. No bitch bites me and gets away with it,' he snarled as he pushed her violently into the car.

'Hey Si. Cut it out. Don't be such a pig.' Nigel was feeling more and more uncomfortable.

'Get the fuck in the car Nige and shut up will ya. I've had enough of your sniveling. You're as bad as her.'

'Where are you taking her Si?' Nigel tried the reasoned approach. 'Back to Rob's house? Leave it for him to deal with her.'

Topaz was now jammed in the back seat between them, so tightly she couldn't move. Her head was ringing, and she felt woozy from the blow. She wanted to throw up. Simon started touching her up as she sat slumped in the seat stunned.

He whispered to her, 'we're going somewhere you can't be seen or heard.'

Nigel looked sideways, now apprehensive. 'What'd Rob tell you to do? I thought we were just to pick her up and take her to him.'

Simon sneered as he looked down at the sobbing woman. 'He told me to sort her.'

Through the fog in her head, Topaz heard the threat. Fear bubbled up almost drowning her, and she opened her mouth to scream only to find Simon's hand clenched over it once more.

'You're not going to bite me again bitch,' said Simon's voice in her ear as they drove off in Jono's V8 with a roar of the engine and a squeal of the tyres.

'Easy mate. Don't want to wake the street,' said Simon.

She was trapped, heart beating in her chest and desperation in her eyes. Jono was driving, fast into the countryside. Thomsons Bush was their destination and at the speed Jono was going they reached it in double quick time. With a scream of the brakes and a big wheelie he brought the car to a stop well into the bush, hidden from the road.

The quiet and serene forest of remnant Kahikatea was used in the summer for trekking and walking. A place for families to visit and picnic, where dogs and kids could run freely amidst the majesty of the statuesque trees. But at this time of the year it was still, gothic, and forlorn with the residual early morning mist gradually dissipating into the nascent sunlight. Today there was menace and oppression in the air. All the love of last night with Ben was now forgotten in her terror.

Simon dragged her out of the car by her hair, and with terror etched on her pale tearstained face she fought for her life as Simon pulled her into the deepest recess of the bush.

'Simon what the hell is going on here?' Nigel shouted.

'Rob wanted her taught a lesson before he dumped her. You coming or not? Stop being such a pussy. Want to be in the gang then man up will you. You can have your turn after me.'

'I didn't sign up for this shit Simon. Cut it out. She's scared enough now. Let's just take her back.'

When Topaz screamed this time, Simon let her. There was no one other than her captors to hear her out here. No one to save her. Simon held her down while she fought like a tiger, clawing at his face kicking for his. Simon's strength eventually overpowered her.

Nigel hung back wondered how he could stop this without putting himself at risk. He couldn't. In the end he just waited by the car. 'Coward,' he muttered to himself.

He chose not to help Topaz. He stood back ashamed of himself and what he'd become. He didn't watch the rape, but he heard her cries. Nigel could only imagine her fear as he held his hands up to his face. He didn't see Simon's rage as he held Topaz face down, or see her struggling for breath, her face against the ground as she lay under the weight of Simon. Topaz felt hands around her throat before she slipped into unconsciousness. She had stopped feeling the pain. Her last thought was Ben's smiling face and his gentle hands. Her last feeling was one of regret before the darkness took her. She stopped feeling the pain. She was now limp and unresponsive. And then the darkness took her.

Silence descended when the men finally finished.

Simon nodded to Jono, 'zip up and go get the spade.'

Jono looked at Nigel leaning against the car hands in his pockets.

'We need to dig a hole. You coming to help?'

Nigel just shook his head, swallowed hard to keep the gorge from rising, but followed Jono. *I need to get out of this. Simon's changed. Turned nasty ever since we've been with Rob.*

He wanted to see where they had buried her in case he decided to go to the cops. Jono dug a shallow grave, and Nigel looked on in disgust as Simon rolled her in the hole. He refused to help. He ignored the sneering laughter of Simon and the words, 'wuss,' whispered to him. They covered the grave with the fallen orange leaves of autumn. The fresh grave they'd created looked natural in its gloomy surroundings. Just a slight hump in the ground looking as if it had always been there. They left a scene as calm and serene as it was when they first arrived.

Nigel dragged his heels, looking over his shoulder as he tried to come to terms with what had happened. *Thisis not for me, this new violence of Simon's.*

'Good that I knew about this spot. I come here rabbit shooting with my dog,' said Simon as they sauntered back out to the car. Now they were safe, and nobody had seen them, he shrugged of any his earlier worries about being caught. Job done. They drove off without a backward glance or care in the world. Nigel had his arms tight across his chest, eyes closed.

'We'd better go home after we've reported to Rob and clean up just in case. You need to have a shower Jono to make sure there's nothing on you to tie you to this.'

'Nobody will find her for months. It's too cold now for anybody to be rambling about here.' Jono didn't like showering, didn't intend to take Simon's advice.

They drove back, Simon in good spirits, Nigel subdued, and Jono, normally the quietest of them, was full of himself. His uncle Rob had only ever been a shadowy figure spoken of in whispers when he was a kid. Jono knew that the others barely tolerated him and only allowed him to hang around because of that connection to Rob, that, and the fact that he grew bloody good weed. It was his one of only two talents, those green fingers of his, that and his ability to drive fast. He drove carefully for once, not wanting the cops to stop them.

'We're not going to tell Rob everything Jono, so keep your trap shut,' said Simon as he opened the door. 'He doesn't want to know. He said he needs deniability.'

'What do you mean deniability?' asked Jono.

'So he can't tell the cops anything and we're all safe. Right Nige?' Simon turned and glared at Nigel in the back seat.

CHAPTER NINETEEN

Ben came home from work later that day, feeling hope in heart. He hadn't felt this keen to come home for years. His happiness turned quickly to worry. There was no sign of Topaz. No sign that she had even been back to his flat. He rang her. No answer. Just a crackling noise. He drove around to her place. It was locked. There were letters in the box. Her car was there in the driveway locked. He looked through the windows. Nothing. He tripped over the broken phone when he rechecked her car. *Oh shit.* The worry changed into vice-like alarm stooping his breath. It was like an octopus with its tentacles wrapping around him as he fought the urge to panic. *Be calm. It may be nothing.* He raced around the back and tried the doors and windows. Nothing broken and all closed tight. Maybe the neighbours?

'Hi. I'm a friend of Topaz. Have you seen her this morning?' he asked her next-door neighbour.

'No nothing sorry. Don't see much of her these days. Baby's a bit of a trial so I don't get out much. Is she in trouble?' Her voice trailed off. She looked worried, but the baby then started wailing again, and harassed and harried she hurried off to attend to it.

'Thanks,' he muttered, and rushed to his car. He drove quickly round to Rob's place hoping he might catch a sign of her to reassure him that she was at least there and still alive. There was no sign of life at Chelmsford Street. The curtains were drawn, and the place looked deserted. Brigit's car was still where he'd seen it yesterday. *Where was Topaz? Was there anyone even in there? Had she gone back to him? Willingly or forced? He reached for his phone.* So many questions flooded his mind.

'Craig Arnold please.' he asked when connected.

'Arnold.'

'It's Ben. I know this is strange but....'

'But?'

'I met up with that woman I told you about yesterday. The one just sitting outside in her car. Bumped into her at the pub last night and we got talking. Her name's Topaz and I expected to see her this evening. But…' he paused unsure of how much he should confess to just yet.

'And? What else? Go on.' Craig sounded impatient.

'I think she's disappeared and maybe in trouble. She may have been abducted. Her car is in her drive, her phone smashed on the ground but there is no-one home. The neighbour doesn't know anything.'

Ben took a deep breath and fessed up. He recounted the last twenty-four hours, the time he had spent with Topaz, the phone call from Rob, the implied threat. He passed on the information she had given to him about Rob. There was nothing to lose now. Her safety was more important than fear of breaking confidences. He described in detail her early distress and her fears about Rob's part in Brigit's's death.

'She was scared that she'd be seen as an accessory to murder,' he added.

Craig listened to all of this with a mixture of interest, hope and concern. Interest at the wealth of new information which filled in many of the holes the police currently had, hope that maybe, just maybe, they might be able to get a conviction this time, especially if Topaz would be a key witness for the prosecution. They'd have to offer her immunity and safety for her to agree to that. And finally concern that she was in danger as Ben had suspected, and her disappearance was troubling.

'You know we can't act on this just yet. There's no evidence of foul play even though I agree with you. Rob was released yesterday and will be busy calling in favours and debts. He'll be sorting out his gang problems, finding out what happened in Bluff, and protecting himself from us, the courts and his disaffected mates.'

Craig continued. 'He'll also be tied up trying to get in on the act regarding Brigit's funeral and estate. He's aware now that her sister, Georgia and son, Dr Niall Smithson are here and that they're the beneficiaries of Brigit's assets. So, he'll be working on how to marginalize them and get them off his back. Probably go to court that one.'

'Niall is the son of the deceased?'

'Yes. You know him?'

'Yes. As a GP. I've come across him in my work. But we used to play a bit of cricket together too.'

Craig nodded and picked up his train of thought.

'But he'll be pretty nasty to Georgia and Niall to try and scare them off. He'll also hope that time is on his side and they won't want a long court case when he challenges the Will, which I'm fairly sure he'll do. I'm just thinking this whole thing through out loud.'

Ben could hear him breathing as he mulled over the possibilities. 'Topaz is a risk for him now. No doubt about that and what she told you is extremely helpful. Let's see what we can find out. Call you back.'

Craig clicked off, rubbed the stubble on his chin. He'd had no time for a shave yet and he desperately needed to get home and shower.

'I'm going home to have a shower and clean up.' he said to the others.

'Good job,' called back Philip to laughter.

'Barbara. Just as a matter of interest have you had the chance to check when Brigit's death notice was lodged?' Craig paused on his way to the door.

'Yep did it as soon as you asked. It's here in the file. Just a mo.' She rifled through papers until she found her file note. 'Yep here it is. It was sent through by email at 3.45 am on the day of her death.'

'Thank you. That's the confirmation we were looking for. He did delay calling the ambulance and he did lie to us about what happened.'

Philip looked at the file note. 'Enough to pick him up again Craig?'

'Not yet. Let's get all the evidence together then let's go to the judge, lay it out and get a warrant. I want the courts behind me for this one and he's not going anywhere fast. I'd like to keep him locked up and away from Georgia and Niall so he doesn't interfere with them, but it's more important to get the file absolutely in order so he can't wriggle out of this one. Would you two work on the papers and get a time in court while I'm gone please?'

'Ok boss. Will do. It'll be here for you when you get back smelling as fresh as a baby.'

He left to gales of laughter thinking that he'd check out Topaz for Ben while I'm out and about.

CHAPTER TWENTY

Rob peered through the curtains and smirked. He'd heard the car arrive and watched as Ben parked. He saw Ben lower his window down, use his phone. The curtains, grey with dust were now tinged with the yellow brown of nicotine. His nose twitched, but the curtains gave him cover. It suited him to live his life unseen and grubby curtains gave him the all-important privacy he needed. Clean ones would open him to the world, and he worked better in the dark without the cleansing light of sunlight shining down on everything he did. *Let's have some fun.*

He strolled out, lit a ciggie and leaned on the car, nonchalant. 'Looking for someone?'

Ben waited. Years of being a paramedic taught him the virtue of patience. He looked coldly at Rob. Remained silent. Still. Waiting.

Rob knew only provocation, not the gentle art of waiting for the answers. He broke first. He couldn't help himself. Anger at the news of Topaz's betrayal with Ben, had him at boiling point. He still had to work out how he could get at Ben for stealing her.

'Topaz's done for,' he smirked as he prowled around. 'You'll never find that bitch.' The menace in his voice was unmistakable.

'Thought she was yours for the taking, did you?' He stubbed

his ciggie out on the bonnet and waited for a reaction. Ben sat unresponsive, fist balled tightly on his lap. Nothing showed on his face as he watched confusion and anger on Rob's.

'Nobody dumps me, even for a one-night stand like you' he snarled. 'She's gone and you'll never find her. I've sent her away to keep her from you. You thought I wouldn't find out about you two?' His mouth hard in a thin line.

He stalked around the car waiting for a reaction. None came so he continued goading.

'My three lads had fun though. Bet you didn't know they snatched her when she came home this morning.' he added. 'But then she's always liked a good three-way fuck.' He laughed as he went back inside.

Ben inhaled deeply and closed his eyes for a moment. He called in to St John's. 'I'm off colour today. Must have eaten something iffy. Feeling a bit queasy so won't be in tomorrow.'

Rob's boastful goading confirmed for him that Topaz was dead. He waited to see what Rob would do when the police eventually drove by. He knew that Craig would guess where he was if he wasn't at home or in the cafe. The unmarked police car pulled up beside him, motor idling.

Craig lowered his window. 'Anything?'

Ben got out of his car and got in beside Craig. He repeated the conversation, word for word, and added. Craig cut the engine.

'He didn't exactly say so, but he's had her killed. I don't know where or how or where he's dumped her. He implied that he'd sent her away somewhere. He also suggested his lads had raped her. But I know he's had her killed. I can sense it and he's gloating.'

Ben knew that women in the gangs were particularly vulnerable. He had treated them, dressed their bruises, and cuts, reset their dislocated shoulders, tried to rescue them and watched them return to their abusers, until next time. It was an endless circle. It was rare for a woman to be allowed to leave and he knew the risk that Topaz had taken. He didn't expect such a quick reaction from Rob, or that he would find out so soon. *Must have sent his lads looking for her.*

'Keep out of it Ben.' Craig warned. 'I don't want to have to pick you up for doing something rash. Nor do I want to find your body. Leave it to us. We don't want you compromising this case Ben, so stay away. I mean it. We have enough evidence now about the timeline and his delay in calling the ambulance to have him charged so don't go cocking anything up.'

'What evidence? Tell me. I won't do anything stupid.'

'No Ben. You might do something which could prejudice the investigation into Brigit's death. Apart from the information we've now got about the time he lodged the death notice, we have precious little to go on.' he warned, 'so go have a coffee or something to eat and calm down. Topaz's disappearance for now is a secondary investigation. We'll look for her.'

'What else do you know about the events that night?' Ben was still probing, hoping for a glimmer of information.

'It's coming together,' said Craig. He was the policeman, not the friend here.

'When did he advise the newspaper?'

'3.45am.' Ben was surprised that Craig had answered.

'Long before he called us then.' Ben said.

'Yes. He must have been anxious to get it into the paper quickly. Lodging his claim perhaps?'

'What do you mean?' Ben was curious.

'He described himself as her partner.' Craig started the car.

'Not his landlady?

'Ben, enough of your questions. Go,' said Craig. 'Go and calm down.'

Craig waited until he saw Ben drive off. He felt weary, despondent. The local force had known about Rob Bennet ever since he'd come to Invercargill. They'd been forewarned about him. Yet for all their attempts and all their skills, Rob had so far made them seem incompetent. Craig's team never seemed to catch a break over Rob's activities. Mouths clamped shut tightly at the mention of him. No-one in the force had succeeded in breaking this wall of silence. *I know someone in the force is helping him. Is it Brendon? Maybe when confronted with the evidence of a crime he could be convicted for, he'll give the rotten apple up just like he did in Sydney.*

Craig sighed. It was another long day and he wasn't going to get much sleep for a while. He needed that shower and a top up of caffeine.

He got back to the station half an hour later, nicely cleaned up and ready to sit down in the situation room to discuss everything over coffee. The three of them sequestered themselves away with files, notes, and a white board and over brewed filter coffee discussed the possibilities. Someone had thoughtfully produced muffins from somewhere.

Philip's fine eye for detail was always valuable and Barbara added an extra dimension as well, helped by a degree in psychology. *That's always useful if you're in the police.* Her skill as a profiler based on her studies had helped the team immeasurably over the years, and a lot of the station's success rate was down to the three complementing skills they possessed. *Shit, I hope I'm wrong about her partner. That might just destroy her personally and professionally, and she was too good a cop to lose.*

'I'm a bit concerned that Ben's going to go off halfcocked,' he said to them.

'Why? What's he done?' Barbara paused pouring a cup of coffee as she asked.

'Lurking around Bennet's place. I told him to get lost. He's a bit compromised now he's confessed to me he's had a one-night stand with Bennet's girlfriend who seems to have gone missing.' Craig added, 'We don't need any more complications.'

'Wheew,' breathed Philip. 'What else did he confess to?'

Craig filled them in on what Ben had said.

'So, we also need to investigate his fear that she's missing, presumed dead?' asked Philip.

'It's an informal notification that she's missing so we need to be mindful as we progress with Bennet,' said Craig.

'Ok,' Barbara said, 'I'll put the wheels in motion on that. Some juniors can go and do a door to door.'

'Why does Ben think she's dead? Because she betrayed Bennet? Is that enough to kill someone?' Philip asked.

Barbara looked over her shoulder as she left and said 'He'd do that I reckon. That would fit the profile of a violent narcissist.'

'OK, put your thinking caps on, look at different scenarios. Look for inconsistencies. Look for coincidences. Do it for a couple of hours and then get home. We'll meet back here in the morning for a strategic review. It's going to take dogged footwork and we need to start now so you can all get some family time. So, heads down and go over everything with the proverbial fine-tooth comb. What have we missed? Where are the holes? How do we fill them in? Who do we need to talk to? Draw up a list when you've finished that go see your families. Get some rest and we'll start afresh in the morning.'

'Ok boss.'

'And Barbara, draw a chart for us will you. Something visual will help us,' Craig added as he walked to his office.

She nodded and Philip put his head down, buried his nose in a file until finally he got up stretched and said to Barbara.

'I'm off home to mull over all this. See you tomorrow.'

Barbara nodded and took her time looking through the paperwork of some decades. She went over the files, all the information they had on Rob Bennet. She drew her chart, looked at it, and relooked at a file. She frowned, reached for her bag. Looked around and then left the room quietly. She slipped out unnoticed. If Craig had seen her face and what she'd been reading he'd realise that it was too late to keep his fears of a mole in the force from her.

Barbara didn't know what the hell she was going to do.

But Craig had already picked up his jacket, brow furrowed. He had a further worry. One he didn't want to articulate yet to his team. *What will it do to our friendship if I catch Ben acting outside the law? Or for that matter his chances of retaining his job or joining the force?*

'I need my own plan.' he said out loud to himself as he walked to his car. *I need help. I also need a wine and decent food. Then sleep, ready for whatever tomorrow brings.*

CHAPTER TWENTY ONE

Ben hadn't wanted to go home after leaving Rob's house. He needed the sound of people talking and laughing, not the cold emptiness of his home. Hunger was also gnawing at his belly.

Do I go off 'half-cocked'? Do I seek out my own information with which to help the cops?

Whatever he chose to do, Ben wanted Rob convicted of Topaz's murder or at least of her abduction. And secondly to find Topaz's body so the police could tell her parents something definite, and give her a proper funeral. If they still didn't want anything to do with their daughter even when dead, then he would arrange it himself. He also wanted to get vengeance for Topaz. One way or another he'd try to do that at least.

He went to his favourite café. He was finishing his first glass of wine, barely hearing the chatter of a crowed café, when Georgia Chappel and Niall Smithson walked in.

It was an unlikely serendipitous moment as if Ben was watching in slow motion through a mirror. Three people happened to conflate at the same time in the same place, each of them with revenge on their minds. But Invercargill is a small city. Disparate people pass by each other every day, knowing of them, if not actually knowing them. Enough to nod a passing greeting even if they don't stop for chat. Good cafés are few and far between and this one was the best in town.

Although Georgia didn't know Ben, Niall did. He nodded at Ben and looked around the crowded café for a table. Ben called them over.

'It's a bit crowed in here this evening Niall, and I've got room here. Why don't you join me?'

Ben's thoughts rapidly crystallised. If he wanted revenge, he needed support. What he needed to know now was what did Brigit's family feel? *Carpe diem. Seize the day.*

'Thanks Ben.' They settled themselves down. Georgia was looking strained, the lines deeply drawn on her pale face. Niall was grim, his mouth a tight line. The waiter came with a menu. Niall nodded his thanks.

'Niall, I've not long learned that the woman I attended this morning was your mother,' he held out his hand. 'I'm sorry for your loss.'

'Thanks Ben. This is my mother's sister who arrived down here today to visit Brigit.'

'Hi.' Georgia was tentative. 'Thank you for offering your table to us. We needed something to eat after today. Didn't feel like cooking. Needed to get out.' Her voice was soft, staccato, strained as if she couldn't put two words together without faltering. Ben could barely hear her.

'I'm sorry about your sister. I'm the ambulance officer called to her and I failed to save her. I'm sorry.'

There was an uneasy pause as they gazed at him unblinking. Georgia barely looked at the menu. Ben could see her emotions fighting with each other. The anger, sorrow, and fear all plain on her face. Her breathing was shallow, rushed as if she'd just run a marathon.

'I don't want much Niall. Just a wine and cheese rolls.' Niall nodded. It was if he couldn't speak. He was rigid as he went to place their orders.

Georgia, desperate for information, filled the void with chatter, holding back the questions which still remained in her mind.

'Brigit's death was so unexpected. She was supposed to be

coming back to Auckland with me. I don't think it was natural.' Georgia burst out, turning to Ben.

'Easy George,' Niall said. 'We don't know who's listening.'

'It's just that nobody has said anything. Nobody's explained anything. I need to know if that bastard killed her. Do you know anything?' She turned to Ben. 'Can you tell me anything?'

Niall looked surprised. 'Paramedics are not doctors, Georgia. No offence to your skills Ben.'

'None taken. But we do get to assess the scene before it's contaminated by lots of people arriving,' Ben said cautiously. 'Why do you think he killed her Georgia?' he asked.

'He's always threatened her, directly and indirectly and he's been behind all her accidents. I'm sure of that.'

'I've attended some of those as well,' Ben said. 'This is what I can tell you.'

They listened as Ben told them about his visit in the early hours of the morning and how he also felt that things were slightly off key. As he spoke, he sensed an increasing level of agitation from them.

'Bastard's going to get away with it isn't he?' Niall blurted it out. Although he and Georgia had talked about their options, he was keeping that close to his chest.

'No evidence to show that anything untoward happened Niall. Just my gut feeling and that's not enough,' said Ben.

'You said you didn't know Brigit?' Georgia said.

'No.' He waited a beat. He then segued into another stream of thought.

'Did you know a woman called Topaz, who was having a relationship with Bennet? I came to know her well. She's disappeared and I suspect has just suffered the same fate as Brigit. There's no evidence there either. But I reckon Rob had a hand in that as well.'

'We hated him and were trying to get Brigit away.' Georgia was forceful in her condemnation. 'And yes, we all knew about a relationship with a woman although we didn't know who it was. There were always signs when she'd been visiting.'

'The faint aroma of perfume. The bed. The unwashed extra

coffee cup. That sort of thing,' added Niall

'I'd come down here to help Brigit clean the place up and arrange all the necessary stuff for selling up. She was going to move up North with me and I wanted to make it easier for her.' Georgia put down her cup and looked faraway in the distance, towards the gracious trees in the park opposite, standing ghost like and leafless as the moon slowly made its appearance.

'We'd organised for an estate agent to come while Georgia was down here to arrange the sale.' Niall said.

'That's why we think her death is suspicious. He wanted her house. And now he's claimed he's her partner.' Georgia sucked in her breath before continuing. 'Brigit never was. She hated him. She was scared of him even.' Georgia looked back at them tearfully.

They all sipped, eying each other, wondering about trust, wondering how far either party was prepared to go. Wondering even should they all be sitting here together looking like a mini mafia cabal, as if they might be plotting and planning?

Georgia looked around anxiously checking to see if anybody was watching them. No-one seemed to care. Everyone was engrossed in their own business, enjoying their own meals. The noise of chatting and laughing floated around them. Reassured she turned back to Niall and Ben. *Should we? Shouldn't we?* Each of them engrossed in their own thoughts of revenge.

How to start talking about what they were planning on doing? Niall was fidgeting.

All of them seemed to recognise the anguish in each other and the desire for action, even if it was unspoken. It seemed initially like an impasse.

Niall and Georgia looked at each other, looked at their coffee, and took a deep collective breath. Ben observed them shrewdly waiting for one of them to break the silence. He thought he'd prompt some action.

'You want to do something, don't you? Do something to avenge your sister and mum?'

'We've been talking about what we can do to get Brigit justice.' Niall chose his words carefully.

Ben leaned forward his hands clenched tightly around his mug. 'I've been sitting here all evening thinking. I'm going to get Topaz justice. While he may not have directly killed her, she died on his orders. He found out she was having an affair with me and Topaz had just told him she wasn't coming back to him. She told me about his plans to get rid of Brigit and claim her house. Said she'd never thought he'd act on them, that his bragging was all big noting. A game. And now because of me, she became a risk and one which he needed to silence. And I can't just let that go,' he said fiercely.

They looked at each other. Niall and Georgia surprised at the vehemence and frankness of this statement.

'There'll be no evidence for either event. It's too coincidental them both dying within 24 hours of each other, both with connections to the same known crim. You can join in or not, but one way or another I'm going to put that bastard out of our collective misery.' Ben added voice low and tightly controlled.

Ben paused as he eyed them. *Have I just blown it? Oh well, in for a penny.*

He continued, 'the police won't be able to do anything. There isn't enough evidence yet, in spite of what Craig says.'

'Craig?' Niall asked.

'The lead policeman and an old friend. We went to school together.' Ben paused for a moment collecting his thoughts. 'If that bastard's done away with a woman I had come to like, I can't bear to just sit on my butt waiting for justice to grind its way through the system while he laughs at us all.'

Georgia was still, mouth open in surprise. Niall thoughtful, gazing steadily at Ben.

'At the same time,' Ben continued relentlessly, 'he'll be planning how to take your property and get rid of me. It's galling to know he'll do that. He doesn't care for the lives he's ruined.'

He stopped and sucked in his breath looking anxiously around. That was the most impassioned speech he had ever made. His legendary calm had deserted him. He was hyped up from too much coffee, lack of sleep, guilt, and anger. A potent mixture of emotions. He rubbed his hands over his eyes and sat back waiting.

'And he won't stop if he gets away with it.' Ben watched their own nervous looks as they considered his outburst.

Georgia looked down at her hands, unconsciously rubbing her misshapen thumbs, eyes crinkled as she did so.

'Sorry, I shouldn't have said that. Forget it. All that angst bottled up all day just came out in a rush. I should've known better to speak when I'm tired and a bit emotional. Perhaps I should have waited some. I'll leave you now. That's a bit unfair on you both.' He was about to get up and leave when Niall spoke breaking the long tense silence. He kept his voice low and slow. He didn't want to be heard by anyone.

'Georgia and I have been thinking what we can do. We know the police are limited in how they act. I understand both their caution and their need to do things slowly and correctly.' He looked over a Georgia who just nodded at him as if to say yes you can speak for me as well.

'Brigit has told us so much about him over the years. We know his threats and the way he uses people. Like you I have heard many rumours and Brigit has told me some things, and I've treated some of his victims in my practice. But they were always too scared to do anything.'

He waited a beat, eyes shut tight, breathing deeply. *I think I trust this guy. He wouldn't have told us all that if he didn't trust us. So here I go putting my career at risk.*

'We know from her what his daily routine is so we feel we can work with that. Also, I'm a doctor, so I can get drugs. But more importantly I've had leukaemia. I've had a stem cell transplant. I don't know if you understand the significance of that?'

'I do. You now have two sets of DNA. Your own in your skin and saliva and your donor's in your blood.'

'And that' said Niall, 'is going to make the perfect murderer.'

Ben nearly choked. Georgia passed him a napkin.

When he recovered from his coughing fit, Ben asked, leaning forward on his elbows, 'what do you have in mind? My access to drugs is limited. Even as an ambulance officer they're controlled so it will take me a long time to get hold of enough. St John's has an audit process every afternoon at close of play.'

Georgia put a hand on Niall's arm.

'Hey guys,' she said. 'It's too public here. Let's go to Niall's. I'll go with Ben to show him the way.'

They nodded, paid up and left, cheese rolls congealing untouched on the plate.

Craig, on his way home had seen Ben's car at the cafe and had just pulled up outside. *Ah, a drink with Ben will set me right for the evening.* But he wasn't quick enough. He saw the three of them leave together. And so did Rob's mob who had been ordered to keep an eye on Ben because Ben was to be their next assignment. All of them wondered at this serendipitous event which had brought three strangers together, and why were they leaving together? What was in their minds of these three unlikely conspirators?

Craig felt a tingle of apprehension. Rob's mob just looked at each other.

'What the fuck?' breathed Simon.

CHAPTER TWENTY TWO

Niall was in a morose mood as he sat in his kitchen looking out at the parterre he'd designed to grow his herbs and veges. As he waited for his visitors he remembered how he'd become such a good gardener. While his vege garden was productive, his special interest was reflected in the gardens surrounding the house with lushness suited to a country manor. He was especially proud of the roses and paeonies They remined him of his parents.

His adored adoptive parents. Veronica and Michael, had given him a fabulous upbringing. He had wanted to be a landscape architect. His headmaster tried to persuade his parents that he was too clever for that and had described the profession dismissively as being little more than a gardener. Niall had mounted an eloquent defense and they had finally left him to his dreams. They thought that over time he would probably change his mind anyway and that forcing the issue in his teens would only cement his desire.

They'd decided to let him work the desire out of his system. They let him loose in their garden.

He redesigned it and planted it up with plants they'd never heard of. Their trust in him was fulfilled when each spring the garden would come alive with trilliums, meconopsis, hellebores and those fabulous old-fashioned roses. The blue of the meconopsis sitting along-side the white of Mme Hardy rose, was a scene of pure beauty. The white trilliums, flowering under the Snake Bark Maple, and alongside purple Duc de Cambridge was another eye-opener.

'What are those little white three-pronged things? And those blue poppies?' His mother had asked him, glass of wine in hand while walking through the garden together one evening.

'The whites are the trilliums, a woodland plant which is why they are happy snuggling up to that maple. The blue ones are indeed poppies. They are called meconopsis and are from the Himalayan Mountains.'

'Oh, how did you know about them?'

'Books mum. Books.' He'd laughed at her astonished face.

His mother had loved those big blousy Victorian peonies which grew like weeds in the Deep South as they infiltrated every Southland garden with their lushness. His dad had liked trees especially Maples, and grew a wide variety of them, and the dark vibrant Gallica roses. They had placed a huge bunch of them on his coffin when he died suddenly in November from a heart attack.

Niall also loved those wonderful old-fashioned roses with their intriguing names and always planted then with the gentle, insignificant, soft coloured crane's bill geraniums. They weaved their way in and out of the garden creating a tapestry to bring the whole garden palette together.

'And those?' his mother had asked, pointing to a small plant with soft blue flowers nestling along the edge.

'Crane's Bill Geraniums. The true geraniums. Those garish things you grow in pots are pelargoniums.' She'd laughed at that.

'I'll probably still call them geraniums anyway. It's what we all call them at the gardening club. Perhaps you should come and give us a talk.' He had quailed at that suggestion hoping it was just a joke. In his early teens he wasn't about to go lecturing little old ladies. He'd never dare call them that, but his mum did describe some of the old timers that way.

A sudden illness at the age of sixteen changed him dramatically.

His view of the future narrowed. Leukaemia hit out of the blue. He learned about things no sixteen-year-old should ever have to learn. Things like, potential death, of life in and out of hospitals, of isolation and of feeling so ill that death seemed a good solution. But he'd also learned about resilience, and the kindness of people as they nursed him, treated him, visited him, or brought him treats.

His life shrank to the confines of hospital and home. He was kept out of school and out of sport. He could barely keep on playing the piano. The different phases of his treatment and progression of the disease had changed him irrevocably. His many near death experiences when he was undergoing his stem cell transplant turned him from a carefree young boy into a much more serious young man. He spent a year or two after he was cured learning to be a teenager, having fun and making up for lost time, until he decided that he was going to use his gardening skills and knowledge for pleasure, and use his experience as a patient to help others.

He turned his mind to becoming a doctor.

Getting into Otago University had been easy. Leaving his newly bereaved mother had been harder.

'I'll be back mum. I'll come home often, and for the holidays and I'll find a job at Kew when I've graduated.'

'I know. I know. But I will miss you and I would never dream of forcing you to stay home. I will have to get used to living alone. I've always known I'd have to one day and I'll start by buying a smaller house. One that I can manage properly. And I expect you to come and design the garden for me.' He had done that and smiled at the joy of his mother's face whenever he visited.

Since his divorce, Niall lived alone, happy with his general practice, music, and garden.

'I've made a difference to people's lives,' he said aloud, 'and in the end I made a difference to Brigit's life even if I couldn't save her.' Brigit had filled his life with new meaning. And now she was gone.

He was forced away from his memories by the ring of the

doorbell. Georgia and Ben had arrived. Surrounded by trees, the gathering was very private and secluded. There was no danger of being overheard here in this secluded haven. No one in this discreet neighbourhood would have given them a second glance.

While they may be sitting in a scene of urban quiet, warming themselves by the little pot belly fire, they themselves were far from complacent. The three of them settled down in the warm while Niall brewed some Colombian coffee. They decided on coffee rather than wine although Georgia was in desperate need of a fortifying drink. *Later. We'll have a wine later.*

While the delicious smell of brewing coffee filled the room, and they were sipping their first mugful, he also quickly whipped up a batch of drop scones from his adoptive grandmother's recipe.

'We left the café before we ate so I thought I'd whip up a little snack for us. Irish drop scones made with soda water, cooked quickly in a frypan, are delicious with cream cheese and salmon. Add some black pepper and lemon juice and it's a meal for kings.'

He was a dab hand at cooking, a form of relaxation with listening to music when he got home in the evening. He'd perfected drop scones when a boy and they became the 'go to' food for hungry students in his flat when he was at uni, even though it was with butter and jam, not salmon. Quick, easy, and filling.

They sat there in his kitchen, the three of them, together but apart, unsure of where this meeting would take them. They were a troika, those three finely drilled horses all pulling the carriage of retribution, just pacing at first, in no hurry to proceed. But were they pulling the carriage of retribution together yet?

Well we're at war. War against a single person and death certainly was on my mind. Is it on theirs? Niall looked at them.

Ben, ever restless when not on duty prowled like a tiger around the kitchen as Niall prepared the scones. 'Y'know I've never thought of hanging art in a kitchen,' said Ben, studying the paintings on the walls. 'But it works doesn't it? Looks good.'

It was a displacement activity, cooking scones, brewing

coffee, and chitchatting about anything unrelated to the reason they had gathered. They were skittish, unsettled, afraid.

'That one I call *the ghost children.*' said Niall. 'It's painted by a Dunedin woman who eventually went blind. That's an awful thing to happen to an artist. Imagine never being able to paint what you see in your mind again. Pure torture, I reckon. It's in the kitchen because I love it, and this is where I spend my time.'

He got up and straightened it. 'The sun streams in those French doors through to the patio and my garden of herbs. On fine days I have the doors wide open. It almost feels Mediterranean on a good day.' He laughed. 'If you can believe that in Invercargill. Cooking is the way I wind down, although it's only me to cook for most days.' he added.

While in the kitchen at the back of the house mentally circling each other, they were unaware of the events outside or that they'd been followed. Not by one car but two. The alert and curious Craig had noticed an older V8 car pull away from the café and follow them, and on impulse he too had followed. The V8 was now parked outside the house. Craig peered through the foggy windows, more interested in that car than in the secluded, sequestered group inside. *Why is it here? Too coincidental. I don't like coincidences.*

The rumours from his sources about the emergence of a new gang and members being recruited by Rob had piqued his interest, and he wondered if the occupants of the car were members of Rob's gang. he knew what young gang prospects had to do to earn their stripes and become fully fledged. He drummed his fingers on the steering wheel. *Young men. In the pay of Rob? Following three key players in Brigit's death? Must mean something.*

He got on the phone. 'Number plate check please.' He rattled off the number to the junior on duty at the station. He waited. He watched.

He rang Philip at home and cut to the chase. 'I think Bennet is having the three of them watched.'

'The three of who?' asked Philip

'Ben, Niall and Georgia. They're all together at Niall's house.

I'm outside watching a car which followed them here to Niall's home,' said Craig.

'He must be worried about Ben. He probably thinks that Georgia and Niall are no threat to him but maybe he feels differently about Ben? From the sound of it, Ben was suspicious at the scene, and Bennet may be concerned about that: the way Ben acted there and the fact that he called us rather than just the funeral director.' Philip was thinking out loud. He paused a while, so Craig carried on his train of thought.

'I don't imagine he knows that the three of them have met up yet. I suspect he's already rumbled to Topaz's all too brief liaison with Ben, and that's the reason she's disappeared. Would be good to know who actually his target is this time.'

'And what is being planned,' said Philip.

'By him as well as by those three inside.'

'Do you think they're planning something and not just three unhappy people taking solace together?' Philip asked.

Craig growled, 'I think they're up to something. It's just too cute to have them meet suddenly like that and then all go off together and meet up here. Never mind Rob's people.'

'Whoever Rob's interested in we can be sure that he's dripping his vituperative venom into the ears of willing cohorts.'

'Hold on. I'll talk to you later. There's another call coming through.'

'The number plate is for Jono Anderson – a known Rob ally. He's a bit of a lad.'

'Interesting. Anything outstanding on it?'

'He's got a history of speeding but warrant and rego are up to date.'

'We wait then.' Craig settled back to watch.

They all remained there until the V8 eventually drove off to report back to Rob.

'We need to get back to Rob,' said Simon putting his foot down hard on the accelerator. 'Something fishy is going on there and nothing's likely to happen anytime soon. Let's go Jono, I'm feeling twitchy about this.'

'Why. What's bothering you?' Jono was curious. Nigel was

silent.

'Well stupid, we killed Topaz for Rob because she had a fling. The man who she had a fling with is now talking to Brigit's family. Why has the paramedic ended up with the dead landlady's family? That's worrying me.'

'Rob didn't kill her though did he? Thought she'd just died 'cos she was old and stuff. We only killed the chick. So, what's to worry about?'

'You're so dumb Jono. Better not say anything to anyone about this.'

'Well they can't do a thing now can they? It's all done, and nobody knows about us anyway.'

'Shut up Jono and just drive.'

Simon turned to Nigel. 'You've been bloody quiet all day. You need to buck up. Either you participate or you ship out Nige. We can't have nonparticipants here. We're all in this together. You, me, and Jono. Just don't forget that.'

Nigel remained silent. Turned and looked out the window. He closed his eyes as he thought.

Craig also drove off to another 111 call. A distressed family out on an evening walk had found something and were having hysterics about it. Homicide had been called in.

CHAPTER TWENTY THREE

Niall, Ben, and Georgia were beginning to relax.

'Everybody had enough?" asked Niall, 'Let's talk before we have a drink. I'll open a bottle of Pinot to breathe. We can have it later with a bite to eat.'

'We're safe to talk here. No-one will even know we're together or wonder why.'

Georgia was hunkered down, shoulders hunched, hand still tightly grasping the mug. She closed her eyes and tried to still her heart. She wondered if the others could feel it thumping in her chest. She sneaked a peek at Niall. He was sitting still, eyes wide open watching her.

'Are you ok George?'

'My hearts thumping like anything. I'm finding it hard to breathe deeply to try and slow it down.'

'I thought you did yoga and meditation George,' said Niall. 'Doesn't that help?'

'I do and yes it usually helps stress, but I've never had a dead sister before or thought of harming anyone. And that's what we're here for isn't it. To talk about killing someone?'

'Me neither, but when I think of the times Brigit was hurt, I harden my heart,' said Niall. 'I am trying to resolve my role as a doctor. And what's more I'm finding it hard to reconcile the thought that I may become as nasty as Rob.'

Ben then took a deep breath. 'Shall we? Should we start talking then?'

'Yes,' said Niall. 'I think the time's right. Are you ready George?'

'Will I ever be ready for a talk about what we can do to avenge Brigit?' She looked at them both. 'But we're here for that reason, so let's start and see where we get to.'

They both nodded.

'You may know some of this Niall, but Georgia won't. I have treated many women who have been mistreated, abused by gangs, often becoming victims to preying male members.'

'I agree,' Niall said. 'I see them in my surgery as well.'

'I think Topaz is their latest victim. She's disappeared.' He gazed into space, hand shaking as he told them about the brief affair, how he first saw her waiting in front of Brigit's house while he was there. When he described her Georgia interrupted.

'How strange. I think I've met her once at Brigit's place, when I was down visiting. One of the many times I was trying to persuade Brigit to sell and come up north. Fat lot of good I did.' She smiled ruefully. 'That woman, Topaz, was there dropping something off to Rob. She seemed uneasy and sad. But then Rob always had that effect on people They always lost their spark.'

She waited a bit before continuing.

'I think you're right Ben. And I'm sorry Topaz's missing. I think he must be involved somehow. I know he never allows anyone to get out of his control. It's what he did to Brigit. Drained the life out of her. Emotionally, and now physically.'

Ben continued his story. 'I've been a paramedic for nearly 15 years since I finished my Health Science degree. I grew up in Invercargill. I really love the job. I like teaching the young ones as well. Perhaps there'll an opportunity later for teaching,' he said. 'I'd enjoy that.'

He waited a beat, then asked, 'What do you know about Rob and his past?'

'Brigit told us lots,' said Georgia. 'Rob thought that she didn't know what was going on, but she did. She was always the smart one. Not at all doolally as he always said she was. That was his way of demeaning her.'

'Rob grew up with his dad.' Niall continued when Georgia paused. 'His dad was a policeman and according to Brigit, corrupt. Rob used to boast to her about him and how he had learned how to use the cops from him.'

'Rob told her how he hated his little sister. He was so happy when she left with his mother and he and his dad were left to their own devices. That's how Rob became the criminal he was. Learned it all from his dad, Eddie,' said Georgia.

'Were there just the two of you?' Ben asked instead focusing on Georgia.

'No, we had a younger brother, but he died young, in his early thirties.' She became pensive, looking out the window, a dreamy look on her face, for a moment all tension gone, the worry lines lifted. 'We went to Catholic schools. Not a good experience. I think that's why we always rebelled, Brigit and me. The nuns would say whenever we got into trouble, which,' she smiled, 'was often, that there can't have been a lot of virtues in our household.'

'Lots of hope, a bit of faith and precious little charity, is what Brigit always joked to me.' Niall cleared the table.

The gentle, almost intimate conversation seemed to ease the strain. It was like a first date as they got to know each other.

'She was the rebel. I think I was the quiet revolutionary. Sedition under their noses. I stuck my nose in books all day or played the piano. The piano was my release from any tension at home and there was a lot of that. On reflection, as more and more is known about post-traumatic stress, I think both my parents suffered from it to a degree. That might have explained the tough life we had.'

'Where did they meet?'

'In the Middle East. She was a nursing sister in the RAF and dad was in the NZ army. She was English and always complained about the shock it was coming to Invercargill. We all left home as soon as we could, and we all went north to Dunedin. Mum wanted me to be a nurse like her. She said it would be a waste of money becoming a doctor because I'd just get married and have kids, so it wasn't worth financing me. Ha - she was not impressed when I fell in love with a woman and had kids by IV. Called them little bastards.'

'Very unchristian of her,' observed Niall

'Eventually I went up to the Far North and lived in a commune near Russell. That was so different to my years at home. Such freedom was bliss.'

Niall laughed. 'Well Brigit never told me all that.' He then became serious. 'Are you ready to talk? Are you ready to solve the problem of Rob?'

He turned to Ben. 'I am going to be open with you both and I hope that you will be as well. I also hope that this conversation remains confidential or as the Romans used to say, sub rosa - *under the rose.* We are now all in this together. If anyone has qualms before we carry on better say them now before we commit.'

There was a sudden stillness in him. He paused for a few moments collecting his thoughts and, speaking carefully and quietly, he started. Georgia found she had to strain to hear him.

Niall continued, 'I don't believe the police will nail Rob on this. I've watched him since Brigit and I first met. She didn't want him to know about me. I couldn't understand it until I heard and saw what he was like. He acts with impunity. The police never bother him. That always worried me, and I wondered why? Although we have no proof that he killed my birth mother, I reckon he played a part.'

He held up a finger as he identified each option until there were three fingers in the air.

'Either he killed her by actively doing something, or, by not assisting her when she was struggling for breath, or by not getting the ambulance in time when she needed it urgently. Any which way you look at it he is responsible for her death.'

His fists were tight, his face contorted and his stance rigid. Ben and Georgia could see it was a struggle for him to contain his anguish.

'He'd always got the ambulance before when she had a bad respiratory attack in the night, but things changed when she told him she was selling up. Although we warned her not to say anything, I think she let slip that she was selling up, or maybe he came across an estate agent's report. She probably gave him notice a couple of months ago when she finally decided to leave. Now, inexplicably, she's dead and he is claiming he is her partner. He's got a gall to do that without talking to George. He never knew I existed. We felt it was safest. But he did know about Georgia because Brigit said he always sneered at the very mention of her.'

'He described me as being unnatural.' Georgia interrupted his narrative and gave Rob the fingers in his absence as she described her anger at his treatment of her sexuality. 'He was deeply conservative and Catholic himself. He had extreme unction before he had his heart bypass. Unbelievable that a man with his criminal history of rape and corruption would resort to old catholic beliefs when he wanted to. He didn't contact me after Brigit died because he wants her property. That's why she's dead.'

She traced the patterns on Niall's table with her finger as she said slowly, 'he's always wriggled out of jail in the past. They managed to nab him when he lived in Sydney but even then, he only got a short sentence because he ratted on his colleagues. He had to leave Aussie after that. There was a contract out on him. We know that some of the police are desperate to convict him.' She sighed and turned to Niall, 'I don't think that'll happen either Niall.'

'Before we start on what we can do to change that, tell me what you meant by two DNAs, and how it will help with 'the perfect crime', if they were the words you used.' Ben had some knowledge but no direct experience. He was interested in why Niall thought he could do the perfect murder.

'I was 16 when I got Leukaemia.' said Niall. 'That's when I finally met up with Brigit. We needed to check the family for compatibility as the various chemotherapies hadn't worked. After about six months of chemo we had to go to Plan B – a bone marrow transplant. We had to find out if there were any matches in the family, so my mother asked Brigit. Fortunately, she, my adoptive mother always kept in touch with Brigit although I didn't know the specifics of my natural parents at that stage. I had never felt the need to explore too deeply.'

'And therefore, he found me.' added Georgia.

'Yes, I found a family I didn't know I had. That's been great. Both sisters started donating blood but unfortunately we had to look at a bone marrow transplant and neither of them was compatible.'

'There wasn't any compatible bone marrow available in the international donor banks either.' Georgia added.

'So, I had to start getting my mind around a stem cell transplant. This was grim and pretty scary for me, as essentially, they had to kill off all my bone marrow to make sure there weren't any leukaemic cells lurking around. They apparently hang around hiding in your brain and testicles. While all this was going on George and Brigit were constant companions to me and my adoptive mum. We couldn't have managed with just the two of us. Dad had died a couple of years earlier so my mum was terrified she was going to lose me as well. They took a load off her.

'A match was found in some placenta blood lodged in the International Donor Bank. A baby born in New York. The transplant itself was pretty ho hum. Just a cupful of blood through IV into a vein and then it's just waiting to see if it will take or not. I had three months at Starship and Ronald McDonald House. Both mums came when they could. And my life was saved by the kindness of strangers to quote Tennessee Williams.'

'And as I lived in Auckland then, it was no issue for me to do my share of being with him.' added Georgia. 'While it was pretty dreadful for Niall it was fascinating for the rest of us to see his blood results over the days and weeks as his red cells crept up and up. We charted it all on a graph. It's a miracle really. We both continued to donate blood regularly, as one thing we learned was that kids like this need blood transfusions, lots of them.'

'So that's the long explanation of the two sets of DNA, mine, and the donor's. But it's also the reason I became a doctor. It was my GP who was canny enough to ask for a blood test when all I had was a sore hip. I wanted to be able to do the same for someone else. Save them before it was too late.' Niall paused, clenched his fist, and whispered, 'and now I want to kill someone.'

'Wow.' said Ben. 'That's pretty dramatic. But how'll that help us?' he puzzled about it. 'I guess that if we do kill the rat, as the police so aptly call him, and you shed some cells you can give a blood test to exclude you. Is that what you're thinking?'

'The police call him the rat as well? Funny I always think of Rob like that. Dirty, smelly and sneaky,' said Georgia.

'Think it's a safety net really. If we do knock him off, we'd better not leave anything around to identify any of us. But with what I have in mind I don't think that's going to be an issue.' Niall rocked back in his chair, armed raised over his head, stretching, wriggling his shoulders.

'Besides,' Georgia added, 'Niall and I have legitimate reasons for being in her house, and you, Ben were there as the ambulance officer.'

'We'll be doing it there?' Ben started. He stopped abruptly when there was a knock on the door, a pause and Sam George walked in. She and Niall exchanged a quick kiss on the check as she greeted him.

'Just popped by to collect my gym gear. Wasn't in my car so I must've left it here last time. I won't interrupt you for long.'

Niall responded by pointing to her gym bag near the hall door and introducing her. 'Washed it for you,' he grinned as he said it. 'What a good little housekeeper I am.' He turned to his guests.

'This is Sam and the love of my life. Sam this is Georgia and Ben. You've heard me talk about Georgia. She's staying here for a bit. We've had a big day and we're now just chilling out. I'll tell you about it later if you are still planning on staying over tonight.'

'Hi all. Any leftovers for me? I've got a few moments before I head off to the gym and face the dreaded personal trainer. She's a witch that woman. Almost breaks me. But I've had a busy day as well so the gym's my winding down time. Been the duty lawyer today and there's a lot happening.'

'Sam left a big firm to set up on her own a few months ago and is working hard to get herself established,' said Niall.

'Well I've just started employing extra young female lawyers as I seem to be getting a lot of business. You know all the publicity about sexual harassment and bullying up north? Well it happens down here as well and that's why I left my old firm,' said Sam.

She poured herself some coffee, dressed a scone, 'any lemon to put on this?'

She chattered on while she quickly ate although she was very aware that her presence had interrupted something.

'Actually, I really need something stronger than this, but that'll have to wait. Had to swallow my disgust at getting a creep released yesterday and I still feel bad about it. Sometimes doing this job sucks when you find yourself as the duty lawyer for the nastiest of criminals in Invercargill. I'll have to work that one out at the gym. The punch bag is going to get a beating tonight.' She laughed dryly. She missed the glances of the other three as they looked quickly at each other, a flicker of concern on Niall's face.

'Sorry I should be more discreet than this. Can't really talk about it and I should let you get on with whatever you were discussing. See you later Niall.' With a cheery wave she grabbed her bag and flew out of the house for her date with the dominatrix at the gym.

Niall said after Sam left, 'we need to be careful to keep her out of all this. As an officer of the law she could be easily compromised.'

They nodded their agreement.

'Time for some wine I think Niall,' said Georgia.

'Hell hey, the thought of killing someone is still freaking me out.' He jumped up, eager to move and got the wine and glasses.

Georgia took over while Niall was opening and pouring. He swirled some around the glass, looked at it under the light, smelt it and took a sip. He nodded to himself.

'The reason I've suggested we all meet here is because I don't believe in coincidences. I couldn't help my sister in her life. I'm going to do so in her death. He abused her in life and is now abusing her in death. He's not only taken her life, but he now plans to take her assets. I'm doing this because she's my sister and because I can. I may have been brought up a Catholic and lived a life that's cherished and supported others, but I've seen the harm he's done. To Brigit and to others. It has to stop. The police have tried and failed. Also, I've got nothing to lose unlike you two. I'm now in my 60s with a frail body, grownup children, and an anger eating me up. If we make a mistake then let's agree it'll be on me. Anyway, judging by the way I feel at the moment, I'll probably be dead before it comes to trial.'

'We all have variations of the same reason. The bullying and abuse of women, knowing he killed Brigit, and knowing that he has always been far too clever to be pinged for anything.' Niall added thoughtfully, 'but that makes him cocksure, too confident with a feeling of entitlement and a sense of impunity. That's his Achilles heel. That's what we can use against him. Pander to his invincibility. He's always got away with stuff before so let's allow him to think 'why not again'?'

For the rest of the evening over the seductive effects of wine, they talked, tossed ideas around, considered options, discarded some and settled on what for them was the most obvious, and hopefully for them, the safest.

CHAPTER TWENTY FOUR

This was not going to be a quick and dirty murder. This was going to be well planned. Well executed. It would leave no evidence. Preparation was crucial and each had a role suited to them. When they'd finished, well sated and more than a little drunk, they saluted the 'murder club' and what they hoped would prove to be a finely executed theatrical performance to an audience of one.

They refined their plan, went over it again and again, nutting out fatal flaws until they were convinced that the plan would work, and they could all do it until finally George called it a day.

'I'm too old to be up at this hour and be this drunk.' she said. 'But man, oh man, I feel better and more alive than I ever have before thanks to all of you, the wine and the delicious food. I'm off to bed.'

She paused and looked at them.

'We have a plan. Thank you both. I'll rest easy tonight and I hope you will as well.'

With Georgia's departure Ben also rose and, as he was about to lurch out of the door, Niall called to him, 'Hey Ben, let me call you a taxi mate. You're too pissed to drive safely, and we'll need you around for a while yet. Pick the car up tomorrow.'

'Good thinking.' He plopped down again in the chair to wait and disappeared quickly enough when the taxi arrived.

'Fīat jūstitia ruat cælum. Let justice be done though the heavens may fall,' said Niall as he showed Ben out.

CHAPTER TWENTY FIVE

Niall was cleaning up when Sam arrived back from the gym. She joined him in this familiar task, not talking very much just waiting for a cue from Niall, but he seemed focused on his own thoughts. There was gentle brushing of hands as they went through the mechanics of clearing the table and wiping benches. She didn't pry or try and break his silence. *Hope Niall isn't too preoccupied for the late-night games for two I have in mind.*

She needed the warmth and physical love of Niall tonight after her rugged day dealing with the aftermath of her visit to Rob yesterday. Her assistance to him as a legal officer still weighed heavy on her and the punching bag at the gym hadn't entirely worked it out of her. She needed to cement her commitment with her body as well as her mind. *Tonight's going to be the night when I make a commitment. And hope that he does as well. But what's happened here tonight?*

She didn't want whatever had happened today to destroy their burgeoning relationship. *I'll just wait until he's ready to tell me.*

'Let's listen to the news before we go to bed.' He turned and smiled. 'Sorry I've been a bit preoccupied about today's events. We'll talk about it later in bed. Afterwards.' He grinned at her. She breathed a sigh of relief.

Niall turned the radio on for the evening's bulletin as they loaded the dishwasher.

A body has been discovered in Thomsons Bush just north of Invercargill by a family walking their dog this evening. Their dog had raced away from his owner and started digging. By the time the family caught him the dog had uncovered what appeared to be a human hand. The police have now cordoned off the area. The family is receiving counseling. And that is the end of this news bulletin. Now for the weather.

'Ben – oh shit.' cried Niall. He turned to Sam. 'That's one of the reasons why Ben was here tonight. I think that may be his missing girlfriend.' Sex went out of their minds.

'I'd better call him.'

'Shall I wake Georgia?'

'No leave her to sleep. She's not had a lot of that lately.'

'What were the other reasons?' Sam asked as she watched Niall dialling.

'My mother's dead. Brigit that is. That mother. My birth mother. Georgia's sister.'

'Oh, poor darling. Poor Georgia.' She went and held him while he waited for Ben to answer.

The phone rang for what seemed ages until Ben answered. 'Sorry was dead to the world. What's up?'

'Heard the evening news bulletin?'

'No thought I'd just go to bed and sleep the worries of the day away. Why?'

'You'd maybe like to come back here mate. They've found a body in Thomsons Bush. There's no other information.'

Ben dropped onto a chair dazed, clenched his hands then rubbed his eyes. He put his head in his hands and slumped over the table. His shoulders shook as he tried to control himself. Niall just waited silent phone in his hand.

'What exactly did the news say?' His voice was barely a whisper.

'Not much. Just the bare facts. A family out walking with their dog which uncovered a hand and the police have now cordoned the area off.'

Ben was silent for so long Niall was prompted to ask, 'want me to come over and get you? You can stay here with us.'

'No. I'll ring my friend Craig,' he said. 'See what he knows.'

He was calmer now and resolute. Niall sensed a hardening in his voice, a resoluteness and determination. Ben's fears were right. He had no doubt that this was Topaz. Retribution was now definitely on his mind.

'He might be in bed off duty.'

'No, he'll be there. He knows about Topaz missing. He'll suspect it's her. I'll be in touch.' He hung up and dialed.

'Ben you can't get involved.'

'Just tell me if it's her.'

'I haven't been here long Ben and we haven't yet started processing the scene, so I don't know. Nothing will happen until daylight. We can't uncover the body until we've processed the surrounding area and collected any evidence and taken photographs. I can't let you know anything.'

Ben interrupted, 'but you'll know if it's a woman before then won't you?'

'There will be a lot of preliminary work to be done before we remove the body and that will take time Ben. The body can only be disinterred slowly and carefully, one trowel at a time with careful brushing away of the soil. We need to work out what damage the dog did to the scene. Also, there's a lot of roughed up earth around the grave. Signs of a lot of activity. Tyre and shoe marks. We need to take casts of them. I can't tell you anything yet.'

'I need to know. I need to see if it's her. I need to see her. I want to identify her.' Ben found himself pleading.

'Do you think that's wise?' asked Craig

'There's no one else who could do it and if it is Topaz, I don't want that bastard doing it. I'll drive out now,' Ben said.

'No Ben. Stay away till the morning. I'll ring you when it's safe for you to come. That's an order as both the lead policeman on the scene, and as your friend.'

Craig looked down at the scene: at the strands of long black hair showing up out of the dirt. He knew it was Topaz but would not tell Ben that until the proper process had been gone through. *I don't want any cock ups with this one.*

'If you come out here now you'll be in the way and we won't be able to do our jobs properly. We'll have a better chance of gathering evidence for a conviction if the scene is not compromised any more than it is now. We must keep the scene secure for forensics. Just wait Ben. Keep away. I'll be in touch.'

Ben stood up, wide eyed, fists clenched. He paced muttering to himself. 'I'm now committed. All doubts gone. No guilt. Just resolve.'

He would be Rob's nemesis, never faltering, always in pursuit. But now it was time to sober up. Meanwhile he contemplated his fleeting relationship with Topaz, how warm and tender she had been, and now, the possibility of a life without her was now a reality. He waited until just before dawn to collect his car and drive out to Thomsons Bush.

CHAPTER TWENTY SIX

On the other side of the city, the news bulletin had prompted a change in Niall. Sam sat with him, holding his hand, waiting, watching.

'I'm ready to talk.' He turned to her. 'It may come out all jumbled and not the way I wanted to tell you, but now's the time.'

'Glass of water?'

'Yes please.'

'I'll start with Brigit, my birth mother and the all too brief time I've spent with her. She told me so much about her life, her travels, teaching special needs kids, and her time living innocently with her killer under her roof. She'd had such a fabulous time until recently. I met up with her only a few years ago but she was in good health and happy. That all changed about five years ago. And recently I've found her confused and despairing about her life'.

And Sam watched him and sensed a change. A flicker of resolve she hadn't seen before. She was good at reading people. Her life in law, with lawyers and in the court, dealing with criminals had left her with an ability to read people quite accurately. She could read lawyers as well as she could the accused, the guilty and the innocent. *This is more than just an innocent meeting of three people joined together under one roof, all of whom had a part to play in his mother's life.*

'Sorry that's all jumbled. Let me start at the beginning. I'll get a brandy.'

She waited until Niall poured them a brandy they sat on the sofa and she listened in silence to his life's story.

'I found Brigit when I got leukaemia. You don't know about that part of my life yet. Georgia whom you met tonight is my aunt and Brigit's sister. She's staying here.'

Over the next hour, with her head resting on his shoulder and his arm around her, he told her all about his discovery of Brigit, when trying to find a genetic match to cure his leukaemia.

'I'd wanted to wait until we had been together for a bit longer before I told you all this. I was always sure of my feelings, but I didn't want to scare you off.'

'Why would I be scared off?' She spoke gently afraid to break the mood.

'Because I really want a life with you. I want kids. I want my home filled with their laughter. I never had that. I didn't want to rush that until I was sure you could accept the fact that the chemo made me sterile and that having children with me would involve a lot more than just having unprotected sex. I wanted to give you time to be sure first.'

'I'm sure and have been for ages and I guessed you were infertile, when I stopped taking the pill.'

'You did that?'

'Yep. It actually wasn't deliberate. The time we went on holiday together I found I'd forgotten the pill and so I thought oh well what will be will be. When nothing happened, I just didn't go back on.'

She sat upright, held out her arms to him and together they just sat, softly discussing their future.

'I want your kids Niall. And the way you've always talked I knew you did as well. We'll just deal with that when we're ready.'

But Niall was not yet ready to confess the plans to kill Rob who was, he'd just found out, technically Sam's client. *I might just need her wisdom. And I don't want to compromise her.*

They eventually went off to bed, cuddled and collapsed into fitful sleep until the phone rang in the morning. Early, just before dawn.

It was Ben. 'Let's do this.'

When Niall and Sam got up and left for work, Ben's car had gone.

CHAPTER TWENTY SEVEN

Day Three

Ben slipped unseen into the depths of an ethereal Thomsons Bush. Ducking in and out of trees in his grey track suit, he remained hidden in the bush. Leaning against a dripping tree, he was unnoticed by the police forensics team and the pathologist. Ben felt as if he were in a gothic mystery. The eerie drifting mist fitted the scene as did the white clothed and masked team of workers moving slowly as they worked. The mist seemed to be amplified by the bright lights, necessary for the technicians to work in.

Ben stared, frowned, as the pathologist called Craig over to where he was bent over the body. *What's he found?* He inched forward trying to hear the gentle murmur of words. He needed to be there in the centre of the action, although in truth there was hardly any action at all. Just the gentle slow zombie like movements of the team as they bent, placed red flags, photographed, picked up, bagged, and labeled anything of interest. *Hope there's something there to catch whoever did this.* Ben's thoughts raced. He wanted the murderers caught. He knew that it wasn't Rob but maybe whoever did it would dob him in as a plea bargain. They'd hope for a lesser sentence if they did.

'What ya got?' As Craig's lanky frame squatted down, his knees creaked and groaned, protesting in the cold. *Shouldn't have played all that rugby. My knees'd be in better shape now.*

Dr Liam Duckworth pointed at the body. 'This is a woman of probably late twenties, early thirties. Although I won't know for sure until I get her in the mortuary. You can see her clothes are torn and that there are bruises on her arms and inside her thighs. There's evidence of rape.' He swallowed. *I hate rapes above all.*

'See the imprint of hands as if her legs have forcibly held apart,' he continued. 'These are only my visual observations here and now. I'll be able to tell you more after the autopsy. We may need to use dental records to identify her if no-one can.'

Craig made no comment. *I know who she is. Good job Ben isn't here. He'd have gone mental at this.* Ben's description of Topaz was good enough for him to know for sure who he was looking at.

'If you look at her body,' Liam carried on, 'there are signs of a struggle. Her hands are already bagged to catch any evidence under her nails. She must have fought back.' He stood up ashen faced. Liam faced Craig. 'This is dreadful.' He shook his head.

'We don't want whoever was responsible for this to be out on the street. They won't stop y'know. People who do this enjoy it. No, these lads had their fun with this poor lass before she died. And I know there was more than one because of the hand marks on her body.'

Liam instructed the forensics' team. 'Leave nothing unturned lads. This is a nasty one and we have to catch these bastards.' One of the 'lads' turned and hissed to her neighbour, the forensic anthropologist of the team.

'Doesn't he realise that its 2019 and women do this work now?' Dr Patrick O'Connor nodded and whispered. 'I have tried to tell him, but he simply doesn't see it as sexism. It's the way people have always acted in Ireland.'

Grumpily she returned to her job of combing the environment and picking up anything that would help catch the murderers.

Patrick was the leader of the forensics team. His doctorate was in forensic anthropology and the Invercargill police were lucky to have him. He'd left a teaching post in Ireland to be with his partner Liam. Invercargill CID was relieved that Patrick was around on the day when this body was found. He was often away lecturing at the Dunedin Medical School.

Once the scene had been carefully searched and photographed and all evidence bagged and labeled, the team started the delicate task of preparing the body prior to the removal. It was only then carefully placed in a body bag and zipped up ready for removal.

Liam took off his gloves as he walked to Craig. 'The scene has been well photographed. Let's get her off to my mortuary. I will tell you more later. Oh, and make sure that the team takes special care of the area under her body. There's often good evidence to be found underneath a body. Criminals always forget that. They make an effort to clean up on top and around but not always underneath.'

'Will do.' Craig looked grim. 'What time will you start?'

'Give me a couple of hours to record the crime scene. Say, after coffee, 11am?'

'See you then.'

Craig turned his attention back to the scene. He just observed, standing slightly to one side. The ghostly figures of the white clad technicians gave it a sense of the unreal. He did not move but his eyes swept slowly over an imaginary grid. Looking for anything out of place. Anything unusual. Anything that jarred with what was normally a beautiful and peaceful scene of trees, shrubs, ferns, and birdlife. On this morning there were no birds singing. No dawn chorus. The sun was low in the sky, the clouds ominous.

He'd a photographic memory, something that had served him well in the past. This was his domain just as Philip and Barbara were better in the interview room. They could sense a lie in a suspect's statement, just like a rat, or dog could sense meat. He could sense the lie in a scene. *We're a good team, the three of us.*

He took his time before finally strolling carefully over to the now empty grave. 'Can I enter here now Patrick? I don't want to disturb anything.' He walked over and stopped suddenly, senses went on high alert, and he caught the lie he was looking for. Almost out of sight near the edge of the shallow grave, he bent down and carefully moved the soil away. *What the fuck?* He called the photographer over.

'Did you get a shot of this?' he asked the police photographer and turned towards Duckworth as he just got into the van with his assistant, giving a cursory wave over his shoulder as he did so. *Too late. I'll talk to him later about this.*

'Missed that on our first pass over. Good eyes you have there. Thank goodness you saw it. It's so small it could easily have been covered over as we worked.'

'Just the way the early morning light caught it. Clouds must have just moved a bit and the shadows changed so I caught a glint.'

With an anxious hover, he watched as the team carefully bagged what might prove to be crucial evidence.

'To the lab with that quickly please. This is high priority.' Craig cast a last glance at the scene before he went to his car. He stopped as if to pick something off his shoe as he watched out of the corner of his eye, a hooded figure slipping quickly out of the mist and into the bowels of the bush. Frowning he wondered. *Ben? Same build. Or maybe the murderer back at the scene to check up on us?*

Craig was thoughtful as he drove to collect his team to attend the autopsy.

'No problems moving the body?' Liam asked the technicians back at the mortuary.

'No all good. Enough ready hands to help.'

'You gonna to be ok with this one?' He turned to his new assistant.

'I reckon so. I need to get used to it sometime. I plan to have your job when you retire.'

'Ha,' said Liam, 'not for another eight or nine years.'

'And by then I will be well trained up and ready.'

'We'll get started in half an hour or so,' said Liam before heading for his office.

Liam had finished his preparatory work and was having his long black when Craig arrived with Barbara and Philip.

'Time for coffee? Any preliminary observations?' Philip as usual was crisp and was all business.

'All in good time young man.' said Liam. 'All in good time. Just sit down and I'll give you my observations from the scene if you wish. Or you can wait for my written report.' He raised an eyebrow at Craig. He had worked a lot with him and recognised his ability as an investigating policeman.

'What were your observations?' Craig was curious. Their forensic backgrounds were different, but invariably they noticed the same things and came to the same conclusions. Although nobody could ever accuse them of collaboration, defense counsel had many times tried to trip them up accusing them of just that. Consequently, when at a scene they tried to keep out of each other's way and wait for a detailed report. This was why Craig tended to observe from the edges and ask permission to enter the dead zone.

'I think, let's wait for my final report. Let's err on the side of caution with this one,' said Liam.

Craig nodded concealing his disappointment. *Wanted to get a quick heads up. Damn.*

They gowned up and went into the cold aseptic mortuary room., all stainless-steel drains and bright lights. Liam's assistant had set everything up and ready, placed the instruments and turned on the recorder. Liam always talked to his bodies. It gave him a sense of calmness and ensured the logical flow of an autopsy, as well as reminding him that these bodies were once alive, humans with a life, family, and emotions. It was a form of respect he gave as he talked softly in his Irish lilt through the grim work of an autopsy.

'11am on Wednesday 18th April 2019.' Liam put on his gloves as he said it. 'This is the postmortem of Jane Doe found in Thomsons Bush at 7pm last evening. She was removed from the site at 9am this morning following a detailed search of the scene. My notes and observations of that scene are recorded elsewhere.'

He stopped, turning to his young assistant. 'Paul, do you know why unidentified bodies are called John or Jane Doe? No? Well let me tell you while we work.'

The three police grinned at each other. Liam was a real history buff and his knowledge of the strange and odd was legendary, as was his propensity for telling whoever was in earshot, whether they wanted to know or not. Paul's eyes crinkled and he smiled behind his mask.

'Well it dates back to Edward III, the Black Prince of the 14th century. The name came from the British legal system called ejectment. It was about the rich and powerful against the less fortunate. English landlords could take court ejectment action on behalf of a fictitious tenant against another fictitious person who had allegedly evicted or ousted him, as a device to rid themselves of an unwanted tenant. Jane Doe and originally John Roe were used to name those fictitious tenants. Nowadays only the term Jane Doe is used. John Doe is also used when there are two unknown bodies. Doe as in the female deer, and Roe as in a species of deer. If it sounds complicated that's because it is, but to put it simply, it was a means to get rid of somebody legally. The rich against the poor. The aristocrats against the commoners. And ever since, any body found unnamed, is called by those fictional characters. Now back to the business at hand.'

His movements were smooth and fluid when he turned back to the body.

'Assisting me in this autopsy is Dr Paul Carkeek and in attendance as observers are DIs Arnold and Johnson and SS Adams. Dr Carkeek is carefully cutting the victims garments off. I am assisting him to remove them. The clothes are now being bagged, signed, and dated for further forensic testing. I note there are no knickers. Craig did you find any at the scene? No?'

There was a brief pause while Paul did all that and carefully placed the bagged clothes on a nearby trolley. While this was being done, Liam was silent as he just looked down at the battered body of Topaz, hands by his sides.

'We now can observe the body. This is the body of an apparently healthy female aged in her late 20s or early 30s. Her hair is black and long. There are no obvious birthmarks or scars on her. I note that there is blood on her scalp, on her torso and legs. There are bruises all over her body. There are signs of earth in her nostrils and under her fingernails. Samples from under her nails, as well as her hair are being placed in a sample bag for testing. There is a koru tattooed on her wrist.'

Another pause while Paul attended to that detail. 'I am now taking samples from her vagina, rectum, nostrils and mouth to check for semen and other foreign bodies. I note there is quite a lot of semen. I will ask if they could see if it came from more than one source. Make a note of that please Paul.'

Paul nodded, made a note, and returned to his sentinel place at the foot of the autopsy table.

The police watched and listened impassively as Liam narrated his observations, checking every part of the body. He paused, checking his audience. 'OK over there?'

'Yep' Craig said grimly. The other two just nodded, keeping their emotions and stomachs in check while holding their distaste for this murder tightly inside them.

Barbara unconsciously wrapped her arms tightly across her chest as she observed the bruises on the body.

'We will now start the internal examination.' Liam paused while his assistant placed the head on its rest to make it easier for the neck and head to be examined. Paul then handed him the scalpel to do the Y incision. As Liam went through the grisly process of cutting, snapping the ribs with garden shears to expose the inner organs, he kept up his patter of what he was doing and what he observed. Paul weighed each organ as it was removed, recording everything vocally so both his and Liam's observation could be transcribed later. Liam, ever aware that this was being treated as murder was scrupulous in his narration. Samples were taken of tissue and blood for further examination.

When Liam came to dissecting the skull, he again paused, collected his thoughts, and described the indentation in the head.

'The indentation is the size and shape of a large flat object. Did you find anything like that at the scene?' He looked over towards his audience.

'Nothing yet to match that description.'

Liam's voice faltered as he narrated, even he, as an experienced pathologist seemed to be emotionally moved by what had been done to the young woman now in his charge. He then fell silent as he took the Stryker saw to expose the brain.

'In spite of the blow to the head there is no obvious trauma to the brain. But with a blow like that which left such an indention on her scalp, she would have been rendered unconscious.'

After he had finished his part of the autopsy, he removed his gloves and silently left the room. The police followed him. Paul Carkeek replaced all the organs, sewed the body back up making sure that everything was anatomically correct and that the body, should it be viewed was as peaceful as it could be. He carefully cleaned the face a look of despair on his face. *This was not going to be an easy viewing if there is anyone prepared to do so.*

He then wheeled the trolley into the chiller. As he left the room he paused and looked back. *What a terrible way to die.* He whispered a brief Karakia for her. He'd noted the koru tattoo on her wrist as he prepared her for autopsy, but he had never seen her at the Marae. He felt comfortable saying his prayer to her. He suspected that there was probably no one else to do it.

Kia koa koutou
Kia tino tika,
Kia mārie te ngākau,
Kia kotahi te whakaaro,
Kia mau te rongo.
Tērā te Atua o te aroha
O te maungārongo,
E noho ki a koutou. Āmine.

If Liam can talk to her as he works, I can at least say a prayer for her as I leave.

He removed the recording disc, went to his computer, slipped it into it and pressed start. Paul waited, eyes closed in silent contemplation until the computer had finished transcribing and then worked on formatting the report and filing it. Dated and signed, it would now be part of the official record ready to be used at the coroner's hearing and any future trial. He printed it out and left it on Liam's desk for final checking and countersigning. And then to his final job, cleaning up the mortuary.

The three detectives left silently, each with their own thoughts and not one of them ready to face lunch. Barbara broke the silence, 'suggest we meet at 4pm to review where we are and to work out who is doing what.'

They went their different ways, Craig to ring his wife.

'Sorry, I'll be late tonight. Have a nasty murder here. Don't wait up for me. Kiss Lucy goodnight for me.'

'Ok. It'll give me a chance to catch up on some work. Lucy will be sad, but she'll cope.'

Craig liked to get home for dinner to help. He remembered the length of time it took for them to conceive and therefore how special this kid was, but it was tough on Beth, working from home as a freelance feature writer while Lucy made the usual demands of a pre-teen when home from school. What's there to eat? When's dinner? Can I use the computer? Can I go out to Di's place?

Sometimes her deadlines caused a bit of trouble in her usually impeccable timing. He gave a silent chuckle at the mental picture he conjured up. Now that would make a good cartoon, *a harried woman hunched over her computer and a kid making mischief all around her.*

CHAPTER TWENTY EIGHT

Barbara went to her office to set up a roster of what to do and who would do it. She had hoped that keeping busy would keep her mind off that poor abused and murdered woman. Her hand moved methodically as she set about readying for the four o'clock meeting. The whiteboard was there, the timeline already drawn on it. She stood pen in hand thinking about adding the latest events onto it. *Was this death related to Brigit's? Did the two of them fit here together? I think I'll wait.* She replaced the pen.

She was orderly and worked systematically, but Craig was much more of a free spirit who worked with his gut and his extraordinary memory. This was often difficult for her orderly mind. He was much harder to pin down than Philip, who, like her was much more systems based. *Still you can't ignore Craig's uncanny ability to solve the seemingly unsolvable. He was like a hound dog. He went with his senses until he found his bone. And invariably his senses were right.*

It was Philip and she who put it all neatly together for the prosecutor to get a conviction. Barbara couldn't put her finger on what it was about Craig. She had just learned to trust him. She had joked with him that he was a psychic and he had snorted in derision.

He went on in his soft burr, 'I'm just an ordinary Mr Plod, with my hands shoved in my pockets, snooping like a bloodhound, and doing my beat. It's just that I am observant, blessed with a good memory, and that makes me seem better than I am. We all share the glory of a job well done and I couldn't do your part of the teamwork as well as you do.'

He had laughed. 'Just look at my desk.'

That's just what he did just then, looked at his desk, ignored it and shoved his hands in his pockets and walked out. He thought better when he walked, visions and ideas swirling around his mind like those bloody winter Southland mists. Swirling slowly around as he sorted and mentally boxed what he had seen, what impressions were there in his mind's eye and how to piece it all together. He was puzzled this time. The jarring note he had found in the grave. It didn't fit and what the hell was it? It was obviously a gemstone of some sort, but it was very unusual in style and shape. He had his favourite thinking walk and his feet automatically found their own way as he puzzled over what he had seen. He knew it would come to him in time, as his feet found their way to the lab. The divine revelation didn't come as it so often did.

'Am I allowed in?' he asked as he pushed the door open. 'It's cold outside.'

'Been up to your old walking and thinking routine, have you?' The laboratory assistant turned and smiled at Craig.

'Yep. Any chance you've had a look at my oddity?'

'A brief one. I've photographed it and put the image into the computer to see if it can find a match. May take some time. But I think it's old, an antique. And I'm not sure if it's a ruby or a garnet, but it is not cut in the traditional way. It certainly is foreign. I think it's from a ring and has some significant meaning like used in a cult or triad,' he said as he walked towards the machine. Craig followed him.

'Is it related to this case?' Craig stopped shaking his head. 'Of course, it must be. It was under the body.'

'Yes, but newly under it. There's no ingrained dirt in it to suggest it's been there a long time.'

'But how is it relevant and can we find the owner?' Craig rubbed his chin.

'Maybe, maybe not. Let's wait and see. I'll email when I know.'

Walking back to the station, Craig got on the phone.

'Ben? Hi. What were you doing at Thomsons Bush this morning?' He didn't know for sure but thought a bluff may get an honest answer. Ben answered straight up, didn't try to explain, or obfuscate.

'I needed to see what was happening. You know it's her, don't you? When can I see her?'

'Yes. I'm afraid it is, you can see her when the autopsy is done. I'll let you know. But you must keep away from Rob's place. Any sight of you there and I'll charge you with obstruction. We'll be visiting him to talk about the discovery of an unknown body.'

'Why? Why visit him?'

'Because she is a known girlfriend of his, even though he tried to pass her off as his daughter. He'll expect it. But we'll dodge around a bit for a while if he wants to identify her. He'll want to and will claim it as his right, and we won't be able to stop him. That doesn't mean to say you can't see her, either to say goodbye or whatever you wish to do. We'll let you know when.'

He ended the call and Ben sat thinking.

Not if I have anything to do with it. He won't get near her again.

CHAPTER TWENTY NINE

Craig asked Barbara to accompany him to Rob's house. He noticed a couple of cars parked outside. *Visitors?*

'Shall we wait and come back later?' Barbara asked.

'No. Let's do it now. I want to see who his associates are. Call in those number plates first.'

He noticed one of the vehicles was very dirty; the tyres caked with mud.

'Notice the mud?' Barbara asked Craig as she pointed with her chin to the car.

'Yep. We'll try and get some on the way out for analysis if we can.' Craig said.

'Get some now. Don't know what's going to happen inside,' Barbara said as she pulled out a plastic bag and spatula.

'Yes. Good idea.' He bent by the car as if to tie a shoelace and unseen by anyone knocked some of the sods into the evidence bag. He shoved it into his pocket.

'Forensics can tell exactly where earth has come from these days,' he observed.

Jono answered the door.

'Hello Jono.' Craig outwardly expressed no surprise when he saw him. *Well, well. That streetcar racing scallywag is now a gang prospect.*

'We've come to see Rob. I presume he's in.'

'You can't see him. He's in bed. In shock.'

'Why's he in shock Jono?' Craig asked the question mildly.

'Topaz's missing.' Jono stumbled over his words to get them out quickly, backing away as he spoke.

'Topaz?' asked Craig.

'Yeah his girlfriend.'

'Girlfriend?' Barbara looked surprised.

'Yeah.'

'Not his daughter?' Craig asked.

'Nah. His daughter's named Amanda, but he never sees her,' said Jono.

Craig and Barbara looked at each other their minds clicking, joining the bits of the puzzle together.

'Not in shock about Brigit then?' Craig was still mild. Non-threatening.

'Oh yeah, that too.' Jono shrugged nonchalantly.

They moved seamlessly into the hall and Jono was forced to shuffle back and let them in. They followed as Jono went into the main bedroom. Craig raised his eyebrows in surprise to see Rob tucked up in Brigit's bed. Nothing had changed since they were here last when Brigit was lying there. *Looked as if it's even the same bed linen, same blanket lying on the floor.*

'What d'ya want. Can't you see that I'm still in bed? It'll have to wait till I'm up. I'm gonna lay a complaint about you harassing me.' Belligerent as usual and Craig wasn't surprised at the reaction.

'It's the afternoon Rob. We thought you'd be up by now.'

'It's been a tough couple of days. First Brigit dying, then you guys hauling my ass into the nick and now Topaz has disappeared, off somewhere else instead of being here. Just when I needed her to help now that's Brigit's gone.'

'Well we're here to talk about Topaz. Jono said to us that Topaz, your girlfriend is missing and that you were worried,' said Craig.

'Yeah, well she's not here and she should be. She said she

was coming here when I rang her, but she hasn't arrived, and nobody's seen her.'

'You asked to ring your daughter when we were first called here the day before yesterday. You called her Topaz. So, first question. Is she your girlfriend or daughter? We can check with the ambulance officers of course. They will have recorded it on their call sheet,' Craig continued mildly.

'Yes, well I didn't want to confuse them by admitting I had a girlfriend. They'd have suspected the worst then.'

Craig let that admission pass and moved on with questions.

'Where do you think she is?' Craig asked.

'Don't know. Sent the lads round to her place and she wasn't there, was she Si?'

Simon shook his head. Jono jiggled about. Nigel stood stoically and silent.

'We think we've found her,' said Craig

'What? Where was she hiding? She's all right?' Rob tried to look surprised.

'Can we sit down to discuss this?' Craig moved some clothes off a chair and sat down hiding his distaste at the recent squalor of the room. He noticed the beer bottles and fish and chip papers. *Celebration?*

'Ah. I think we'll leave you to it?' Simon was quick to try and extricate himself and together with Nigel and Jono, got up to go.

'Just remain where you are. We'll need to talk to all Rob's associates to see what they know.' Craig looked at them frowning, his voice sharp.

'Yeah.' Rob shouted to them. 'Just bloody well sit down where I can see you all.'

'What for?' demanded Simon. 'Why d'ya think we'd know anything?'

'Did you just check her house, Simon?' asked Barbara. 'I'm sure Rob was so anxious about Topaz he would have had you all looking out for her everywhere.'

Barbara was smooth as she stood by the door. They didn't even try to get past her. She wasn't big in height, small and sturdy, a body builder. She stood like a boxer and ready to out box them if they tried to hustle past her. They stood sullen, shuffling, looking out the windows, at their hands, anywhere but at the police. Only Rob was cool, gazing at them all in complete feigned innocence.

'Why do you think it's her? I haven't reported her missing until just now when you asked about her.' Rob said. Jono put his hand to his mouth. Craig turned slightly and looked at Jono who immediately dropped his gaze.

'No, you didn't Rob. Someone else did. Which begs the question? Why did you not report your girlfriend missing? We know you rang her when Brigit died. We know you rang her the next morning. Weren't you worried about her when she didn't turn up? Did you expect her to?'

'How do you know that?'

'Phone records.'

'You checked my phone records? How are you allowed to do that when I'm not charged with anything?'

'A judge gave us a warrant. The courts are always helpful when we report a suspicious death. Especially when the Police Gang Unit is involved.' Craig said.

'Nothing suspicious about it. Brigit died in her sleep. I told you all that and here you are again harassing me. That's illegal y'know? I'll call my lawyer now. What's her name again that pretty little piece of arse?'

'No need for that Rob,' said Craig. Barbara's lips tightened in disgust.

'Why are you talking about Topaz anyway? Thought you were interested in my fiancée Brigit.' Rob demanded.

'Brigit is an ongoing investigation, but Topaz's investigation is just starting.'

'What investigation? You don't investigate a missing person till after a couple of days. Even I know that. Is she dead as well or something?'

'Why do you ask that Rob? Do you know something? Want to tell us anything?' Barbara asked.

'No. You're just fishing,' said Rob defiantly.

'A body was found in Thomsons Bush early this morning and we believe it to be Topaz.' Barbara looked keenly at Rob. Craig watched the others.

Craig was relaxed, just hanging loose as he watched the three of them squirming. He noticed the scratches. Jono's face, Simon's strong hairy arms, one scratch on it so bad it needed a plaster but nothing obvious on Nigel. Jono was unconsciously fiddling with his ring.

'Interesting ring Jono,' said Craig suddenly. They were all startled at this segue. Barbara just watched, impassive.

'Yeah it's antique. Friend gave it to me. Chinese. Did him a favour didn't I? Gave it me as thanks.' Jono was bullish. Simon held onto his arm as if to warn him to be silent, knowing he would blab if pushed too hard. Good driver but no balls.

'Leave it to us,' Simon whispered in Jono's ear.

'Your car out there Jono?' Another unexpected segue from Barbara.

'Yeah. So what?'

'Yours the dirty old dunger?' asked Barbara. Craig watched on.

'Well I do a bit of rally driving and haven't had a chance to clean it.'

'And the other?' Craig turned his attention to the other two.

'Mine.' Simon said.

'How come you can afford a big V8? Can you explain how you got it when you have no record of employment?' asked Craig.

They all found it a bit disconcerting all this toing and froing from one topic to the next. Didn't give them time to think properly.

'So, you're all here to give Rob some support, are you?' Barbara had moved into the room as she asked, wrinkling her nose as she looked around.

She took over after Craig gave her a slight nod. He got up and started prowling around the room. Everyone except Barbara watched him as he drifted slowly around the place looking at everything. He didn't touch a thing, kept his hands in his pockets like a nonchalant schoolboy trying to pretend he was one of the cool kids.

What the fuck's he up to? Rob was unsettled. He knew this game of Craig's. He knew he would suddenly fire off a comment or a question out of the blue, rapid fire like an automatic weapon. He knew that this copper could unsettle the unwary. Rob knew to be on guard but the other three? *Especially that fuckwit Jono. No wonder his slang name was Dumbo.* Rob sat still, like the cat watching the mouse waiting for the right time to pounce. Except Craig was the cat and Jono the unwitting mouse.

Craig was casual and soft when he suddenly asked the question. 'There seems to be a stone missing from your ring Jono. Where did you lose it?'

Fuck. Rob turned and scowled at Jono. *The bastard's found it. But where? If it's been found at the scene, we're in deep shit. Did the little twerp even know he had lost it?*

Jono looked at the ring on his hand. It was an ugly thing; a silver dragon's head with two red stones as the eyes. Except Jono now noticed to his horror that one of them was missing.

'Well it's antique in'it. Could've been lost anywhere, anytime. Why'd you think I lost it and not the old geyser wot gave it me?'

'I don't think anything Jono. I'm just asking?' Craig looked at Johnson, nodded and moved to the door. 'I've just come to tell you about the body of a woman found and wondered if you would care to come to the mortuary to identify her as we think she may be Topaz. You said she was your girlfriend and we're not aware of any family?'

'Na. I'm too sick and devastated about Brigit. I need to arrange her funeral an'all. Get someone else.' Rob pulled his sheet up and waved an arm at them.

'Fine. I'll ask Ben McGregor.'

'Not bloody likely. That ponce isn't going near my Topaz.' Rob yelled in outrage. 'I'll come by later when I'm feeling better.'

'One hour's what you've got Rob. Any longer and I'll get Ben,' said Craig.

'After all, we need to get cracking on the investigation,' Barbara said.

Craig and Barbara got ready to leave. As they sauntered

though the bedroom door, Craig looked back at Jono.

'Oh Jono. We just might have found your stone. Call by and collect it. See if it matches the others and if it fits.'

'Or you might just like to give us the ring and we'll check it out.' Barbara added.

Jono rocked back, mouth wide open and eyes darting from them back to Rob, face paling in terror.

'Not bloody likely.' He held his hand tightly closed.

Rob held his peace. Now was not the time to erupt. Let the filth go because he had words to say to his incompetent team. This was not going to end well, and it would not be his head on the block. He knew what had to be done. It'd been done before and he had no qualms about dealing with problems quickly, efficiently, and in a way which wouldn't get back to him. He gazed balefully at them. They waited in trepidation for the inevitable outburst.

He needed to send a strong message to his fledgling troops that any cockups wouldn't be tolerated. As he was about to speak the home phone rang. He was puzzled. Nobody ever rang. Even after the news of Brigit's death, nobody had rung him to offer condolences.

He picked it up.

'Hello,' he sounded querulous.

'I know it was you.' It was a quiet voice, one he thought he remembered from some time ago. One with the perfect vowels of an educated woman now deepened as she'd aged.

'Who the fuck are you? What the fuck do you think you're doing ringing me now with that sort of message? And what the fuck do you mean by that comment?' he asked.

'I've kept an eye on you Rob. Not out of any concern for you. Nor out of any desire to know how you are faring. No, I've watched you to keep my daughter Sarah, your niece, safe. To keep her from knowing what a violent shit you are. To make sure she never comes across you and that you never have a chance to abuse her or use her as your father did to me and our mother.'

Rob was silent. He had never given his sister another thought after they had been booted out and he lived with his dad. He was shaken. What did she know to prompt her to ring just now, out of the blue, and from where? He was puzzled. He didn't like that feeling.

He didn't like knowing he had been watched. Didn't like not knowing he had a niece he'd never heard of. *How would Becky know anyway?* Her name came back to him. *Did she have a spy down here? Was Brigit the link here? Did that treacherous bitch blab about him behind his back to his sister? How the hell did she even know about her because he'd never said anything?*

'How do ya know about me anyway? Where do you live and why have you never been in touch? What happened to mum anyway?' Unbidden questions kept tumbling from him.

'Somewhere you'll never find me Rob. I read the newspaper, listen to the radio, and have friends you'll never find out about. And I know from your history and that of our dad's, that you did this to that poor woman and also your lately departed lover.'

'I'll find you and you'll be sorry.'

The last he heard from her was her laughing as she hung up on him.

Simon, Nigel, and Jono sat in silence as they watched the deepening reddening of Rob's face and the vice like grip he had on the now silent phone.

CHAPTER THIRTY

He looked at them balefully through gimlet eyes, fists clenched. They waited for the inevitable explosion. They could see the temper rising. His colour changed from puce to purple in a flash, like an overripe tomato. Already on a short fuse since the cops left, that phone call had sent him into overdrive. His explosive temper was about to erupt. They instinctively took a step back.

He turned on them, his temper barely in control now the police had left. 'Why the fuck didn't you bury her deeper?'

They whined. They shuffled. They tried to blame each other. *God they're all fuckwits.*

'It was cold and misty. The trees dripped and the roots were everywhere. Did the best we could.'

'Why the hell there? Why not deeper away from the walking paths?' Rob roared in anger.

'We needed to keep away from the other sites. Didn't want to go digging up anything nasty.' Simon tried to be placatory.

'Besides, we were getting cold.' Jono added. 'And she was struggling too much.'

'Yes, and so it was a bit of an effort getting her that far in at all. Especially as we didn't want her making a racket for everyone to hear,' Simon said smoothly.

‘And bloody Nige was no help at all,’ cut in Jono. Simon scowled at him. Jono quailed and shut up. Nigel stared straight ahead, silent, and unmoving, hands shoved in his pockets.

‘Never know who’ll be out and about at that time of the day.’ Simon moved on quickly keeping Rob’s attention from his mate Nige.

‘Thought at this time of the year it’d be too cold for people to be walking out there, but we needed to be quick. In and out like a rat up a drainpipe.’ Jono said.

‘And besides, fucked if I know why anyone would be out in the late afternoon anyway with a dog and kids when there was barely daylight.’ Simon shrugged as he said it and strolled over to the windows to check outside.

‘What did you do to her? I told you to sort her and get rid of any evidence. What else?’ Rob was beginning to wonder what the idiots had done. ‘What did you do? Hit her or anything so there was blood around? Was she scratched when you dragged her, so the dog smelt blood? Those bare branches can be pretty vicious. Any other body fluids for the dog to scent?’

‘What do ya mean body fluids?’ Jono was puzzled by that phrase.

‘Semen you idiot. I reckon you probably gave her a good doing over before you killed her. All of you?’ Rob raised his eyebrows. He looked quite comical as he tried to scowl and raised his eyebrows at the same time. Jono suppressed a snort.

‘I need to know what you did before I get there to identify her. So I’m properly prepared to be surprised and devastated. So out with it what did ya do?’ They shuffled, squirmed, waited for Simon to start.

‘Well yeah. We did play around a bit. But we thought they wouldn’t find her for ages and wouldn’t be any telltale signs.’

‘What?’ asked Rob struggling to control the pitch of his voice.

Jono and I had a bit of a go. You know I’ve always fancied her but kept my hands away out of respect for you,’ Simon said.

He kicked Jono when he saw him open his mouth. ‘Shut the fuck up Jono,’ he snarled under his breath.

‘There seems to be evidence now to tie at least one of you to the scene if we believed the throwaway line from the cop.' Rob stared at Jono, pointed a finger.

'Thought it would be ok to have some fun with her. Always wanted to when she was yours. It seemed like the only opportunity.' Jono was now whining, hands automatically rubbing together.

'She fought a bit,' Nigel ventured. 'Scratched them both a bit.'

'You didn't want her anymore. We may have overdone it a bit. But you can trust us, we'd never dob you in,' said Simon all bravado. Simon unconsciously scratched his groin as he stared back at Rob. *Silly old man What'd he expect us to do.*

Nigel said nothing more and just let Simon do the talking. The last couple of days showed him he wasn't cut up to be a member of Rob's mob. *I don't care anymore what Simon says. He can tell Rob I didn't join in for all I care. I'm outta here. I don't understand how Si's got so nasty now.*

Rob leapt to his feet as quickly as his dodgy knees would let him. 'So, you're telling me you raped her. Si, I just asked you to get rid of her,' he said with menace in his voice.

'But she's so beautiful,' Jono said, 'and it was so easy. I could never have someone who looked like that usually.'

'Shut the fuck up Jono,' snarled Simon.

Rob looked at them, his hands tight in his dressing gown. He felt a mixture of anger, resentment, worry and an emotion he'd never had before. Pride. Pride at Simon. *I shouldn't be surprised. I've trained Si like my son to be just like me.*

'Those scratches on your faces could be a problem if any DNA could be retrieved from under her nails,' he said.

He noticed Nigel standing silently with his back to them looking out the window. He also noticed Simon frowning at him. *What's up there?*

'And what about the semen? Did you use a rubber?'

'Didn't think of it Boss. Weren't in a position to get one. Y'know things kinda just happened.' Simon shrugged again.

'Numbskulls. Fuckwits. Do I always have to think for you?'

They were a bit surprised Rob was so pissed off. He had after all told them to sort her out.

'Hey Boss,' Simon protested. 'You wanted rid of her, so what does it matter what we did?'

Rob glared at them. 'Go get me some coffee. Need to think what we do next.'

Rob waited in the bedroom until they left. As he dressed, he was thinking, taking his time. *That's it. That's what we'll do. That'll get us through the next few days. Need to make sure Jono doesn't blab.*

He first had to deal with Brigit, and the cops thinking he killed her somehow. There was also the old slut of a sister, never mind the bastard son to deal with, but that'd be down the track after he claimed the house. He needed a new lawyer after Olds let him down. He'd use that nice little lawyer for that, and also if the cops tried to do him for Brigit. *She'd done well getting me out of the clink yesterday. Got to sort Olds as well.*

'Got a plan of action. In three parts but we're smart so we can handle this.' He strode into the kitchen, the big man self-assured again. 'Simon do a bit of sleuthing on that lawyer chick. What's her name? Sam George. Check her out a bit just to be on the safe side.

'What I'll do is arrange Brigit's funeral and claim her assets as mine.' Rob was talking to them loudly as he walked back into the kitchen. 'I'll let the executor know that everything's mine when I go to the Will reading. There should be no surprises there as I let Brigit know I expected the house if she died before me. Stuff the son and sister. They can just bugger off to where they came from.'

'Stupid poncy names anyway,' said Simon passing Rob a cup of coffee. 'Here, just as you like it.'

'Then we need to manage the Topaz business. I need to get to get to the mortuary now and identify her and then arrange her funeral quickly. Who's going to drive me? Nige? You'll do.'

'It would have to be a different funeral home to the one used for Brigit.' They watched him uneasily.

'Wonder if I could put a stop to the autopsy?' He wondered aloud as he looked around the kitchen. Strangely, Rob really couldn't bear to think about Topaz there with the pathologist doing his dicing and slicing and investigating.

'Doubt it. It'll be a police decision. Part of their investigation.' Nigel hoped it would land them in jail.

'Who raped her last?' He surprised them as he had appeared deep in thought. They jumped at the sound of his rasping voice. He'd watched them from the doorway, before he came in, but they weren't talking to each other. Simon the coolest one was just sitting eyeing Jono with a frown on his face. *As well he might 'cos I've got a job for him.* He noticed Simon didn't jump. *Nerves of steel that one. I'll have to watch him. Make sure he doesn't get ahead of himself.*

'Me. Held her for Simon first. He said it was his right to go first as he's older. Nige didn't join in the fun.' Jono said. He sniggered at that. *Wuss.*

So that's it between them. But why? But I need to find out why Nige wasn't up to it That might be a problem to be sorted as well.

He noticed that Jono jumps right in without thinking. He'd have a quiet word with Simon. He, of all of them, had his head screwed on right. The real problem was the semen.

'We'll need to act fast if the filth get a warrant for DNA from you. Make sure you're far away and can't be found.' *But then, if the only external evidence was linked to Jono and not the other two, it'll be ok. If they'd both had her then all their semen would be mixed so perhaps, they wouldn't be able to identify whose was whose. Maybe it'll all be ok then.*

'Nige let's go to the mortuary now. You'll have to stand by me and help as I act the distraught lover. You others can go and get some beer and grub for when we get back.'

As they all moved outside, Rob motioned Simon aside. 'Deal with him,' he whispered as he nodded toward Jono.

'We'll be back here in about an hour or so get going. Got lots to celebrate.' *Brigit, Topaz and Jono – problems solved.*

Nigel observed the little exchange between Rob and Simon as he sat in his car fiddling with the ignition. The silence was heavy and foreboding as they drove in silence to the mortuary.

. He hadn't like seeing Topaz there. Although her eyes were closed and she looked peaceful, he felt as if she was staring at him, calling on her ancestors to condemn him. He'd shivered, shaken the feeling away with a toss of his head and defiance in his eyes as he'd said so quietly the watching police could barely hear him. 'Yes. That's her. That's Topaz.'

Later, after they returned from the mortuary, Rob was tetchy and the four of them ate and drank long into the night. By the time they left they were all well drunk. They'd had a raucous night, bonded together just like blood brothers. Even Nigel had set aside his disquiet at the day's events after a few beers. *I'll have to talk to Simon sometime about this, even at the risk of being mocked. But we've been mates for ages so that must count for something.*

Simon had been watchful and thoughtful. *God, Rob was such a braggard.*

'Ever told you about my time with Mr. Asia?' shouted Rob over the din. 'It was when I was in Sydney,' and he proceeded to regale them his spicy stories of making it big time.

That was when Nigel went quiet. Pretended he was too drunk to keep his eyes open. His head flopped on his arms on the table. *I know he ratted on his colleagues to get a soft sentence. He'd sell his own mother to save himself. Well, he's not gonna sell me out.*

'I moved here with wifey Blanche down to Bluff, after I left Auckland. Had gone there after jail in Aussie but it didn't work out for me. Proved much better anyway. She had family there. Her old man was good to us way back then. He helped us get settled, bought a house for us with all the money he got from his fleet of Bluff boats. Good little earner that was, and now that's been fucked up somehow.' Rob was now rambling.

'No-one'll trust him now that cocaine had been found on one of his boats. The courts would probably confiscate his fleet.' Rob waved his arms in the air, 'but he doesn't know anything about it.' He cackled. 'I did it behind his back. Even Blanche didn't know. That's how clever I am.'

Rob was idly swirling his drink around in the glass as he drunkenly thought out loud. 'She's a difficult bitch, that Blanche but she should know which side to be on. Maybe she'll have to come crawling back to me now that I'll have this big posh house.'

Simon was seeing Rob in a new light. He was just an old man trying to talk big. And that quiet conversation with Rob when Jono went to get the beer was an indication that he was losing control. *I'll take over this lot in time. Just need to be patient. Nige will work for me then, no trouble. We'll take over the drug dealing. Rob can't even manage that properly. Fancy getting caught out with that large haul in Bluff.* He let his mind wander freely as he imagined taking over this house and using it as his headquarters. *Just need to keep in good with him so he sees me as a successor and not as a threat.*

'Here's to you Rob,' he shouted as he raised his glass. Nigel didn't join in the toast.

They left when the booze ran out and Rob was so drunk, he fell asleep.

'Let's go. No need to stay any longer.' Simon was on his feet. 'I'll go with Jono.'

'What about him?' Jono pointed to the slumbering Rob sprawled on the couch, legs apart and dribbling.

'Leave him there. Can't be bothered getting him into bed. Anyway, we'd probably all fall down.'

Jono sauntered off, reeling as if on a ship, as he carefully placed one foot in front of the other.

The other two just looked on, giggling slightly at him. Simon muttered to Nigel, 'If Jono can't hold his liquor, we are going to have to watch that, but Rob's given me the solution.'

Nigel paused, waited a beat, took a deep breath, and walked to his car. 'Night.'

'Here tomorrow lads. 10am sharp.' Simon was already acting as the boss, issuing instructions to his underlings. Behind his back Nige scowled and gave him the fingers.

They'd stumbled out into the night shouting and laughing and making such a noise that Moira and Stephen couldn't help but hear them. They peeped through the curtains grumbling to each other that things were sure going to take a turn for the worse now that Brigit wasn't here.

'Such a racket. Hope this doesn't happen every night.' Moira mumbled.

'Might have to complain to the cops if it does,' replied Stephen.

'It looks as if they're celebrating. Wonder when her funeral is?' Moria asked, her mind turning to Brigit.

'Said in this morning's *Southland Times* that it's on Friday. Notice put in by Rob claiming he's her partner,' said Stephen crossly. 'Now they're gone let's get some sleep. It's after midnight after all and we're not spring chickens anymore.'

Nigel was worried as he drove home alone. He'd noticed the exchange between Rob and Simon. *What they did is going to haunt me forever. It's her name, Topaz, that got to me.* He remembered back to a friend of his mum's when he was a child. He'd seen her on the street when he was walking home from school, crying about losing her ring. He'd helped her look for it all along the footpath. It was her grandmother's ring she'd said, and it meant a lot to her. He remembered she'd said that to lose that ring would mean the connection between her and her gran would be lost forever.

He'd found her ring eventually. It was a topaz one. He remembered the look of joy on her face and how she had swept him up in her arms and danced with delight. He hadn't felt like that for a long time. Not since secondary school when he met up with Simon.

He drove home carefully, pulled up into his garage and sat there thinking until the cold got to him. Chilled to the bone he climbed into bed knowing what he had to do. He was about to break gang protocol. That didn't rest easy with him after his long friendship with Simon. But then neither did the rape and murder of Topaz. His mind made up he slept easy.

Jono was also careful. Simon sat in silence. Jono glanced at his forbidding face. Jono was scared.

'What? What'd I do? What's wrong?' Simon didn't answer.

When they arrived at Simon's house, he got out, turned, and said, 'thanks Jono. See you tomorrow.' He walked through the gate.

Jono breathed out long and slow. He was shaking as he drove off.

CHAPTER THIRTY ONE

As the three of them left, giggling and stumbling, they didn't notice the waiting Mercedes coupe or that the windows were steamed up. They were too busy getting to their cars. They were long gone when two people got out and went into the house.

They found Rob slumped in his chair totally out to it, so fast asleep he didn't notice Georgia's light fingers as she deftly checked him to make sure he was fast asleep and wouldn't wake. Niall glanced at her and nodded a slight smile on his face. They stood on either side of him and pulled him up, none too gently.

'Who you?' he slurred barely coherent and so drunk he'd didn't register who they were or why they were at the house. Georgia kept out of his line of sight. He'd never met Niall, but he would know her if he saw her.

'Time for bed,' said Niall. 'Your friends called us and suggested we help you. They said they were too drunk to get you to bed safely. Come on now. Up you get.'

'Need to piss.'

They manhandled the stumbling Rob to the loo and then to his bedroom. Although he was older and skinny, he was still a big man. Niall had to do most of the holding and manipulating. Georgia did the balancing and opening of doors as the trio danced a grotesque cha-cha-cha. With side shuffles and front and back movements they fought to keep Rob upright. Rob was hardly aware that Niall helped him into the bedroom, pushed him down on the bed and took off his socks and shoes. Gently, he placed a blanket over the top of the snoring Rob, and then stood silently at the door watching, making sure he was asleep.

They took their time inspecting the place and removing more of the important items they felt shouldn't stay: the things that held memories for them both, and the things they could easily transport out of the home without anyone becoming suspicious. But what they wanted was more of Brigit's papers which would be useful tomorrow. They might need them for proof down the track should there be a fight for the property. Brigit's solicitor had requested a meeting of them all together with Rob. The reading of the Will was scheduled for tomorrow afternoon.

Georgia was busy looking through files, cupboards, sifting through a lifetime of papers. 'It's such a quaint concept that – 'reading of the Will' – all Victorian in a Gothic way,' she said to Niall as she shuffled through papers.

They wanted to be prepared so inspected every room, every cupboard, and every drawer. They packed the things that mattered now and noted everything else. With luck Rob's family wouldn't notice the items removed, like the files containing Brigit's papers detailing her history with him. They found these in the washhouse, an area Rob never went into. They left noisily laughing loudly as they did so. It was now nearly one in the morning. They were sure that the Taits would hear them. They wanted to be heard. They wanted the time noted.

'Curtains twitching,' said Niall.

'Good. Let's hope they note the time.'

The Mercedes engine, so finely tuned, sped off, stopping just around the corner. They waited for Ben to arrive.

'Give us a couple of hours at least.' Niall had said earlier when they were planning. 'We'll go in after midnight or when the others leave. When we're sure Rob will be asleep.'

'Why don't we do it when you first go in after they'd all left? Why the pretense of coming and then going?' asked Ben.

'Niall and I need to be seen coming and going. We can claim the right to be there. You can't, and we want the Taits to know we'd come and gone,' replied Georgia.

'You need to come later, much later.'

Later, they all gathered silently.

'Sure?'

Ben nodded. Georgia nodded.

'We can do this.' They left their cars and then quietly walked back to the house, pausing to check the neighbour's window. All in darkness. They opened the door and slipped inside. Waited a beat, breathing quietly, checking to see if Rob was still asleep. The sound of snores reassured them.

Rob had underestimated Niall and Georgia. He really didn't know much about either of them. He'd never bothered with Brigit's family. They were irrelevant. Ben had never entered his thinking until he had hooked up with Topaz and only then to work out how to get revenge on the man.

He didn't appreciate how easily he had been fooled. He didn't know about their tenacity of purpose, or their single-minded determination for justice. Vengeance is a powerful motive; even more powerful than greed and the retribution extracted is balm for a troubled emotion.

They left as silently as they arrived, walking in the stygian gloom of the starless night. They were unobserved by the sleeping community. Not even a dog barked to announce their presence. They were somber and tense and each of them dealing with their own guilt. All of them wondering how they were going to reconcile their actions with their consciences.

CHAPTER THIRTY TWO

Niall returned to his house with Georgia. They didn't talk, both of them dealing with their own internal moral dilemmas; Niall, with his oath for saving lives and caring for his patients, and Georgia with her Catholic upbringing. Both in need of a stiff drink.

Georgia sipped her brandy, feeling the tension slowly leave.

Niall sat opposite her, swirling the brandy round his glass enjoying the aroma before he took a sip.

'What are you thinking about George?'

'That we have dealt with the old and a new day has begun. I am beginning to feel less fretful about our actions, but my conscience is still pinging there in the back of my brain. I'm still uneasy about it.'

'I think it was just. Probably not right, but just. Not legal, but just.'

Likewise, Ben, who had chosen to go to his home rather than back to Niall's, felt no remorse. He knew that Rob was behind both Brigit's and Topaz's deaths even if he hadn't laid a finger on them. He knew there would never be enough evidence to even arrest him, let alone convict him. He wasn't worried about leaving any signs behind him at Chelmsford Street. *There may be fibres left from our clothes but mine can easily be explained being there as a paramedic at Brigit's death. We have a good story if anything from Niall and Georgia is found. They have a right to be there, and the police gave them the keys anyway. But I don't think the police will act.*

Ben didn't regret his part. Like Niall he was involved in protecting life, but he needed the sense of justice that tonight's activities had given him

Surprisingly, Ben always quiet, still, and professional on duty, was usually a restless soul. He fussed about his home. He'd not spent much time there lately and it now seemed a cold and lifeless place. He took the sheets from the bed, sniffed them to get the last lingering fragrance of Topaz and broke down. He sobbed for the loss of two women, neither of whom needed to die.

He sobbed for the woman for whom he had felt responsible, even after knowing her for such a brief time. He sobbed for the wasted years of Brigit's life trapped in a cold lonely home with a vile bullying man. He felt remorse that he didn't escort Topaz home and guilt that he might have prevented her death if he had, but he did not cry for his part in Rob's death. He silently thanked Georgia and Niall for having the guts to go through with it. He vowed to protect them if necessary. He lay down on clean sheets and eventually slept, waking abruptly in the morning refreshed. No ghosts had visited him in his dreams.

Craig and his colleagues also felt rested as they arrived at the station that morning. Philip had got home in time to read to his daughter and eat supper with his wife. Barbara found herself alone at home wondering where her partner Brendon had got to.

All of them felt they were getting the feel of Brigit's death. All felt they would get enough evidence this time. All had picked Jono as being the source of that evidence.

CHAPTER THIRTY THREE

Day Four

Nine o'clock in the morning was always team talk time. They settled into the daily situation breakdown. Coats had been shrugged off as the station warmed up. Someone had thoughtfully brought in some Danish pastries from the new shop around the corner.

'Want to discuss who is doing what?' Phillip asked.

'Yes, where are we up to with all the open cases?' Craig asked the assembled group. The two cases which took the most time, with animated discussions from everyone involved in the station, were those of Brigit and Topaz.

'Why do you think Brigit's death was murder?' a junior constable asked. Craig went through it all. It was a good discipline as it gave everyone involved a chance to pick up on any flaws in the logic. It was also a chance to remember things which get forgotten in the adrenaline rush of the moment. Craig ticked off the reasons. Barbara and Phillip nodded their agreement.

'Ben McGregor, the paramedic,' he added for the benefit of rest of the team, who had not been so involved to date, 'mentioned a car. Any luck tracing that? The neighbours,' he checked his notes, 'Moira and Stephen Tait, reckon it was a dark car. Hard top, saloon and they think there was the letters C and M with a number which looked like a six or an eight on it. They said they were not particularly good on makes.'

'Anyone checked it out yet?' asked Philip.

'Yep. Put it though the recognition software last night. Results are just in. Belongs to a Topaz Rauwiri. Anyone know her? She's not on our database,' a junior PC answered.

Craig, Philip, and Barbara looked at each other unsurprised.

'Yes, that's our victim number two. Found yesterday morning in Thomsons Bush. Brutal assault and murder. Former lover of Bennet. We'll get to her in a minute,' said Craig. 'Anything else about victim one?'

'Preliminary forensics are in from the house but don't tell us much. Samples are being tested now, but with such a lot of activity from paramedics and police, they could belong to anyone. And most of them had legitimate reasons for being there. There'll also be many from visitors over the years and besides, Bennet lived there for about five years since he came down from Auckland. So, you would expect his DNA and related evidence to be there,' said Barbara.

'There is absolutely no evidence of foul play. Dr Duckworth can't find anything to suggest this was anything more than a natural death from asthma. Much as he tried, he just couldn't find anything to pin this on anyone as murder,' said one of the juniors, anxious to get into the homicide squad and away from traffic duty.

'Is this one that's going to be a closed unsolved case, even though the paramedic, the pathologist and all you three have doubts? How do we classify it? There's simply no evidence of a crime,' another junior commented.

'Not if I have my way. I don't give up so easily.' Craig got a supporting nod from Philip.

'Ok, let's put that one aside for now and concentrate our efforts on victim two, Topaz Rauwiri. What do we know so far?' Craig continued leading the meeting.

'We know her name, where she lived, that she had a relationship with Rob Bennet, and just recently, a brief relationship with Ben McGregor, the paramedic. We have samples of semen that the pathologist is putting through his databanks. We know her car was outside Chelmsford Street.' Another junior read it out from the fact sheet.

'And don't forget we have that red gemstone from the scene of her death,' Philip added.

'We also know that Jono has a ring which is missing a stone similar to the one we found at the scene. He also has a very dirty car. We have supplied a sample of the mud from it for forensic testing. We have applied for a warrant to take it to the yard for forensic testing,' Craig said.

'And we know that the owner of the ring and probably the found gemstone is an associate of Rob's, with a list of minor offences,' Barbara continued the analysis.

'Mainly speeding, car conversions and growing a prohibited substance for distribution,' said the junior, reading from the file.

'We also suspect that the mud collected from the car is likely to be the same as samples taken from Thomsons Bush where the body was found. We have taken casts of the tyre tracks to see if they match,' Philip said.

'So, unlike Brigit's case we know a lot, and we have evidence which could stand up in court. We also know that Bennet's associate, young Jono owns that car and a ring missing a stone. I want forensics all over it. I want samples of anything and everything. See if they can get clothes samples which we can match DNA to. I want the tyres compared to the prints we have of the tyre marks at the scene.' Craig started issuing instructions.

'OK boss. On it.'

'And I want a warrant for Jono's arrest. We have enough to satisfy a judge. Barbara, will you get us a time with the court? With a judge I think rather than a JP or registrar. I want this absolutely legal with no holes anyone could wriggle out of.'

'I'll do it right after our meeting,' she said.

'Meanwhile let's keep him in our sights. I don't want him slipping the net before it's closed up tightly. Everyone clear?' Craig asked.

'On it.'

With that Craig closed the meeting.

The young coppers left the room to arrange the watch and check the casts of the tyre marks against the national data base, while the three senior coppers discussed strategy. They had just refilled their mugs with the station coffee when the call came in.

'Dead body in Chelmsford,' said dispatches. 'Ambulance is already on the way.'

The three of them looked at each other astonished.

'What the hell?' said Barbara. 'You two go and I'll do the follow-up paperwork and get a time with the judge. Keep me informed. Another body at a Chelmsford Street address? Is there a number? This is just too bizarre to be a coincidence.'

'Same address.' Philip looked at the dispatch,

'I don't believe in coincidences,' growled Craig.

They didn't rush to the scene. The dead would not be going anywhere, but they did worry about who had called the death in and what part they may or may not have played. Would the ambulance also have been called?

Craig was suddenly tired, his early freshness drained, and he needed to close off the two deaths they had already before having to deal with another unexplained one.

CHAPTER THIRTY FOUR

Ben breathed deeply as his got into the ambulance. The 111 call had come in at 10.30am. It had already been a busy morning with a major road traffic accident and one death and two serious injuries.

'I feel exhausted already and the day had only just started,' he said. His deep breathing was not one of tiredness or despair. He was tense. He knew this address. He'd been there twice before in the past three days: when Brigit was found dead, and last night with Niall and Georgia. He'd hoped for a little more time before the body was found so that someone else would be on duty. *I can fake the surprise, the concern, the care.*

He knew the scene was clean so all that mattered now was for him to hold it altogether. *I'm not sorry. I feel empty. And besides, Topaz's killers are still free. That'll be my next focus.*

He put on his ambulance officer face, steadied his nerves, and prepared for his star appearance at the theatre of his own crime. *It needs to be an award-winning performance.*

He glanced at Tom riding shotgun in the ambulance. Tom looked a bit pale, his handsome face with deep worry lines, his hands were clenched, gripped tightly around the safety belt.

'You OK Tom?'

'Yeah fine. Just a bit tired. We know that address, don't we?'

'We were there a couple of days ago at the death of the woman who lived with Rob Bennet. Remember you spent a lot of time with him consoling him in the kitchen while I cleaned up the scene.'

'Oh yeah, that's right. Too much happening lately and I'm too tired to remember everything.' Tom looked down at his hands now curled tight into fists.

Ben and Tom rushed into the house. The three of Rob's mob were standing there visibly shaken, Simon rigid, Jono ashen and Nigel looking as if he didn't want to be there.

'When we arrived, he didn't answer the door even though he was expecting us,' said Simon.

'We broke in and found him in bed, dead.' Jono was speaking, rushing in like a fool, letting his tongue do his thinking.

Simon went silent. *Let them condemn themselves if necessary, especially Jono. We're going to get rid of him anyway. If there's a problem we can land it on him, and he can take the fall.* He nudged Nigel, put his finger on his lips. Nigel nodded.

Ben went to the bed, looked down and bent to check the pulse, felt the coldness. 'Long dead.' he said. 'Looks like natural causes. But we'll leave that for the doctor and police to decide.'

Tom just stopped deathly pale at the door. *Fuck. What the hell. I'm not ready yet.*

'What'll we need to do?' Jono blurted out. He was scared. He knew there were still signs of their party last night.

'We'll leave him here undisturbed until the police arrive. They'll need to see this because of the death the other night. They don't like coincidences.'

And neither do I. Tom finally moved and took his father's hand as if to check his pulse. In reality, he was saying a silent farewell to a man who had groomed him in his likeness. A man who had been as brutal as he himself had become. And the man, he was now going to take over from, if he could only keep his identity secret.

They had moved into a pristine kitchen to wait. Simon stopped puzzled. They hadn't cleaned up last night, yet everything was spotless. Glasses washed, ash trays emptied. No sign of the shindig they held last night. Just the empty bottles all neatly arranged in the recycle bin. *WTF.* This was just a bit freaky. Nige and Jono hadn't noticed yet. Jono was still babbling on inanely to Ben who remained silent, just watching, thinking. *Let them prattle in fear. They don't know what I've done. And my paramedic teammate has no idea either. But he's gone very pale and quiet. Wonder why?*

Last night, the three silent assassins had been scrupulous to leave no traces of themselves. Their excuse, if the Tait's had seen them, was that Niall and Georgia had come by late to see if anyone was up so they could collect Brigit's clothes to dress her for the funeral. They'd seen the lights still on after the others had left and that they had ended up staying for a few drinks. They'd wanted to discuss the funeral with Rob, they'd say to the police if asked. They'd stayed on to clean up the mess after they put a very drunk Rob to bed.

If Ben wasn't worried about this tangled web, Simon was. The more Jono prattled the more he became convinced that Jono had to be dealt to. As he listened, ciggie in hand, he wondered when he'd do it to Jono.

Ben went to let the police in. Simon hissed to the others. 'Shut the fuck up. You appear nervous, Jono, and the filth will be suspicious. Let me do the talking.'

Ben nodded to Craig. Philip was silent as he observed everything.

'The doctor is on his way. It's just a locum who won't know the victim, but he was dead when I arrived. It seems it happened when he was in bed asleep. No sign of any activity. Just him in bed.' Ben said.

The police remained silent as they looked.

'Who found him?' asked Craig eventually.

'His three mates. Said they had an appointment here at ten to plan Brigit's funeral.' Ben was packing up his equipment.

'What do you think Ben? Got your usual feeling about this one?'

'No, not really. It looks pretty much as they said.'

'Which was?' Craig asked.

'That they were drinking last night and left him asleep in his chair.'

'He got himself to bed then?'

'Must have.' Ben was packing his gear away as he spoke, head down away from the quizzical gaze of Craig.

'OK. Let's wait for the doctor. Where are the lads?' Craig asked.

'In the kitchen waiting for you.'

'Who's going to do the talking?' Craig was now brusque as he entered the kitchen. Jono and Nige jumped up. Simon who remained seated answered.

'Nothing much to say really. We had a booze up last night to help Rob ease some of the stress of losing his old lady. We had a meeting arranged for this morning to discuss the funeral and Rob didn't answer the door, so we broke in. The patio door's a bit wonky so it wasn't hard to push it open. Dead in his bed, he was,' said Simon.

'She wasn't his old lady as you well know, so cut the pretence.' Phillip cut in. 'When did you last see him? What time did you leave?'

'Left before midnight, last night. Rob was well pissed by then. He needed us around because he was upset at Brigit and Topaz's deaths. We didn't feel we should leave him by himself. We left him asleep in his chair. Didn't want to disturb him. He must have woken up to go to the loo after all that beer we had and then got himself to bed. He didn't get changed into his PJs and it looks as if he just tumbled into bed fully clothed.'

'Yeah.' said Nige. 'We made a bit of a noise when we left. The neighbours saw us go if you need proof of the time.'

'Nosy bastards.' added Jono joining in. He was suffering from a hangover and was whiter than his usual pallor this morning. He was having trouble putting it all together. It just didn't make any sense to him. He worried about his position now that Rob was dead.

'I'll have to arrange the funeral you know. I was his nephew,' Jono said nervously.

'Probably you should discuss that with his wife and daughter, Jono.' Craig said.

'No, he has nothing to do with them now. He's only been interested in me as family.'

'Where'd you go when you left?' Craig, hands shoved in his pockets and left Philip to look around.

'I went with Jono in his car. He usually drives me and Rob. Acts as our chauffeur. Nige drove himself home,' said Simon.

Philip nodded to Craig. 'Perhaps you should pop next door and see what they have to say. You talked to them last time so it's better if they see you again. I'll check up here.'

On his way out, Craig passed the harried looking doctor. 'First on the right.'

And, as Ben had predicted the locum signed off Rob's murder as natural causes. An older man dying in his sleep. He didn't even order an autopsy on the body or think it worth going to the coroner's court.

'Does he have family?' asked Philip.

Jono silently cursed. Simon just smiled. He'd already thought about the property and there was no way the ex and the daughter would get a look in. His take-over plan had come sooner rather than later.

'An ex and a daughter,' said Simon.

'Do you have any details? Address or phone number?' Philip asked eyebrows arched.

'You'll probably find them on Rob's phone.' Nigel said. 'They live in Bluff and the surname's Hunter.'

'Thank you, Nigel. I'll ring them.' Philip walked outside, and phone to his ear he took instructions from Blanche.

'It's out of your hands Jono. Blanche is arranging it all. She also lost no time in claiming the house and contents.' Philip said as he walked back inside.

Nigel held Simon back at that. Philip continued. 'They'll use Spry and Sons. They'll arrange that first and then come here as soon as they get up from Bluff.'

'What about his daughter?' Jono asked.

'Blanche will advise Amanda, and also her old man, but he's

out with his fleet of boats at the moment. Unsurprisingly she didn't sound upset. They want us to lock the property when the body is removed, and her instructions are to keep you lot from coming in.'

'Bitch.' Simon looked surly at that and shoved his hands in his pockets to stop Philip seeing them curling into tight fists.

'She doesn't seem to like you lot, either' Philip commented. 'We'll be locking the property up and advising Brigit's family that the house is now unoccupied. They'll need to come round and secure it. It'll be nothing to do with Blanche, or you Jono.'

'In the meantime, you lot, get yourselves down to the station. Detective Johnson will expect you. I'm about to ring her now.'

Tom just listened, slightly removed from the activity around him. Ben was too busy to notice his silence, his stillness. Tom knew of his half-sister and her mother, but they didn't know of him. Rob had never let on to Blanche about an affair which had resulted in a pregnancy. He didn't like it that they were to arrange his father's funeral but couldn't do anything about it without blowing his cover too soon. *They'll learn soon enough. They're going to get a shock soon when Dad's Will's read. Meanwhile I need to secure my rights to this place. That's in his Will but those two bitches who betrayed my dad by kicking him out when he was down, will fight it. No way will they ever get anything.*

'Why do you want us down there? Nigel was surprised. 'We haven't done anything.'

'You need to give us a statement of your actions for our records in case there's a problem. Besides, you all just confessed to us that you broke into the house, didn't you?' Philip turned and went outside to phone the station.

'Barbara. The old crook really is dead. It looks like natural causes. Rob's family's on the way. We'll wait for them. Meanwhile the three sidekicks are on the way to give you statements. They're in two cars. I want Jono taken off by himself as soon as he arrives. Keep him isolated. Take Jono's statement last. I want to question him myself about Topaz's death. I think he's a bit shaken at what's going down and he just might crack and give us everyone else's heads on a nice big platter.'

'Ok. What's Craig up to?'

'Talking with the neighbours. The lads claim they saw them leave last night after a party.'

Craig heard all the details from the Taits. The party, the noise, the drunken departure of the three associates, as they called them. 'Know who they were?'

'Oh yes they're often around visiting the house. Friends of Robs.' Can't tell you their names though,' said Stephen.

'It's them three in there though isn't it?' Moira looked at her husband.

'Yeah I reckon it's them.'

'What time did they leave?' Craig asked.

'Around midnight. It was all quiet then, so we went to bed.'

Moira and Stephen looked at each other. By silent and mutual consent, they didn't mention the later arrival and departure of Niall and Georgia. They knew exactly who they were because Brigit had introduced them as her son and sister when they visited once. They reckoned she was worth protecting if necessary.

Craig returned next door thoughtful. This is one he wasn't going to investigate too thoroughly. It seemed simple enough, but his gut told him otherwise. He suspected the doctor would place the time of death long after those lads had left. *Maybe Rob's got his just desserts. I'll leave this one alone for the moment.*

He returned just as the three left. He noted the time as he and Philip watched them leave, Jono in his usual position as driver to Simon, and Nigel in his own car.

'Must make sure we confiscate Jono's car while he's at the station.,' Craig said to Philip.

'Already done. Barbara will seize it when they're there, being questioned.'

Once inside Jono's car, Simon swiveled towards him. 'Want to do a bit of a detour Jono before we get to the nick if you don't mind. Need to take the dog for a run and check out Thomsons Bush again to make sure everything is ok there. If the police have gone, we'll go and have a look-see so we can get our stories straight. Brute likes Thomsons Bush. I can take him off the lead there and let him run freely.' Jono nodded.

CHAPTER THIRTY FIVE

Off they drove, with Jono chattering nervously.

'Never been to your house, Si. Where is it?'

'I'll give you directions, Jono,' Simon said rolling his eyes at Jono chattering on like a simpleton. 'What's Jono short for?'

'Jonathan. Hate it. Sounds too poncy and it's hard to spell. Jono's good for me.'

'Can't you spell Jono? When did you leave school? How old are you now?'

'Couldn't manage school. Couldn't read and so I can't write either. Mum and Dad gave up on me. I didn't get extra lessons or anything. Kids made fun of me, so I just didn't turn up.' Jono didn't sound unhappy.

'How old were you then?'

'15. Did odd jobs after that until Uncle Rob gave me the job of driving him about. That was cool. I'm good with cars. Always fixed the cars for the olds,' Jono said.

'The olds?' Simon asked surprised.

'My drunken mum and dad. Always called them the olds 'cos they looked so old, being drunk and all that smoking.' Jono put his foot down as he swerved around a corner. Simon rocked a bit beside him grabbing the door handle.

'Steady on Jono,' he said.

'Uncle Rob found I was good at converting cars so that's what I did for him. I'd either drag race them and dump them or if they were posh enough Rob would flog them off. That's how we got Topaz's car.'

'What else did you do with them?' Simon asked.

'I like to hoon about on the beach doing wheelies. That's where I practiced so I could drag the cops and beat them. Would then dump them in the dunes.' Jono was driving fast as he spoke.

'Don't drive so fast Jono. We don't want to be picked up.'

'Aren't the police a bit busy with all the drama we've given them?' Jono laughed.

'If we're not careful they could ping this on us Jono. You realise we'd be in a heap of trouble if we don't get our stories straight. Just drive cool like.'

Jono thought he was already driving cool as he overtook, swerved, and raced along Queen's Drive.

'Next right. Third house down on the left. You wait here and I'll go and get Brute.'

Jono first look at Simon's house caused his eyes to pop.

'Hey Si, pretty cool. Maybe one day I'll get a house like this. And a dog too. Yeah when the olds finally die and I get their house, I'll get a dog. Can't be too far away judging by the state of them. Maybe we can help them on their way a bit like we did Topaz? No-one would find out.' Jono blabbered on. Simon stared straight ahead.

He wanted to peek over the tall fence. but could see through the iron gate that there was no garden to bother with. He heard the dog barking, a deep, angry sounding bark. He wasn't worried though. He liked dogs and they seemed to like him as well.

His thoughts bounced around his head like beads in a baby's rattle.

He turned the radio on while he waited. More stuff on the news about the murder. The media will be talking about it for a while.

Simon came back out with the dog on a strong lead. His mind was focused on the job ahead. His major concern was preventing

Jono letting things slip to the cops. He got in the back.

'I'll sit back here with Brute just to keep him from getting excited. He loves going in the car because he knows he's going for a walk. You're not scared of dogs, are you?'

'Nah. Been around them often enough at home even though we don't have one now. The olds can't be bothered anymore. And all the lads seem to have them. That's a pretty big one. Rottweiler isn't it?'

'Yep. Had him since he was a pup. He's pretty easy and not as fierce as he looks and sounds. Good dog for me. I've left him entire because I'll breed from him. Lots of people want good Rotties and Brute's a goodie. I'll get heaps of cash for the pups. They're smart and easy to train. Used to be used as herding dogs until the police discovered that they were good on the beat.'

'Cool.' Jono laughed.

'Good guard dogs too. I'm happy that when he's at home no one will ever break into my house. Nazis used them, keeping the prisoners all together in the concentration camps.' Nobody knew about Simon's Nazi insignia tattooed on his butt. Didn't need the aggro of anybody thinking he was alt-right.

On the drive out to Thomsons Bush they chattered. The dog sat quietly, ears pricked up, sensitive to the nuances in Simon's voice. Jono was telling him about his lack of girlfriends.

'I've never managed to keep a girl long enough to do it. I never really knew what to do except what I'd seen on porn sites. Yesterday with Topaz was my first time.'

Simon grunted, mentally preparing himself as he stroked Brute.

They arrived, parked in the same car park, jumped out and walked into the Bush. It all looked peaceful even though the police and forensic team had been through it searching everywhere carefully. The Bush was recovering. Jono just stood scratching his head wondering what they were looking for. He looked at his ring fretting about that missing stone. Did he lose it here? If you believed the copper, then he must have when they were at it with Topaz. Bugger that. It really spoiled his ring. *Wonder if I can ask for it back?*

'Rob had asked me to check that there was nothing left which will tie us to Topaz. I think, even though he's dead it's a good idea.' Simon seemed to read Jono's thoughts. 'Sure, you've got all the other stones in that ring of yours? Where'd you get it anyway? It's an ugly thing.'

'Nicked it from a Chinaman. Did over his vege store and saw it lying by the sink, so I just nicked it. I put it in my pocket whenever I see someone from China around. They all stick together, and he might have spread the word about it.'

Brute was straining at the lead, Simon speaking softly to him.

'You go ahead. Brute needs to do his business. We'll catch up. Don't mess the scene up.'

Simon was confident they were alone. There were no other vehicles in the park and no sound of voices. He waited a bit then quietly followed. Jono was in the clearing just looking around. He saw his hand go into his trousers. He waited some more while observing Jono from behind. Jono was checking everything, looking around him, head going back and forth, unaware of what was to come. When Simon sensed the time was right, he slipped off the lead and murmured a few well-chosen words to his dog.

Brute needed no encouragement. He bounded off and leapt. Jono didn't know what hit him. As he watched, Simon thought to himself, *great, Brute is now fully trained as an attack dog and he's been trained to hold on until instructed otherwise. Another perfect murder. This will seem like a random dog attack and no evidence left.*

Simon whistled. Brute came to him accepted the pats from his master as he replaced the lead, and together they started on the long walk home.

CHAPTER THIRTY SIX

The walk home was tedious, Brute bouncing alongside him, held tight on his leash. It took an hour to get back to his house, tie up Brute and wash him down before he could drive to the station. He'd changed his clothes so there was no sign of any dirt on his trousers and jacket. He strolled nonchalantly into the police station, hands in pockets.

'Thought you and Jono may have done a runner.' Barbara said as she sat him down to take his statement. She folded her arms as she observed him.

'Nah. Went home to take the dog for a run. Left too early this morning to do it and he gets a bit frisky if he doesn't have his morning exercise. Jono dropped me off on his way here. I'm surprised he isn't already here. Thought he'd be well done by now. What more do you want from us? I told you all I know at Rob's house.'

She questioned him. He was relaxed. Too relaxed as he sprawled in the chair. *All too pat and too much like Nigel's version. They've worked this out between them. Wonder if Jono's will be the same.*

'Thank you,' she said when he'd finished answering.

'That's it? Can I go now?' Simon got up quickly grabbing his jacket.

'No, you need to write a statement out. Then you'll have to wait till it's typed up. And then you'll sign it. And then you can go.'

'I've got things to do,' he snarled. 'I can't hang around all morning.'

'I could arrest you if you prefer,' said Barbara. 'Then you'll have to stay for as long as it takes.'

She passed him pen and paper and left him to it, just stopping herself from asking if he could write. Craig, watching through the one-way glass. turned around when Barbara entered.

'We need to get a car round to Jono's house. You heard that smart arse say he's late because he stopped to take his dog for a run and thought Jono'd be here and be done by now,' she said.

'Agree. However, their verbal statements both match up what the neighbours reported. Maybe both Brigit's and Rob's are natural deaths, but it's all a bit too coincidental for me to feel comfy. With all that's been going down I do feel a bit suspicious.'

'I'll get someone on it now.' She poked her head into the squad room.

'Need a PC to go around to Jono's house and pick him up,' she said to no one in particular. 'Who's free?'

'I'll get on to it.' A young constable stood up and reached for her jacket.

Barbara checked the files while she waited.

'Craig, there's nothing much here. Jono Anderson. Aged 19. A long list of petty crimes from car conversions, speeding, larceny, vagrancy is here. He's been known to the police since he was about 12. Looks as if he was a real tearaway.'

'Easy pickings for a gang prospect.' Craig said.

'I see why you want him separated from the others. He'll be the one to put pressure on if he's a bit simple as these reports suggest.'

'Yes, if anyone's going to crack it'll be him. But first we need to find him,' said Craig.

She had a look at the other two as well while she was waiting. Both had substantial files. She made notes as she read them, looking to see if they had operated before, with or without Jono.

'There's nothing about Simon and Nigel in Jono's file. I wonder when and how they first hooked up together.' She looked up at Craig questioningly.

'Probably Rob was the connection. You ok here for a while? I've got thing to do.'

'Yes sure. You go. No point in both of us hanging about. There's too much happening.'

Craig nodded as he left leaving Barbara nose deep in the files.

She stopped suddenly. She hadn't paid much attention to the signatures at the bottom of the files, but now quickly flicked back and forth between them all, checking. She sat back brushing her hair back and forth with her hand as she thought.

Something pinged in her mind and she didn't like the feeling which had been in the back of her mind since she'd last read the files the other day. She went back into the file room checking that the room was empty. There was no one in sight. She spent the next hour engrossed, and as she read them, she remembered an off the cuff remark Craig had made.

'What was it he said?' she muttered aloud to herself. 'That's it. He wondered how Rob had always walked free and how he'd always covered his tracks so well.'

She was certain she now knew why. *I don't like this one bit.*

Her shoulders slumped as she sat at her desk looking vacantly into space. She couldn't quieten her mind. *What the hell am I going to do with my suspicions? I have always hated crooked cops. They give all of us a bad name.*

'Go slowly here,' she told herself. 'Do what you're good at. Collect the evidence and build a case. Don't tell anybody yet. Don't let on to anyone of your suspicions.'

She had to go outside to get some fresh air. She couldn't quite comprehend what she'd read.

'Out for a minute,' she called to anyone who may be interested.

Could it really be her partner? Should I talk to Craig? Does he suspect Brendon? Can I now go on living with him? No. Absolutely no. Her mind was on a roller coaster, her emotions as well. She felt like being sick. She walked, hands deep in her pockets. She'd left without her coat, but she barely felt the cold.

She walked past the staff car park. His car wasn't there. She didn't break her stride or look around. She just held onto her handbag slung carelessly over her shoulder and walked quickly to the nearest bank. She withdrew some cash and went to the computer place on the corner.

'I'll have that one.' She pointed to an iPad on special and tucked it into her roomy bag before she returned quickly to the station, picking up a coffee on the way. *That'll be my excuse if anybody asks where I've been.*

As she switched her desktop computer back on and waited for it to boot up, she quietly removed her new iPad and locked it in her desk. *He must never know I've got another one.* She then hid the key to the drawer. She'd lost all trust in her partner now.

She left her own files still lying there and wandered into the general staff area. No one who handled robberies was there. Brow furrowed, she looked furtively around, checking behind herself very few minutes. She flicked through filing cabinets, poked around peoples' desks for any cases involving Rob or Brendon. She went to the photocopier room with everything she'd found.

She stayed alone and busy without interruption copying everything until she heard the noisy racket of the Brendon's team going into the cafeteria on their way back to their squad room. She quickly shut the machine down, collected up her own copies, replaced the originals and stealthily slid back to her desk in the serious crimes division. *Safe. No-one noticed a thing.* Breathing deeply, she put the copies into her gym bag.

Meanwhile Craig, ignorant of Barbara's sleuthing, had gone to discuss the discovery of Rob's body that morning with Niall and Georgia. He found them sitting in the patio discussing funeral plans.

'We were called to Rob's house early this morning. It seems he died in his sleep last night.' He watched them carefully.

Georgia gasped and put her hands to her mouth. 'This is all too much,' she said.

'I don't imagine you had anything to do with it but as part of our investigation I need to ask you where you were last night?' he asked.

'We were both here,' said Niall feigned surprise.

'We were physically and mentally and emotionally drained. We had an early night,' said Georgia with a straight face.

'Sorry to ask at this difficult time for you but protocol says I must. We need to know where anyone recently associated with the deceased person was. Anyone else see you here?'

'Sam came over and cooked for us. She then went back to her home,' replied Niall.

'She doesn't live here with you then?'

'No, she stays over sometimes but not last night. She knew we had things to discuss.' Niall nodded towards Georgia.

Craig made a note. 'Now that both your mother's and Rob's bodies have been removed, the scene is cleared for you to enter later today. We'll be finished by about 4pm. I presume you still have the keys?'

'Yes, and we have a copy of the Will. The executor is meeting us there soon. Brigit left the house and assets to us equally with some small bequests going to a couple of charities and $5,000 going to each of my children.' Georgia said.

'You'd better change the time till later this afternoon when we've finished processing the scene. You know of course that everything needs to go to probate before you can dispose of anything.' Craig was leaning back into the chair eyes half closed, the soft sun on his face.

'Yes. We'll just tidy up, get rid of the rubbish, empty the fridge and leave it clean and tidy ready for sale when the time comes. We might put a tenant in just to keep it safe until we sell. You don't think there will be problems from Rob's family, do you?' Georgia suddenly sounded anxious. 'I don't want any more drama.'

'His family now knows he died. They may come around expecting to get in and remove his stuff. Why would there be any trouble? He was just a tenant and had no right to the property or to any of the effects in the house. Presumably, they were all your sister's?'

'Yes, they're all from hand-me-downs from our parents,' said Georgia.

'Well, be forewarned. Change the locks in case they have keys. Ring if you need help,' said Craig.

'We'll just secure anything we need for when then executor comes and then leave it.' Niall added.

We'll also check everything thoroughly just in case we missed anything last night.

CHAPTER THIRTY SEVEN

Niall and Georgia were inside picking through the detritus of Brigit's life, Rob's family foremost in their minds.

'They could make things a whole drama. They could probably claim everything even when they're not entitled to it,' she fretted.

'Yes. They could take us to court claiming that as Rob has said he was her partner and not her tenant, that therefore everything's rightfully theirs as his next of kin.' Niall was worried about that.

'Yep but I can't afford a court case. And I want to grieve. I can't do that while all this is going on.' She rapidly blinked away sudden tears.

'Well they probably can't either, unless they had some money stashed away,' said Niall.

They were desolate as they tried to make sense of what was left. Niall got a couple of boxes and started on the papers, photo albums and anything personal. Georgia got rid of the old dirty bedding in Brigit's room and cleared the bathroom out. She started on the kitchen.

'We should make a written note of what's here in case they break in and nick stuff. Last night we tried to remember, but we'd better be more organised now.' Georgia called out to Niall.

'I'll take photos as well. Thank goodness for cell phones.'

Niall reached in his jacket pocket.

They busied themselves and stopped briefly when the Taits bought over some scones for them. Delicious as the scones were, neither Niall nor Georgia were in a mood to entertain nosy neighbours,

'Georgia and Niall surely seemed upset when we took them over those scones,' Moira was saying plaintively to Stephen as they left the house through the back door.

Stephen laid a placatory hand on her arm as they walked around to the front. They saw to their horror that Blanche and Amanda had rolled up in their truck and close behind were Simon and Nigel, hooked up again after their visits to the police station.

No-one noticed Moira and Stephen reverse and leave through the back gate.

Blanche and Amanda had been to the mortuary and identified Rob's body. 'Just send him to the cheapest funeral home. Spry and Sons. That'll do won't it Amanda?'

'Yeah. Don't want anything fancy. Let's get out of here mum,' said Amanda who couldn't leave fast enough. They drove straight to Brigit's house.

'We need to get to the house quickly before anyone else gets there. You still got the keys you nicked?' asked Blanche.

'Of course. It's how I used to get in and nick stuff when they were out,' Amanda laughed. 'Remember when I nicked that emerald ring? Rob saw it on me but told Brigit she'd lost it. Called her a silly cow for always losing things.'

'It's all ours now Amanda. Both Rob and Brigit are dead, so we need to decide what we want to keep before we sell up. I can feel a holiday in Aussie coming up.' Blanche was cheerful. She got out of the van to be met at the gate by Simon.

'Who the fuck are you?' Simon said.

'Rob's family. We're here to take possession of our property. It's ours now he's dead.' Blanche went to push by him.

'No, you're not. I'm claiming it as part of our gang's assets. So, bugger off. Rob was quite clear that this was where we were going to have our rooms.'

'Not likely. We're his next of kin. It's ours. He wasn't in a gang anyway and he's never even mentioned you, whoever you claim to be,' said Blanche.

'I'm Simon Smart, Rob's right hand man. You don't want to mess with me. I'm warning you. This is going to be our headquarters.'

'Ha.' Blanche was scathing. 'Think you can scare me? My husband's Will says this house was his, and we are the only beneficiaries. My father bought it for Rob. We've got proof,' she bluffed.

'Oh, I know all about your father. The old man in Bluff who allows his boats to be used for smuggling cocaine and just got rumbled didn't he? Think he's going to run and rescue his daughter? He'll be so up to his eyeballs in trouble that even Jack Olds won't be able to get him out of it.' Simon was standing arms akimbo, legs apart, the stance of a mobster delivering an order. 'Think I don't know about you all and your smuggling ways? I also know that he didn't buy this house and Rob always said you were a born liar.'

'Yeah and think we don't know about that shady Jack Olds, kicked out of his firm because of his dodgy business practice.' Nigel joined in but wondering what rights they actually had. He wasn't going to show Simon that he was having second thoughts about all this just yet. *That discussion had to be later over a quiet beer.*

In the sanctuary of their own home Moria turned to Stephen and said, 'better call the police. Trouble's brewing and we need to help Georgia and Niall. That lot can't be allowed to get in there.'

Tom had also arrived, driving quietly up unseen and unheard amid all the malarkey. He watched and listened, judging when would be the right time to step in. No-one knew about him yet. *They're going to get such a fucking big shock. The bitch wife and Simon who thinks he's gonna be boss. They won't know what's coming at them, like a train, on track to mow them all down.*

He smiled at the spectacle. *Police will be here soon with all this racket. The Taits are sure to call them.* He noticed the

Mercedes, strolled by it while thinking it's a bloody good car that. That must be the son's. *He also is gonna get a shock when I walk in.*

The call to the police was answered by the receptionist who noted the call was from the Taits. She put it aside. They were always ringing and complaining about next door. And anyway, she reasoned, Craig and Philip were busy elsewhere.

CHAPTER THIRTY EIGHT

Craig and Philip were once more at Thomsons Bush confronting another distressed family over a gruesome find, the badly mauled body of a young man.

'Jono.' said Craig. 'Not much of his face left but I recognise his clothes and the ring.'

'And the reason he never turned up to make a statement. 'What on earth was he doing out here?' Philip asked.

'He knows we found a stone from his ring here so perhaps he came out to check that there wasn't anything else incriminating,' replied Craig. 'That's his car in the car park. Unlocked?'

'Yes, and keys in it. Let's get it to the yard and see what we can find. I'd like to know if there are dog hairs inside. We know Jono doesn't have a dog.' Philip got on his cell to call for a team and tow truck as he paced around the perimeter of the scene.

While Philip carefully walked around, Craig did his usual. Standing still and letting his eyes do the walking. Philip watched him as he spoke to the dispatcher. *He's freaky when he does that but shit, he's good at it.* Craig flashed back to the scene only a mere couple of days ago. Nothing spoke to him.

'Simon said he took his dog for a walk, didn't he?' Craig turned back to Philip.

'Yes, said that was why he was late.'

'Any idea what sort of dog?'

'No but easy enough to find out. The council will have a record. What are you thinking?' Philip asked.

'Coincidences. Don't believe in them. Simon has a dog. He was late for his statement because he says he took his dog for a walk. Jono's been mauled to death by a dog, a large one by the look of the paw prints. We need to find out where he went for his dog walk. We need to get forensics here, get a sample of that blood. There may be some dog saliva in it or on the body.'

'I asked for a team when I phoned in for a tow truck,' said Philip. 'So, some questions to get answers to. Was Simon here as well as Jono? Did he walk back with his dog or did they come in two cars? I'll get a junior to see if there was a sighting of them walking back to the city. Not going to be easy though. It's quite a long way back into town. We need to time it as see if that fits approximately when Simon arrived at the station.'

'Those are critical questions. All we know from the scene is that Jono used his own car to drive himself. We know that this is his car and that it was dirty with soil from the crime scene where Topaz's body was found,' said Craig.

'Do we know if Simon has a car?' Philip asked. 'We need to check to see if there are more than one set of tyre tracks here.' He bent down to inspect. 'My uninformed eye says only one set.'

'Forensics can answer that. And in response to your question. Yes, he has a Holden Camaro V8. Question is, where does he get his money from? He doesn't seem to have a real job.'

Craig spoke out loud, more to himself than his colleague. 'Was this just an unlucky accident and an unprovoked attack by a roaming dog? Or was this a deliberate assault to silence a key and weak witness, made to look like a random dog attack?' Craig couldn't pin it down yet. He needed more than his gut this time.

'I want this scene secured and combed. We need to find out what really happened. If this was an accident, someone would have called it in. They would have called an ambulance or the police. A responsible person would not allow his dog to live once it had done this.' Craig said. 'When you get the station, ring the vets to see if they have anyone who wants to put down a dog. I'll rope this off before I go.'

He went to his car, got the high viz tape and draped it around the scene.

'I'll stop by Simon's place to see what sort of dog he has, if any. And I might just go past Chelmsford Street and see if Georgia knows. She might know something about Simon from Brigit,' said Craig.

'Will do. I'll wait for the tow truck and mortician's van to arrive and hitch a ride back with one of them. Meanwhile I'll start combing the surrounding area in case there's anything outside the immediate site. Leave some gloves and evidence bags will you.'

Craig left and drove to Simon's house. He parked outside and call the station. 'Put me through to Barbara please.'

'Sorry sir. She left earlier in a bit of a hurry. Looked a bit peaky. Hope she's not coming down with anything.'

'Ok thanks. Get her to ring me if she comes in. Meanwhile I'll let her be.'

He looked over Simon's gate. The place was closed and quiet but Craig rattled the gate. He jumped as an enormous Rottweiler lunged at it. It looked as if it'd been hosed down.

'Well, well,' he muttered. 'This doesn't look good. But there won't be any evidence now unless I can persuade a judge to have him put down and his stomach contents analysed.'

He drove round to Chelmsford Street where he found a fracas was in full swing in front of Brigit's gate. Cars and vans parked any which way, and there were a number of people shouting at each other.

Georgia had suddenly heard the ruckus outside, stopped still, wiped her hands down her sides. 'What's all that shouting outside?' she asked.

'Damned awful racket whatever it is. Let's go and look,' Niall replied. They were quiet as they opened the front door. They glanced at each other questions on their faces and they stood shock still watching mouths open at the scene in front of them.

Craig saw them leaning against the veranda post, arms folded, watching. He slipped by and joined them. It seemed that there were opposing sides wanting to claim the house.

'Locked the back door?' Craig asked quietly. They nodded grateful that the police had come.

Simon was getting pissed off with this virago and her daughter. *Wish I had Brute with me. That'd scare them off.*

'We should discuss this inside because at the moment all we're doing is alerting the neighbours,' Blanche said suddenly.

So finally, as if in mutual agreement they turned and opened the gate to walk inside. They stopped as they saw the threesome watching from the porch.

'What are you doing here at our place?' a chorus in unison demanded.

'Who the fuck do you think you are?' Simon spoke loudly, full of authority and aggression.

'We're cleaning out our house.' Niall answered. 'You're now trespassing on our property.'

'And you know who I am, and I could arrest you all for disturbing the peace and for trespassing.' Craig said.

The curtains next door twitched. It was almost too much excitement for poor old Moira and Stephen. Being a nosy neighbour was so tiring. You had to be on the alert all the time in case you missed anything.

'This is our house.' said Blanche. 'I'm Rob's wife and I'm entitled to it.'

'And I'm his daughter so I am as well.'

Craig was looking at Brigit's Will. Niall had passed it over to him.

'Actually Ms. Hunter. You're a former wife. And this Will, properly signed and witnessed leaves all Brigit's assets to her son and her sister. That includes the house, contents, assets and car,' Craig quietly said. 'And this other piece of paper shows that Brigit owned her house outright with no mortgage. Rob Bennet is not mentioned in her Will except as her boarder, and he is not registered on the land title as an owner or part owner.'

'So, all you thieves can just leave our property. There's

nothing in here of yours. Rob owned nothing except his clothes, and we have packed them already for you.' Niall took a suitcase down the steps and put it by the gate.

'He came with nothing except what was in a suitcase, so he'll leave with nothing but what's in this suitcase,' said Georgia.

'And as for you.' Niall turned to Simon. 'You are not known to me or to my aunt. You appear to be an opportunist as well as a thug and a thief. I suggest you leave now as well before I ask the Detective Inspector here to arrest you for trespass. In fact, you should all leave now.'

They did, full of mutters and threats.

Georgia and Niall gratefully went back into the grand art deco house without looking back at the departing foursome. Once inside, Craig turned to them.

'Young Jono is also now dead.'

'Who?' asked Georgia.

'He and Simon, the big fellow out there, were associates of Rob's and we were about to question Jono about last night's events here,' replied Craig.

'Oh,' said Georgia. 'That Simon seems a nasty fellow. Never met him before. Seems he's taken on the mantle of leader.'

'I think he's been critical to Rob's plans and is deep in this. I also think that it was his dog who mauled young Jono,' Craig said.

'He was mauled to death?' Georgia shuddered. 'This is nothing to do with us is it?' she asked.

'No. This was just advising you, and to alert you to the fact that Rob had many unsavory friends, not to mention his family. But you've already met them.'

'Why would they try and get rid of one of their own?' asked Georgia.

'Probably because he was a bit simple and they feared he was a danger to them. Worried that he might tell us too much. We had evidence to tie him into the murder of Topaz. They wanted to remove any threat. Although setting a dog on him leaves evidence, that will be hard to get without recourse to the courts. A perfect murder really.'

Niall and Georgia looked at each other.

'Ok thanks.' Niall hastily said. *I suspect ours was even more perfect.*

Craig registered the look and chose not to ask what that was about.

CHAPTER THIRTY NINE

Craig returned to a meeting with Philip and the team with a slight tingling down his spine. He shrugged it off and together his team tried to make sense of the events in the last couple of days.

'How can we put all this together and get a conviction?'

'Well,' Philip said thoughtfully. 'Four deaths in as many days, all with a central character. Rob. There'll be no arrest now for Brigit's death, or murder if it indeed was one, as our main suspect is now rather conveniently dead.'

'There might be enough evidence to get a conviction for Jono's death but that would require more leg work,' said Craig.

'Yes, but Brigit's family's not going to get a satisfactory solution to her death as two of the suspects are now dead,' Philip continued.

'And then there's Topaz. Her death is still not solved.'

'I think we'll find that with Jono dead, evidence may be hard to get now.' Philip looked worried as he said this, his hand rubbing an imaginary spot off his desk.

'We need to pull these threads together. So, more work is needed there to tie in Simon and Nigel. Anyone know where Barbara is, or when she'll be back? I need her to put all this in a diagram on the white board.' Craig looked around hoping that she'd just slipped in unnoticed.

Everyone shook their heads. *I need to get to her. Something's wrong.*

'We're up for this people. Just some dogged police work. We're all used to that.' Craig nodded to them all in confirmation.

'OK boss. We're on to it.'

'And as for Rob's death. Well,' Craig was thoughtful and pragmatic about that one. 'I don't think there's much to go on there. Let's not put too much time into that one.'

'Good call,' said Philip. 'He's no loss to the human race anyway.'

'However, all deaths deserve an investigation if it's warranted. So do some work on it. Enough to appease a judge or defense lawyer, but it is the least important one,' Craig said before he sent them all off to their various duties.

'I'm not going to give it any time at all, but the team doesn't need to know that. Maybe Rob's got his just desserts. I'll leave that one alone for the moment,' he said to Philip.

'And we mustn't forget Simon Smart and Nigel Butler,' said Philip. 'Now there are two thugs if ever there were.'

CHAPTER FORTY

As they backed off, away from the Chelmsford Street house, Simon turned to Blanche and Amanda.

'We'll talk strategy off-site. Better to beat a retreat now and come back later. Those two won't be staying here so we can come back tonight. Break in if necessary. Remove anything good and discuss what we'll do.'

He'd already eyed Amanda up as a good looker, young and interesting. *Might be able to have a fling with her. That'll keep her onside.*

'We need to work together on this if we are going to be able to get anything out of it,' Simon added.

The women nodded, each of them thinking the same.

'Joining forces is a good idea.' Amanda looked up at Simon.

Simon grinned down at her. *Gotcha.*

'They won't be able to afford a good lawyer either if it comes to that. Not one as skilled as Olds anyway.' Amanda said. 'Mum and I know him well. He'll help us. Granddad will make sure of that.'

'They won't want a long dragged out case because the sister lives in Auckland. We can drag it out and wear them down,' she added.

'Yes, better to work together for now and then divide the proceeds,' Blanche said decisively, aware of the flirting between Amanda and Simon. *Good move kiddo.* 'Olds would do it for a cut of whatever we could get for the house. Even though he now works for my old man, that shouldn't be a problem. Olds is pretty greedy and unscrupulous.'

They all walked off with Simon saying, 'See you at my place in a minute. Follow me.'

They strolled up to the gate and waited for Simon to tie up the dog which seemed to be ataxic as it wobbled and stumbled towards Simon.

'What's up mate?' Simon stooped down to check him and noticed some meat nearby. *Strange I didn't leave him that.* The dog could barely stand and couldn't bark. He just whimpered but became settled at the sound of his master's soothing tone. He looked around him but noticed nothing else unusual so then he went to unlock the door. He stopped confused.

'What the fuck? I locked this bloody door this morning.' Tentatively he pushed his open door and walked inside wishing he had the dog beside him. Blanche and Amanda were behind, giving the door wide berth. They glanced at each other. Blanche shrugged.

'Who the fuck are you. What the fuck are you doing in my house?' Simon was astounded to see someone standing in his living room.

'Hello Simon. You took your time getting here. I'm Rob's son, Tom Forsythe. I'm here to tell you what's going to happen now that Rob's dead.' He held up his collection of skeleton keys. 'Dog was easy to attend to,' he smirked.

Legs apart, he stood easily, emanating power and menace. Simon started, stopped when Tom held up his hand.

'Don't even think it.' He was standing quite still arms now at his side. Hanging loose in the position of a fighter. He showed no fear, and little empathy. His eyes were those of a shark, cold, cruel glinting in anticipation of a fight. Simon backed off.

'Simon?' Amanda looked inside.

Simon was standing shock still. Even he, known for his

strength and his ruthlessness, felt a quiver of fear. *Hold back for the moment Si. Pick your time and place.*

Tom looked at Blanche and Amanda standing with their mouths open at this jaw dropping revelation. As one, they stormed in shouting. 'No way are you Rob's son.'

'He only has one daughter.' Amanda advanced on him. With a swift side swipe, he knocked her sideways, and turned towards Blanche.

'Back off old woman,' he snarled. Blanche bent to help her daughter up and wipe her bloodied nose.

'Didn't know, did you?' Tom grinned as he said it. 'We thought it might shock you. He quite fooled you both didn't he? Well you can't keep a virile man like my dad down just awaiting your pleasure. We kept it secret from you Blanche, because we reckoned your old man wouldn't like it and Rob still needed to use him.'

He rubbed his hand as he turned to Amanda and snarled, 'and as for you sister mine – well half sister – you just knuckle down like a good little girl and shut the fuck up.'

Blanche sank onto a nearby chair, face white with disbelief.

'He was having it off with someone while I was married to him? That early in our marriage?' Disbelief. Her voice quavered. Amanda sat beside her, arm around the shaking shoulders.

'Rob hated children.' She was stunned that he had another child, just as much as she was stunned that he'd never told her. *You look and act just like him.*

'He wanted a son and you wouldn't give him one. Daughters are useless.' He turned to Amanda. 'He thought you were useless.'

'I know that,' said Amanda. 'I hated him because of it. I'll never grieve for him.' She had in fact quietly celebrated with friends out of her mother's earshot. She glowered at Tom. His opening statement to her was just like her father's attitude to her. Be seen, do as you're told and shut up. No way ever would she succumb to that again. A stepbrother? *Not likely.*

She looked at Simon afresh, eyes half closed as she watched his reaction to this news.

'This is one insult too many. He's not going to get away with this and neither are you.' She glared at Tom. Simon just watched, waited, ready if needed.

Blanche clenched her jaw and unconsciously started grinding her teeth. She'd always done this as a child when she got tense. She let Amanda start the running and she would pick up the pace when required.

'How old are you then? When were you born? Who's your mother? Where is she now?' Amanda had a number of questions, but these would suffice for now. Rat a tat, tat, she fired them off in quick succession.

'Only slightly younger than you, but age doesn't matter. It's what Rob had always planned,' he added to forestall Blanche's inevitable denial.

'It matters to mum,' said Amanda.

'I don't care about your mum. Rob had me and my mum.'

'How could he afford to have two families? He barely kept us in food and clothes? Mum had to go out and find work even when I was little.'

Tom smirked. No way was he going to tell them that. *They might decide to claim the thousands in the bank. Wouldn't put it past them.*

'Well who is your mum then? Do we know her?' asked Amanda.

'Not telling and no?' Curt and to the point. Tom wasn't going to give anything away.

Amanda immediately started asking questions. She strode up to him aggressively, hands on hips.

'So how did you know about us then? Were Niall and Georgia a surprise as well? Had Brigit or Rob told you anything about them?'

'Enough of this.' Simon interjected as his eyes swept around his home looking to see if anything was disturbed. There was nothing obvious. His magazines, cars and porn were as he left them last night, just scattered around the bottles and the glass on the coffee table.

'And how did you know where I lived?' Simon was contained,

the fury at the treatment of his dog well-hidden for now.

While the question and answer banter carried on between the two cocks Amanda was plotting.

Quietly she said to her mother, 'They, Georgia, and Niall, obviously have got the ear of the police. We need a different strategy to deal with them and the house now that this Tom chap is here.'

'You'll have to get on the computer Amanda and do some hacking. Find his dirty little secrets.'

'We need to be patient, mum. Our little nest egg may take longer than we planned. But we can plan, and we're good at waiting.'

Blanche had always been patient. She leaned back against the sofa and stretched her long legs. 'I learned patience by having to deal with Rob.'

And in turn Amanda saw the benefits of timing and place. She had spent most of her life estranged from Rob and had spent those lonely hours in front of a computer learning all she could about the art of hacking people's lives, their secrets, and their little dirty foibles. No-one was safe from her prying eyes. Certainly, Brigit wasn't, although she used her computer very rarely. Rob had taken it over and was writing his life story.

She whispered to her mother. 'I've been into Brigit's computer. Rob had taken it over and I found he'd been writing his story. Badly. No publisher would look at it. Maybe he wanted to make an eBook. But then that would have really got him in the clink. Pity he'd died as I was just getting ready to lay it all out to him for us.'

'Still how did you miss this Tom character? More digging needed.' Blanche whispered back.

'What are you two whispering about? You won't be able to put anything over me.' Tom, finished with Simon, turned his attention to the women.

Simon went outside. Checked on Brute, got him some water and removed the residual poisoned meat.

He took deep breaths as he wondered how he could turn this around. He got on the phone to Nigel, 'get over here quick smart.'

'Why?'

'Just do it.'

He slipped quietly back inside and watched the three of them mentally circling each other. *That Amanda is a cool customer, just leaning casually against the wall. Well stacked. Like it.*

Amanda noticed him eying her up. She almost folded her arms across them and hunched down as she often did when confronted with lecherous stares, but instead she brazenly shoved her chest out. *No qualms about snaring him with my boobs if that's what it'll take to hook him.*

Blanche still appeared shattered at Rob's deceit. 'Why should I be so surprised? I thought I knew all about him and it seems I didn't. What else don't I know?' She looked at Amanda, took a deep breath, stood up and approached Tom as if to give him a hug. He stepped back.

'Don't touch me,' he snarled.

'You have just lost your dad Tom, and I wanted to offer you some comfort and sympathy. We can help each other here. It's hard for all of us.' She stopped, spread her arms open and shrugged. 'Meant nothing by it except to offer warmth from a mother even if I'm not yours.'

'Don't need it,' he bluffed. Rob's death had hit him hard, but he was dammed if he would show any weakness here. He was not about to be seduced by them into thinking they were going to be friends.

Simon strolled into his kitchen. 'I'm going to make some coffee. You can come in and have some and sit down or you can continue sizing each other up in there,' he said over his shoulder.

As he went about the mechanics of turning on the espresso machine, grinding the beans, getting milk ready to be frothed, and putting out mugs and sugar, he considered his position and what he could do. He mentally listed his options.

Firstly, those three were indirectly family, whether they accepted it or not. They were linked to Rob for better or worse. Therefore, theirs was a bond which could become tighter as they got to know each other or be broken when competing aims became strained.

Secondly that daughter could be useful. Not only for sex but also to get her on his side against Tom, a power freak. Simon recognised he was staking his territory just like Brute and every other male dog did. *I understand dogs so I can understand Tom. Let him piss in all corners if he thinks it's gonna help him.*

Thirdly, Amanda could go either way, but she had her own goals and that didn't necessarily mean they were the same as Tom's. Blanche may be a difficulty. The older rejected woman, bitter at being spurned and unforgiving of Rob's betrayal with the sudden appearance of a child she knew nothing about. *Blanche could prove an interesting challenge. But equally she'd be an advantage. She'd fight like a tiger for her daughter and her share now. Am I up to it? Hell yeah.*

'Coffee's ready.'

Simon poured the coffee and placed the filled cups on the table along with the milk and sugar.

Tom went to say something when Simon cut him off with a raised hand. Kinda neutral, like a stop signal. Nothing aggressive about it.

'This is my house, so I think I'll start the conversation.' He faced them, mug in hand, apparently relaxed but inwardly furious.

'Tom,' he said quietly. 'I am pissed off that you would poison my dog. I hope he recovers because if he dies, I'll fucking kill you. I've trained him too well, spent too much time on him to let anything happen to him.' Tom opened his mouth. The hand again. Tom stopped, scowled.

'You three are all family, connected to Rob one way or another. I'm the outsider. That can be viewed as a challenge or an asset. How you want to play this will depend where Nige and I are in this. Nige is on his way here and we are blood brothers. Partners till the end.'

He paused while he stirred more sugar into his coffee, looking at their reactions.

'We need to find out if we all have the same aims and what they are. Tom has already laid out his claim and believes he's going to call the shots. That's what I understood him to have said after he broke into my house.'

That statement got an immediate reaction from Blanche. She balled her fists and shouted.

'He's bloody well not. I'm Rob's wife. That house is due to me after all I've suffered at that bastard's hands. We're the ones who helped Rob when he needed assistance there. Not you, you little bastard.' She rounded on Tom raising her clenched fists. Tom gazed at her fury, the look of a shark as he appraised her.

'Let's hear what everyone has to say about their goals first. Then if they're all the same we can decide on a plan. Agreed?' Simon was all quietness and reason.

Tom was looking mutinous at this turn of events. Somehow the initiative had moved from him to Simon. In the absence of any agreement or for that matter disagreement, Simon continued.

'From what we have learned so far,' he said, 'both Blanche and Amanda believe they have a claim on Brigit's house. They want to have a crack at getting that either through scare tactics, or the courts if the son and sister don't buckle. And we have no evidence that they will just pack their tents and leave. Right you two?'

'Yep we're gonna get that house. Dad kept us short and we need the money,' said Amanda.

'Besides my dad expects something out of it the way he's bailed Rob out from time to time.' Blanche had calmed down enough to respond to the reasoned voice of Simon.

'Ok so that's your aim then. Tom, you have said you are going to be the leader. Is that right and if so, how do you intend to lead and what will you lead?'

Simon was on a fishing trip to see how much Rob had let Tom know of their own plans. Clearly the women didn't know what was intended for the house because they aimed to sell it.

Tom just nodded as if in full agreement. Took a sip of coffee before he answered.

'You obviously haven't been told by Rob that he intended to use the house as a gang headquarters and use Topaz as a honey trap. She's now out of the picture but there will be other women coming on the scene.'

He kept his voice quiet and menacing. He found that worked better at scaring people than a full rant and rave.

There was a lull. The group shuffled nervously as they all looked at Tom who seemed to be far away remembering something by the look on his face. He moved quickly as he reasserted his authority over this lot. He put down his cup and stood up as he spoke.

'I have all the information on you Simon. I know what you did to Topaz and Jono. I know you got rid of them both violently. Don't worry about proof because I have it and anyway people always believe me.'

He smiled slowly as he said it, pointing to his iPad. 'That little telltale machine never leaves my sight so don't go getting ideas. The camera in Rob's kitchen and Brigit's bedroom, filmed all your little chats, so you're now beholden to me for your own safety, and will do as I say, just as you did what Dad said you had to.'

'Why would people believe you and not us?' sneered Blanche.

'Because of my work in the community as an ambulance office. People trust us.' He smirked. 'We're so kind.'

He waited a beat while he watched the reaction of all three. When he sensed mutiny, Tom suddenly moved to Amanda, leaning against the wall. He seized her around the throat with one hand. He slowly pushed her up against the wall till she was balancing on her tip toes.

'Let her go. Leave her alone. You're strangling her.' He held off Blanche with the other arm as she jumped up to help her daughter.

'Back off or I'll pull her up even higher so she can't balance on her toes. She'll suffocate and do you want that on your conscience?'

Amanda tried to struggle free but the more she twisted the tighter his iron grip became and so she stilled herself as she slowly began to lose focus. Her eyes watered, her breath came in gasps, her lips blued. Blanche was whimpering as she watched her daughter dying until finally after what seemed to be eternity, he dropped her like a stone. Amanda dropped to the floor, semiconscious, struggling for breath, and sounding like a freight train as she tried to suck air into her tortured lungs.

Blanche rushed to her, held her, and stroked her back, whispering to her. 'Breathe, just breathe.'

Simon sat in a state of shock; motionless and silenced by the enormity of what Tom had just done and the speed with which he had done it. Not only his strength to hold up a fully-grown woman like that but be so cold as to do it to his own half-sister.

'I can do that to any of you if you step out of line. That was just an example to warn you. My way, or no way.'

Simon finally moved. 'That was unnecessary. And to your sister.' He was appalled.

'Get up and clean yourself up.' snarled Tom as he watched the result of her bladder emptying, slowly spreading over the floor.

'This way.' Simon raised himself to show them the bathroom. He brought them towels and some spare trousers left behind by a former girlfriend. 'We'll talk when you're ready,' he whispered. 'That behaviour is like an animal. Not on.' He didn't see the irony in his comment.

Blanche sat arms wrapped around her daughter watching he chest heave as she gulped in air. The sounds of Amanda's breath sounded like the noise of a steam train. *That's what Brigit's asthma sounded like.* Blanche felt a sudden spasm of pity for Brigit. With her hands now pressed against her chest, the shock of how easily Tom had strangled her daughter and her feeling of helplessness abated slightly to be replace by cold, ferocious anger. The lion mother had emerged in defense of her cub. Amanda felt a sense of utter embarrassment sweep over her as felt the wetness of her trousers. Her face flushed red, prickles of cold sweat formed on her forehead, and she covered her face with her hands. Sobs replaced the tortured breathing. Blanche silently continued to rub her back as the air wheezed in and out. Crouched on the floor together she knew they had a fight on their hands.

Eventually as Amanda's breathing became regular and more controlled, they set about cleaning up. The knickers provided by Simon fitted, even if they were not her style and the trousers were a tad too short for her long legs. But they were clean and dry and for that she was grateful.

'I can't go in there and face them.'

'We have to if we want to get anything out of this.' Blanche said softly.

'My throat hurts.' Amanda was whispering, rubbing her neck as she viewed the red hand marks with the two darkening ones on either side of her throat. 'I'm going to get bruises.'

'You've got some arnica at home. We'll rub it in when we've finished here. It might stop it looking too bad.'

'I'll never forgive him for this. I'll remember every day.'

'I'll never forget either. I'll watch and wait. I'll never forget. Just see me as the elephant in the room.' She laughed grimly. 'Ready?'

Amanda nodded and together they walked back into the lion's den. The circus master was waiting, eyeing her up, checking her trousers.

'If you ever step out of line, I'll do that again. If I hear you plotting, I'll do it again.'

Amanda managed to keep her humiliation in check as she coolly stared at Tom.

'Thanks for the clothes Simon. Appreciate that.'

Simon nodded and gave her a wink behind Tom's back. Tom could hardly keep the swagger off him as he went to her and gently stroked her neck. She didn't flinch under his gaze or recoil at his touch. She was a rock, an island he would never touch again or destroy. She noticed out of the corner of her eye Simon moving towards them. She flicked her hand to hold him off. They stood like statues. Amanda, unflinching and Tom with only his hand moving, gently stroking her neck, waiting for a reaction so he could do it again. The lion toying with his prey. The mother standing by, waiting to pounce.

A knock on the door heralded Nigel. He stepped into the room. It was a tableau, a stage, with the main characters staked out as if in a play.

Abruptly Tom turned to greet him. 'I'm Tom, Simon will fill you in. I've just been clearing up a little misunderstanding here.

We had a little problem before you arrived Nigel. These three have just learned a lesson about who's in charge.'

He sipped his coffee and gazed at Nigel who was looking confused. The silence of Simon, the smoldering anger and fear from the two women seeped into the atmosphere.

'This is where we're at. I'm Rob's son. Although Simon probably told you he was going to lead and use Brigit's house as his new headquarters I'm telling you that's not going to happen.'

Nigel made to move, opened his mouth to comment until a shake of Simon's head prompted him to close it again. He swallowed his words and listened as Tom continued.

'Rob trusted you all so I will as well, to begin with anyway until you prove your loyalty to me. Nigel, Simon will tell you I have all the evidence I need to put you both in jail for Topaz's rape and murder. Never mind Jono.'

Nigel swallowed. He looked over at Simon for guidance. Simon just stared at him. As soon as Tom looked away, he put a finger to his lips.

The only one who looked comfortable was Tom. He plonked himself down in a chair and held court while he told them all his plans for the immediate future. He wasn't ready yet to discuss long term. He needed to be sure he had them on board. He knew how to handle two women; fear would do that, and he'd shown them what he was capable of. The two men he needed to be his front men, if he was to remain behind the scenes as the ever-helpful paramedic. And he needed to keep that job because it was his entry into people's homes and the lucrative sideline of stealing and fencing.

'So, that's it. But let's be clear. I call the shots and I won't tolerate any dissension. What you saw today was just a taste of what I am capable of doing. And no point plotting against me as I'll soon know.'

He stood up, stretched, stroked Amanda's neck again, winked at her, ignored Blanche, and sauntered out.

'We'll meet here at 10 tomorrow. We'll use this place until we get the position of Rob's house. In the meantime, have a think about what, when and how we're going to operate. I have an idea of what we need to do first but let's see if you're up to the challenge and can work something out.'

As he left, he bent down and patted the still slumbering dog. Nigel held Simon back.

CHAPTER FORTY ONE

'No way.' Blanche started until she saw Simon put his fingers to his lips. He indicated to go out to the back garden.

'No Nige. Put that ciggie away. New house rule. No smoking inside. We'll join you out on the veranda for one. You women coming?'

'What?' A surprised Nigel looked questioningly at him.

Confused they followed him outside right down to the far end of the garden.

'What? You know I don't smoke. Haven't done for years.' Nigel said.

'Yes Simon. Why all the secret squirrel stuff? It's cold out here.' Blanche rubbed her arms.

'Remember he said he'd know if we plotted against him. He was already here in my house before we got here and maybe he's bugged the house. Why else would he be so cocky?'

'What'll we do then? What happened in there before I came?' Nigel was becoming increasingly concerned about this group of ill-fated people.

'He showed us his prowess,' said Amanda.

'His prowess? What the hell does that mean? How?'

'He fucking nearly strangled me to death.' She glowered at

him.

'What? How? Why didn't anybody help?'

Blanche told him exactly how it went down, how they were too afraid to move in case he killed Amanda.

'We were terrified he'd kill her. He was laughing as he did it. He was on a high. I could see that.'

'Look at my neck. See the bruising already appearing. By tomorrow I'll be black and blue. How'll I explain that at work? Everyone will think I've been assaulted or having kinky sex.' She was still near to tears.

'Crikey. But where the hell did he come from, appearing out of the ether like that? He said he's Rob's son?'

'Rob's bastard. He's not mine,' Blanche quickly said to the inquiring look from Nigel.

'Fuck me.'

'He'll do that to you an'all.' said Blanche. 'I wouldn't trust him to save myself especially after he did that to Amanda.'

Simon was sitting still weighing up the options. 'We need to see if he's bugged the house. If he has...'

'We'll remove them,' said Nigel quickly. 'I know how to do that.'

'No that won't work. He needs to think we don't know. We look for them and if we find them, we leave them in place. We carry on as normal but anything we don't want him to know we say off-site. Agreed'

'Yep. Let's look for them, everywhere, even the not so obvious places. And while we're looking, we chatter to each other about this and that as if we don't suspect him,' said Nigel.

'OK. Blanche and Amanda, you do kitchen and hallway. Pretend you're cooking up a feed, make a note but leave them where you find them. Nige, you and I'll do the bedroom, sitting room, dining room.' Simon stood ready for action.

'And don't forget the patio and verandas. Wouldn't put it past him to put some bugs there either.'

By the end of the search they reported what they'd found while huddled together bundled up outside in the winterly evening. They all held their hands around steaming hot cups of soup while they sipped and shivered, unwilling to go inside while they talked.

'I'll go first,' said Simon. 'In the sitting room there were three of them. One in the light in the middle of the room.'

'Obvious,' cut in Nigel.

'Yes, so he's placed the other two in less obvious places. It's as if he expected us to find that one and feel secure. Another one is sitting inside that large oriental vase with the dried reeds in and the third one is cunning, lodged just under the doorway between the lounge and dining room.'

'Sneaky,' Blanche was almost admiring.

'In the bedroom there was one in the central light, another behind the headboard of the bed and a third under the chest of drawers,' said Simon.

'Three in each. A pattern? Or just covering all bases for good coverage?' asked Blanche.

'The hall seems clean but I'm uneasy about that. I think we need another look. I expected to find one by the front door. Will check later.' Nigel said.

'We found two in the kitchen. It's a pretty small room so I don't think there are anymore,' said Blanche.

'It doesn't matter.' Simon said. 'All we wanted to achieve was where it was safe to speak openly. Now we know I'm well and truly bugged, we need to be careful.'

'I think when we're talking outside, we need to have that on loud in case there are any out here.' She nodded to the ghetto-blaster playing Def Leppard.

'Nothing will get through the noise of heavy metal music.'

Simon was singing away. 'Love this band. Went to see them when they toured New Zealand.' He started playing his air guitar.

Even Amanda managed a smile at his antics.

'Ok so what now? What'll we do?' Nigel asked.

'We lean on the son and sister, without him knowing. If that doesn't work, we file a claim in the family court as I am still legally married to Rob and as such am still his next of kin. Tom won't be registered as his son. He has a different name anyway so he will have a hard time proving his claim,' suggested Blanche.

'I think it's a battle in two parts. First, we get the house in your name. I'm easy with that because I'll help, and we can come to a formal arrangement between the four of us. I assume that none of us wants anything to do with Tom so are we all in this together?' Simon raised his eyebrows as he asked.

'Yes, agree so far. I won't have anything to do with him.' Amanda unconsciously rubbed her neck.

'OK so if that's agreed let's work up an agreement between us and file a claim because I don't think the son and sister will let us take over.'

'Part two?' Blanche asked.

'Part two is working up a plan to eliminate Tom and secure our future away from him. Do we believe that he still has no-one else apart from us? If we have to get rid of him, we will. No qualms about that,' Simon said.

'What do you mean eliminate?' Nigel asked looking worried. *I'm not up to more violence and murder, or I'm really out of here.*

'Not kill Nige. Don't worry. Just eliminate him from being able to get the house.' *But I may kill him.*

'I wanna kill him.' Amanda put a protective hand to her neck.

'And us?' Blanche asked. 'What about us two in your grand scheme of things.'

'Full partners Blanche. Don't worry about that. I'd never treat Amanda like that.'

'I'm gonna hack his computer. See what I can find out about him,' said Amanda.

'You know how to hack? That'll prove useful. Smart cookie.' Simon smiled at her. 'What about the son and sister? Can you hack them as well?'

'Yep. No problem. I've already been into Brigit's computer and checked up on what Rob was about. If we can find out stuff, we can maybe use that to neutralise them. Don't want to give Tom time to marshal his own plan.'

'I think he already has a plan,' grumbled Simon.

'Amanda, I think we need to get you home to rest. This has been a traumatic day for you and you still look shattered,' said

Blanche.

'Yep. I need to rest and then focus my mind. How can we be sure that that bastard won't break into our houses?' Amanda turned to her mother, fear in her voice.

'Good point. We will need to check that out for bugs as well. But that's for tomorrow.'

'You can stay here Amanda if it'll make you feel safer, although I only have one bedroom.' Simon chanced his luck. 'I know I couldn't help you before, but we now know what he can do, and I'll be more prepared next time he lays his hands on you.'

'How?'

'I have a stash of weapons.'

'Thanks Simon. I know we were all taken by surprise and there is no way I'll go anywhere near him in the future. No to your offer thanks. I need the security of my own bed and my own clothes. I'll make sure the bugs don't bite.' She gave a bitter laugh as she and Blanche went to the door.

'Watch what you say in the car as well,' warned Nigel. 'Cars are easily bugged.'

They drove off in silence. Before they went inside their own house in the less salubrious suburb of Kingswell in South Invercargill, they paused.

'Trust Simon?' Blanche asked.

'Not entirely but more than the other one,' replied Amanda as she gathered her bag.

'You mean Tom?'

'Yes. I could work around Simon. I think he's interested in me or at least in my boobs. Nige is a bit quiet and I don't trust that in men.'

Blanche just gave her a hug. 'Whatever you do, take care my precious girl. I will always look out for you.'

'Do you want to stay here tonight mum?'

'No thanks. I've got an early start tomorrow at the docks. Dad's got a boat landing early.'

'Thanks mum. Night.'

Amanda watched her mother leave for the half hour trip back

to Bluff.

She shut her bedroom door, changed into her nightie. In the bathroom she inspected herself, her face, her body. She slid her hands down her breast and hips. She checked her already reddening neck and rubbed some arnica into it. After she washed and cleaned her teeth, she went to the loo and silently crept back into her bedroom.

She lay still wondering if there were also bugs in her room. She thought of Tom and then of Simon and unconsciously started stroking her breasts. *He liked the look of them. Can I seduce him to work for my benefit?* The more she thought and stroked her breasts the more aroused she became as her hands went lower between her legs and regardless of the bugs, she moaned herself to sleep.

CHAPTER FORTY TWO

Nigel sat up for a while after he got home. He'd stayed and helped Simon clean up. But he felt tense, his shoulders tight, and he was unable to wind down.

He poured himself a scotch and sat in the dark outside. He thought about the increasing nastiness of his old friend. He didn't like the changes in him. It's as if Si's gone schizophrenic. The violence had come on so quickly Nigel had barely noticed it at first. Maybe all those evenings that Si spent with Rob while he was working. What had they got up to by themselves? He sipped slowly as the thoughts came thick and fast. When they were younger and a bit rebellious, they had fun together but now? He didn't want anything to do with this guy Tom. It's all getting out of control. Not fun anymore.

He felt the need for a ciggie. Thinking about Tom and how he had just popped up from nowhere. Did that viciousness come from Rob? Or had it influenced Rob's own nastiness? Nigel knew Rob had a record for drugs, theft, and rape, but he'd never experienced the out and out darkness he now saw in Tom.

He brooded as he sat at the patio. He looked around at his back yard and didn't like what he saw. He heard a Ruru quietly making his nightly calls. They were rare around here and he twisted around to see if he could catch sight of it. There it was, sitting still in the old pohutakawa tree next door; head slightly tilted looking directly at him. Although it seemed to be watching him, Nigel couldn't be sure. He heard an answering call but the Ruru kept quite still, watching him with those large brown unblinking eyes. He felt a prickle up his back as if someone had walked over his grave. That's what his mum always used to say when you got that prickly feeling. She'd be disappointed now. Perhaps it's her spirit up there watching.

Nigel remembered the time his mum had found an injured fledgling Ruru and had nursed it back to health. He'd enjoyed helping her and since then that bird had always been around their garden as a night watchman; just keeping its peace in the stillness of the night. Is this the same Ruru?

As he sat there in the darkening night, alone with nothing but his thoughts, he began to wonder about his life. How did he come to be here like this, scared out of his mind and wondering if there was another way? Was it too late to change?

He sat without noticing the cold as he thought about how derailed his life had become. He knew the police would come looking for Jono. He knew the ever-crafty Simon would implicate him in Jono's disappearance to turn the cops away from him. Nigel had no illusions that Simon would save himself first. Time to get out before it gets too out of hand.

He turned back to the Ruru. 'Hey little wise one. What do you reckon I should do? I think I want a normal life. Shall I talk to Craig Arnold or not? Do you reckon we could come to a deal? What do you think?'

The Ruru just looked, wisely saying nothing.

By the time he stirred, he'd worked through what he wanted to achieve.

He felt he had found a way forward. A way that his old mum might like. A way to redeem himself. He knew the risks but had decided he'd do it anyway.

He went inside after turning off the radio. He'd worked out how he was going to manage the meeting with Tom and Simon in the morning, while he was sitting there in the dark with the brooding presence of the Ruru. He'd be compliant and complicit initially but not deferential. He didn't want to raise suspicions.

This is no time for loyalty.

He wondered about Amanda. He'd like to know about computers, figured it was time he learned about them. If he treated her with a bit of respect maybe he could ask her to help and maybe they'd get on ok. He wondered if you could hack phones. Hackers can still access deleted emails so can they access deleted texts? He needed to find out.

He went inside whistling, feeling lighter in spirit than he had for ages, ever since he and Simon had fallen in with Rob for that matter. It was if a cloud had lifted and he slept soundly that night. He dreamt of his mum and her happy laugh back in the days of the farm. He missed those days. He looked at her smiling face as she hovered over him in his dreamlike state. He smiled back.

CHAPTER FORTY THREE

Day Five

When Nigel got up the next morning, he walked to the public phone booth on his way to the meeting with Tom and Simon and rang the Invercargill police station.

'Craig Arnold please.'

'Arnold'

'It's Nigel Butler here. I want talk. Off site. I'll be at the Observatory gardens at 9 o'clock.'

He didn't wait for an answer, just hung up and returned home. He poured his morning coffee and cup in hand wandered around his garden. He looked at the plants, the walls, thinking as he sipped. He looked for the Ruru, but it was gone. *Off to its own bed just as I'm about to start my day. A new day in my new life.*

He set off for his meeting with Craig. He walked to the Observatory gardens huddled in his jacket. Queens Park was depressing. There was no-one about. He'd bought two takeaway coffees. *Hope Craig takes milk.*

The observatory had been closed after the Christchurch earthquake and there was no one around.. He peered around the deserted garden seeing only a few straggling plants. He turned up the collar of his padded jacket and hunkered down into himself to wait.

He sat and sipped. He'd liked coming here when the Observatory was open to watch the starry arena as it displayed the beauty and magnificence of the skies. He liked the peacefulness of it here. It was another world. The vision made you think how small we were and how possible it is for other lives, other civilisations, other angels and demons.

He jumped when Craig sat down beside him.

'Morena.' Craig's greeting was almost a whisper. He waited.

'I want out. How do I do it?' Nigel was nervous and terse.

'Out from what?' Mildly curious.

"From this life I've found myself in. I want to do a deal. Either I can stay and be your eyes and ears in return for you dropping any charges you may have against me.'

'Or?'

'I can turn state witness in return for charges being dropped and you getting me out of here. Either way I can give you the evidence you need about Rob and Simon, and the murders of Brigit, Topaz and Jono.'

'Anything else?'

'Yes, There's Tom Forsythe.'

'Tom?' *Doesn't Ben work with a Tom?* Craig's face crinkled in a frown at this piece of news.

'Just appeared. Out of nowhere. Says he's Rob's son and is about to take over everything. He's a nasty piece of work. The others will go with him. I won't.'

'The others?' asked Craig.

'The wife and daughter, and Simon.'

Craig was silent as he thought about this unlikely offer. Nigel started fidgeting suddenly scared he'd blown it and that when he walked out there'd be coppers waiting to arrest him.

'I'm interested but I need to think this through. Say nothing. Do nothing. Act normally. Get yourself a burner phone. Leave me the number. Wait half an hour before you leave.' He handed him a slip of paper with a cell phone number on it.

He slipped out and half an hour later Nigel did the same.

CHAPTER FORTY FOUR

George and Niall were left alone for the rest of the day. Nobody came. Nobody rang. It was an oasis of calm business. They sorted, packed, stored, and cleaned. By the time they left in the evening there was a semblance of order.

'We've found enough evidence to support our right to this,' said Niall as he locked up.

'Yes, we've got all the papers necessary to defend ourselves.'

It was with growing amazement they went through Brigit's papers. They found a wealth of information, enough to protect them even if it hadn't protected Brigit. Carefully documented. Carefully hidden.

There were statements from Social Welfare confirming the status of Rob as tenant and not a partner. They found sworn statements from Brigit to the police at the times he was arrested for two rapes in which she clearly stated she was not in a relationship.

They found insurance papers so that if anything was stolen then they could make a claim. They felt they had completed a job, secured Brigit's home, and their inheritance, and found justice for Brigit.

They went back to Niall's exhausted, but reassured. It had

been four days of hell. Yesterday they had attended the funerals of Brigit and Topaz. Today they had sat grim faced through Rob's.

On her final night in Invercargill, before she'd returned home following Brigit's funeral, Georgia, Niall, and Ben, sat in the comfort and security of Niall's home, and raised their glasses in a final salute to Brigit, as they all remembered that night. Israel "IZ" Kamakawiwo'ole's *Over the Rainbow* was gently playing in the background.

Enfeebled by a lifetime of indolence, booze and drug abuse, Rob proved no match for Ben and Georgia who held him down with pillows so as not to mark his arms and legs, while the lethal dose of insulin and potassium was smilingly delivered between the toes by the wily and determined Niall. The drugs would remain undetected by the attending doctor, called to the house the next morning by his surprised friends complete with their hangovers. The doctor would then sign off his death as natural causes.

'Potassium and insulin with a touch of fentanyl in large enough quantities is lethal and undetectable. If he goes for an autopsy, they will never look between the toes. It will appear as if he had just drifted off to sleep while drunk. No sign of foul play. No sign of drunken vomiting. It will just appear very natural.' Niall said reassuringly. 'It's what we use for assisted suicides in terminal illnesses when the patient and their family want it all just to end peacefully. But don't tell anybody that.'

Book Two - A teaser...

THE TANIWHA CALLS

CHAPTER ONE

The watcher was still, leaning against a tombstone on that damp misty morning. Bluff was as dismal as ever, the cold mist which swept in from the sea chilled you like nothing else. It went through your parka, your swandri, your Merino underwear. And still you shivered in the bleakness of the dawn surrounded by death.

The watcher waited for the boat. Old Man Hunter's one trawler out of his fleet of fishing vessels. The wives and children of the crew also waited but they were still warm in their beds unencumbered by the need to know. Secure in the knowledge of a fat pay cheque this month. Not all of them perhaps, but some were. The ones of this fishing trip were. Perhaps they were dreaming of a trip somewhere warm, away from this godforsaken place at the furthest end of the South Island. Bluff, a place where the wind never stopped, and the sun barely registered during the winter and spring months. A place where the equinox caused the population to fret, much like the mistral in France which so unsettled the natives. Those fearsome gales meant a southerly blast coming straight up from the Antarctic.

It was worst when the wind from the south fought for supremacy with the prevailing westerly wind, and there was one hell of a battle occurring out there on Foveaux Strait right now. It was bad enough on cemetery hill overlooking the harbour. The watcher sniffed the snow on the air and imagined the smattering of it on the surrounding hills. She wrapped her arms protectively around her as the wind tried to upend her. It was too early to see yet; dawn was still minutes away. It would be a bleak day. The clouds were heavy, black and thunderous.

The watcher shrugged into herself, mittened hands deep in her pockets. She could hear the noise of the ocean in the Strait as it roiled. *This's one hell of a boat trip.*

A light on the horizon flickered. She pulled out her night vision glasses. It was all she had with her. Nothing else to give her identity away. A darkened spectre in a cemetery, silent, watching, upright like those tombstones. She was still, resolute, and watchful. Her Bushnell glasses had a built-in video camera. They turned night into day, but she needed to wait until the boat was closer. She needed it to be at least 200 metres closer to shore before she could see much.

Soon the chug chug of the engine could be heard, and she tensed. She felt like a snowman so cold and still. But she needed to remain hidden. She puffed into her parka to try and get some warmth onto her frozen chest.

The engine changed gear as it slowed. She raised her glasses. The flickering light on the horizon now tuned into the trawler, men tied for security as they fought the conditions to dock safely. Old Man Hunter stood securely at the bridge as he battled to keep the trawler upright. She could see him clearly now. The scowl of concentration, the thickness of his strong arms as he wrenched the wheel. She could now hear him barking orders to those poor souls on deck as they readied the rope. Dripping and slipping, the deck was a death trap.

She now heard words rather than just the noise of shouting. The cursing and swearing of men under stress. Men tired from long days and nights out catching fish in the troubled waters of Foveaux Strait. They were as skilled and as hard as the rocks along the harsh, rugged coastline where they sailed, and where the winds whipped up a storm between the South Island and Stewart Island. And the tide was adept at throwing the unwary onto the jagged rocks along the shoreline. This piece of water shouted, 'don't mess with me'. and Old Man Hunter was sailing tonight with a skeleton crew. Dangerous. But the fewer who knew the safer it was.

The crew shouted to be heard above the pounding of the waves. Old Man Hunter shouted the loudest as he too fought to keep himself upright. This was no gentle cruise to dock. No graceful glide to the safety of shore. This was man versus sea, and he was out to win. This catch was important for his future and the crew knew it. Except for the lad. He was busy being sick, emptying his belly into the foul waters.

Old Man Hunter was by now bandy from the years he spent balancing himself on the deck in the invariably stormy Foveaux Strait. She could see him clearly through her glasses. Even the waterproofs couldn't hide his shape. All that bracing on sturdy legs as the boat rocked, rolled, heaved and shuddered had done damage to his hips. He now suffered daily. Nights were worst when the pain of his arthritic joints seared up, coming in waves and depriving him of sleep. He needed new knees and hips. But there simply wasn't time for him to take off for surgery. It was the nights when sleep eluded him that his past came to remind him of those early days of poverty as a fledgling fisherman, the long days and nights out catching the elusive and eagerly sought expensive Blue Cod. Never again, he had often thought, would I be poor, hungry, cold, wet and exhausted.

So, at nights he now ate the biscuit. A variation of the old favourite Anzac biscuit, made from oats and coconut, bound together with butter, syrup and sugar, and cooked for him by his daughter Blanche. They had proved a balm, and a source of income. He'd never asked where she got the cannabis from in those early days. He'd just appreciated the peace of painless nights that those biscuits gave him. His aging friends, also casualties of a life at sea, paid him handsomely for his biscuits. Old Man Hunter was by nature a greedy grasping bastard. He'd fleece his friends as well as his enemies. That was why he'd always got on so well with Rob initially.

He shouted a warning clearly heard by the watcher.

'Watch your fucking self or you'll go overboard. Check those ropes. Look out for the lad.'

He'd seen many of his mates lost overboard into the unforgiving coldness of the Strait and now wanted to work onshore. Fishing was a young man's game. The Bluff cemetery, where the watcher now stood, eyes glued to the glasses, overlooked the Strait, and was full of people lost to the fearsome winds which caused the water to roil viciously. Everyone who sailed the Strait lost a piece of themselves when out on that piece of water. He smiled grimly as he watched the lad throw up his dinner. You had to be fit strong and healthy and he paid his young crew well. That way he kept them loyal. But mostly he relied on his first mate. They were in it together. Trust was something they each had, earned over long years at sea. Trust that they would come out of this maelstrom alive, trust that they could do business together on the calmness of the shore as much as they did at sea.

The first mate was the conduit. She watched him as he prepared the ropes. She watched as another man appeared out from behind the pile of crates sitting on the wharf. He was the only man on shore to catch those heavy braids, strong enough to hold the trawler fast against the tides. No-one else was mad enough to be outdoors in weather like this. Even the Harbour Master was at home in his bed unaware of the returning boat. She watched as the shadow caught the rope, looped it over the bollard and quickly move aft for the second one.

She watched him he stepped back into the gloom, his face hidden. Tall and strong she judged from his back view. *He doesn't want to be seen.* His cap was pulled down over his face leaving it in shadows. She caught a glint of his eyes. Seaman blue. Cold and piercing.

She watched. She waited. Still and silent as the tombstones around her, those guardians of the dead with their epitaphs of by-gone days, of grief and release.

She watched as the first mate oversaw the unloading of tons of blue cod. She waited in the interminable cold and relentless drizzle as he counted each crate as it laboriously was craned up from the bowels of the trawler. With the last crate unloaded he gave each of the crewmen a blue cod, their bonus of the night. He walked them to the gate. He saw them off. Old Man Hunter watched all this.

She too remained watching.

When the last of the car lights was seen well away from the port, he looked up at Old Man Hunter. Thumbs up. Old Man Hunter called him back to the trawler.

'Come and get the last one.'

Now onshore Old Man Hunter turned, 'You can come out now.' The ghost like rope catcher appeared like a wraith.

'How much?'

'Enough.'

Trouble?'

'None.'

Together they watched in silence as the first mate lowered the final crate. Walking over to it, the visitor plunged his hand into the icy slurry which surrounded the remaining fish. He pulled it out and looked in its belly.

He nodded.

'Worked then.'

'Yep.'

'Let's get it inside. Too bloody cold out here.'

'Too exposed. But no-one to see us.'

She was still there, a silent sentinel as the three of them manhandled the crate inside.

Sarah had her story.

Made in the USA
Middletown, DE
24 October 2020

22098739R00154